COLLEGE GIRLS

Her tutor seemed to sense the change in her breathing, a cold note entering his voice as he paused. 'So is this what you came here for, Beth? To be punished like the eager little slut that you are?'

'Yes,' she moaned.

But that hurried answer failed to please her tutor. His next harsh slap caught her directly across the top of her thigh, an unexpected change that made her stiffen in pain. 'What was that? Did you forget to call me "sir"?'

'Yes, sir,' she managed to gasp. 'I'm sorry, sir.'

'You came here to be spanked?'

'Yes, sir.'

COLLEGE GIRLS

Cat Scarlett

This book is a work of fiction.
In real life, make sure you practise safe, sane and
consensual sex.

First published in 2005 by
Nexus
Thames Wharf Studios
Rainville Road
London W6 9HA

www.nexus-books.co.uk

Typeset by TW Typesetting, Plymouth, Devon

Printed and bound by
Clays Ltd, St Ives PLC

ISBN 9780352339423

You'll notice that we have introduced a set of symbols onto our book jackets, so that you can tell at a glance what fetishes each of our brand new novels contains. Here's the key – enjoy!

cp (traditional)

cp (modern)

spanking

restraint/bondage

rope bondage/hojojutsu

latex/rubber/leather/enclosure

fem dom

willing captivity

medical

period setting

uniforms

sex rituals

One

Professor Withenshawe beckoned to her as the other students streamed noisily from the lecture hall. His tone was ominous. 'Could I have a word please, Beth?'

Stomach tightening with apprehension, palms clammy, Beth slowly gathered together her notes on his hour-long lecture 'Women in Chaucer' and made her way down towards the podium.

With his tweed jacket, elbows patched with leather, and his fussy gold-rimmed spectacles, Professor Withenshawe was the epitome of a highly respected Oxford academic. Dry as dust and totally absorbed in his own field of research. None of the other students at St Nectan's College would believe her if she told them what he was really like under that stuffy upright exterior. Which was just as well, Beth thought dryly. This was unlikely to be the last time Professor Withenshawe asked her to stay behind after one of his lectures and she was not in any position to terminate such a mutually satisfactory arrangement.

As soon as the fire door at the top had clicked shut behind the last of the stragglers, Beth ascended the podium and dumped her heavy rucksack on the floor.

'Professor Withenshawe?'

'You did not attend my lecture last week,' he said in a cold voice, putting his lecture notes in order. 'Why not?'

She flushed guiltily. 'I was feeling ill.'

Professor Withenshawe looked down at her like a stern parent over the top of his gold-rimmed spectacles. 'You disappoint me. You'll be sitting your Finals next year, Beth. You can't afford to miss such important lectures.'

'I know. I'm sorry.'

'Did you have a hangover?'

'No.'

'Then perhaps you overslept?'

Beth stared down at her feet in dismay, cheeks scarlet and her heart beginning to thump as she recognised the tone in his voice. 'I really was ill.'

'Illness is no excuse for falling behind in your work, Beth. Nor for offending me by failing to attend my lectures. I expect you to make full amends for your lack of courtesy,' the lecturer told her in clipped tones, stony-faced. 'In the usual manner.'

'Here?' she queried, pretending to look aghast.

'Why not here?' His eyebrows arched dismissively as he slipped easily into a role she had come to recognise. 'You certainly don't deserve any better treatment, young lady, and I have no time to find anywhere more suitable. I have to give a seminar on *Sir Gawain and the Green Knight* in less than an hour.'

Professor Withenshawe dropped his hands to the flies of his grey corduroy trousers and unzipped himself. He reached inside the green-striped boxer shorts and extracted an erect cock, its purplish head swollen and already weeping pre-come from the narrow slit.

'Please assume the position,' he said coldly. 'Down on your knees. Head back and mouth open.'

Although her face had turned beetroot-red at his order, Beth obeyed without bothering to argue. From experience, she knew it would only make matters

2

worse to protest. She sank to her knees on the podium, skin-tight jeans straining around her crotch and bottom, white midriff top riding up to reveal a flat stomach below the curve of her breasts. It had become a familiar position over the past few months, down on her knees in front of Professor Withenshawe's gaping crotch, and she adopted it with ease. This time, though, she opened her mouth even wider than usual and clasped her hands firmly behind her back, hoping to pacify his anger by accentuating the submissiveness of her pose.

Forcing her to perform fellatio on him in a public place seemed to be one of his favourite punishments at the moment, she thought, tilting back her head to receive his cock. In the beginning, she had visited the professor in his college rooms once a week, crouched between his legs while he read her essay. Now, though, he seemed almost reckless in his desire to humiliate and exploit her. It was not merely her ignominious position that excited him but also the thrill of potential discovery. Perhaps the professor was becoming a little foolhardy, she thought, recalling how often he had told her that having sex in public was a dangerous business. He could easily lose his position at the university if one of his less understanding colleagues were to walk in unexpectedly.

'Yes, it's a pity you missed last week's lecture. It was on Chaucer's *Troilus and Criseyde*.' He groaned as her mouth moistly circled his cock and drew it further inside. 'You remind me of Criseyde. She would have been just as eager and experienced a little fellatrix as yourself.'

Unable to reply, Beth concentrated her efforts instead on the thick shaft stretching her mouth. He had been circumcised as a young boy – an odd affectation of his mother's, the professor had told her,

3

since the family were not Jewish – and the bulbous head pushed towards the back of her throat without the encumbrance of a foreskin, his flesh mottled among a clutch of greying pubic hairs.

She could still remember her surprise the first time he had pressed her to take it out of his trousers and kiss it. Now she sucked on his cock with only partially faked enthusiasm, her lips a perfect 'O'; a warm slick tunnel into which he could sink and withdraw at will.

Feeling him reach down to push up the midriff top and fondle her breasts through the skimpy white bra, Beth raised herself higher on her knees to allow him better access to her nipples. These encounters were not only about money, she admitted to herself, growing ever more flushed and unable to prevent her hips from moving to the rhythm of his thrusts. It was true that earning extra cash on top of her student grant had been the original motivation for agreeing to suck his cock like this. But that did not mean she was left cold by her own shamelessly filthy behaviour. Quite the contrary, in fact.

'Poor misguided Criseyde,' he continued, holding her head close against his crotch as she sucked. 'A promiscuous young woman was passed from man to man in those days. Once Criseyde had yielded to her uncle and taken Troilus as a lover, there would have been no turning back.'

She tried to remember that Professor Withenshawe was over sixty, as she squeezed and stroked the lower part of his shaft while her tongue slipped backwards and forwards over the bulbous head. Beth had sucked off boys her own age in exactly the same way, of course, and felt the same excitement at her feminine power. But this was a different situation, she reminded herself.

Professor Withenshawe was not another student, tensing ecstatically in her mouth after an evening down the college bar or out at the cinema. He was not even her lover; he was one of her lecturers. And this was a straightforward business transaction, not an act of pleasure between friends and equals. It was important not to lose sight of that fact and get too excited by what they were doing together.

The lecturer dragged his slick cock from her mouth, his gold-rimmed spectacles glinting as he bent over her kneeling figure. 'I think this might be an opportune moment to fuck you,' he said hoarsely. 'Slip those jeans off and let's have you on all fours.'

'I'm sorry, but I can't do that. I never agreed to full sex,' she pointed out as politely as she could, remaining on her knees. This was not the first time he had asked her for sex and been refused; perhaps he thought he could wear her down through sheer persistence. 'Just blow jobs, remember? That was the deal.'

'I'll double your fee.'

'It's not a question of money.' She shook her head. 'I'll suck, but I won't fuck.'

'That's probably what Criseyde said. But it didn't work for her, my dear, and it won't work for you either.'

Professor Withenshawe pushed up her bra without waiting for a reply, exposing her small white breasts. His hands roamed across her flesh, hot and sweaty with excitement, and her nipples began to swell and stiffen into peaks under his manipulative fingers. Beth found herself groaning and writhing as he continued to fondle her, humiliated to realise she could not control her own physical responses.

'What difference can it make whether you give me a blow job or a fuck? You're not exactly a virgin,' he

5

pointed out dryly. 'Come on, out of those jeans and bend over. You know you want to. There's no point pretending you don't.'

'No,' she insisted, pulling stubbornly away as he tried to lift her. 'You can do it in my mouth or not at all.'

'What if I force you?'

'Then you'll just have to find some other student willing to suck your cock for money, Professor Withenshawe. Because I won't be doing it again.' With a defiant look in her eyes, Beth stared up at the academic. Her voice trembled but she was determined not to back down. 'Blow jobs only and no penetration. That was our original agreement.'

'You infuriating little –' The professor stopped himself, no doubt realising from the look on Beth's face that she meant it, and gave a wry shrug. He was still angry, though. She could hear it in the ironic bite of his voice.

'All right, young lady,' he muttered. 'You win. I'll spunk in your throat if that's really what you prefer.'

Beth nodded in mute relief, settling back on her knees and letting her jaw relax so that her mouth gaped open for his cock again. The moment of confrontation between them seemed to have passed and she did not want to risk losing her payment by refusing to relieve him at all. His prick slid back inside with one easy thrust, slick from her saliva. The professor was still quite erect, in spite of their disagreement, and the swollen head of his cock tasted of pre-come which she licked expertly away before beginning to suck again.

'Though I don't entirely understand your reasoning,' he muttered, jerking his hips back and forth as she locked her mouth firmly around his shaft. 'I wouldn't have made you pregnant. I'm not some inexperienced teenager, for God's sake. I could have pulled out at the last minute if you'd asked me.'

She made no response, closing her eyes instead as the thick cock began to swell and harden between her lips, a sure sign that the professor was close to orgasm. It was a moment she had always enjoyed: knowing that she had brought a man to the limit of his self-control and over it, simply by taking his cock in her mouth and sucking.

His breathing was ragged now. 'Perhaps next time? Think about it. You can name any price you like . . . within reason.'

Even though Beth had absolutely no intention of agreeing to have sex with the ageing professor, she gave a stifled moan at his suggestion and sucked even harder, perfectly aware that such behaviour might trigger his ejaculation. It seemed to have done the trick, she thought, for a few seconds later his thrusts intensified and his fingers tangled in her chestnut hair, holding her tight against him as her body swayed under the onslaught.

'Coming in your mouth is excellent, of course. But spunking in your cunt would feel even better,' the professor continued. The end was obviously near. He began to grunt like an animal, pushing himself uncomfortably deep into her throat. 'I'd like to take you from behind one day. Fuck you like a bitch on heat. Perhaps even do it . . . up your splendidly tight arse.'

A sudden hot jet of spunk hitting the back of her throat caught Beth by surprise, even though she had been willing it to happen for some minutes now. Her throat convulsed around his shaft. She swallowed once, twice, and then a third time as his cock continued to pulse its thick white cream into her.

It must have been ages since he had last come. There was too much of the bitter-tasting stuff for her to cope with, and it spilled from her lips and trailed messily down her chin. Her hands clawed at his buttocks through the corduroy trousers, trying to free herself now that he had finished. But his cock was still jammed deep inside, blocking her airway. She began to feel uncomfortable and tried to communicate that by making an urgent mewling noise in the back of her throat. Yet still the professor did not release her, clutching her long brown hair with both hands and clamping her firmly against his crotch.

Darkness drummed unpleasantly against her closed eyelids and for a while she feared she might actually faint. Then the lecturer withdrew and Beth collapsed back on to the wooden podium, spluttering and gasping.

She glared up at him through a blood-red haze, her tone accusing. 'There was no need to be so rough with me. I could have been hurt, the way you forced it down my throat.'

'You must allow me to apologise, Beth.' Professor Withenshawe tucked his damp cock back into his trousers and adjusted the gold-rimmed spectacles which had slipped a little way down his nose in the excitement. He helped Beth to her feet without any outward sign of remorse, and with what she suspected to be a hint of irony in his voice. 'I was under the impression that was how you liked it . . . a little rough and ready? I shall know better in future, of course. But perhaps this will sugar the pill?'

He counted out a large handful of banknotes and placed them inside a dog-eared paperback copy of *Troilus and Criseyde*. After glancing around the lecture room once more, as if belatedly concerned that he might be spotted in a compromising position, Professor Withenshawe passed the book to Beth. 'Plenty there to keep you occupied until the next time we meet. Feel free to make use of any notes in the margin. They're not mine, of course. That copy belonged to a former student. Though he did manage to get a First, so . . .'

'Thank you,' she said dryly.

He nodded, checking again that his flies were fully secured. 'And don't forget to let me know if you decide to accept my offer. If you do, we could meet somewhere rather more congenial. One of those out-of-town motels, perhaps? Simply to avoid the usual tittle-tattle, I'm sure you understand.'

Beth bent to slip the paperback into her rucksack alongside her library books, wishing she had brought something refreshing to drink after their encounter. As usual, she felt dizzy and light-headed now that the lecturer had finished with her. Perhaps even a little nauseous. The acrid taste of his spunk still coated her throat and tongue, with sticky remnants drying on her chin, a constant reminder of what she had just accepted in her mouth. But at least the money he had given her today meant she should soon be able to afford a new laptop.

He turned to assemble his papers, clearing his throat as he packed them away into his briefcase. 'Before you go, I thought you should know that one of my colleagues is interested in meeting you.'

She froze, staring at him. 'Have you been talking about me behind my back? This was meant to be –'

'Strictly between the two of us, I know,' Withenshawe admitted. 'But your secret is still safe. He's the most discreet man in the university as far as this sort of arrangement is concerned.'

'His name?'

'That, I'm afraid, I am not at liberty to tell you.'

Silent for a moment, Beth considered her financial position as she hoisted the heavy rucksack on to her shoulders. She could hardly afford to be too choosy about how she earned her money, she reminded herself wryly, or she would end up owing the bank a small fortune by the time she graduated.

'So what does this guy want?' she asked. 'A blow job?'

The professor seemed pained by her deliberate crudity. 'More like a preliminary chat, I should imagine. Whatever happens after that will be entirely up to you.'

'And when am I supposed to meet him?'

'Tonight.'

She frowned. 'So soon?'

'Can you make it?'

When she nodded reluctantly, the professor gave a little smile and scribbled a few lines on a sheet of paper. He tore it out of his notebook and handed it to her without speaking. She glanced down, reading through the words swiftly, but there were no clues as to the mystery man's identity. It was merely the name and address of a local hotel with a time and a room number beside it.

'Are you sure I can trust this man?'

'Absolutely,' Withenshawe replied without hesitation, gesturing her to precede him up the flight of steps to the lecture hall exit. 'I admit that his sexual predilections may be a little more exotic than my own. But I would never have mentioned you to him if I had not thought you would both benefit from the acquaintance.'

He opened the fire door at the top of the steps and insisted that she walk through first, his brief touch almost proprietorial. 'I'm also sure he would never do anything to jeopardise his career at this university,' the lecturer continued, lowering his voice as they passed a group of students chatting in the corridor.

10

'So whatever he may propose, however outlandish it might sound at first, you should be safe enough in his company.'

'Sounds like a perfect gentleman,' she commented dryly.

'A perfect . . .?' Professor Withenshawe shot her a startled look from behind those gold-rimmed spectacles and hastily shook his head. 'I never said that, my dear,' he muttered, and waved her away at the end of the hallway, checking his flies for the last time before turning in the direction of the staff cloakrooms. 'My goodness me, no.'

Fresh out of the shower, Beth stood naked in the middle of her cramped college bedroom, trying to decide which outfit to put on. She hung her head to towel dry her long chestnut hair upside down, thinking hard as she watched her bare breasts jiggle and bounce with the motion. It had not occurred to her before but she had absolutely no idea what she ought to wear to this meeting tonight.

Would an elegant black dress be more appropriate than the short leather skirt and see-through blouse she had just pulled from the wardrobe? Perhaps the anonymous lecturer would prefer to see her dressed in a T-shirt and hipster jeans, as Professor Withenshawe usually did, which emphasised her youth and the tight curves of her body.

Deciding to opt for the less subtle leather skirt, Beth slipped into a black lace thong and matching bra, then turned back to the underwear drawer with a frown. Should she bother with stockings? It was a warm May evening and she did not relish the idea of walking through town in a short skirt and stockings when most other girls her age would be barelegged or in jeans. But this was no time to be coy. If a man wanted to pay for the use of her mouth, to treat her like a cheap whore, he would probably prefer to see her look the part, too.

She chose her sheerest pair and pulled them on slowly, careful not to snag the delicate silky material on her nails. High black stilettos gave her a few much-needed extra inches in height before she wriggled into the tight leather skirt. Her see-through blouse, some dark-red lipstick and a pair of silver earrings completed the outfit.

Before turning to leave the room, Beth glanced at herself in the mirror and caught her breath. Looking like some common streetwalker, slim legs provocative in black stockings and the tilt of her breasts clearly visible through her blouse, an unfamiliar creature stared back at her from the mirror: sleek, glittering and undeniably available. There could be no doubt in any man's mind that she was out to make money tonight, she thought, and slipped a concealing coat over her outfit in case she bumped into any friends on her way out of college. But the gates of St Nectan's stood silent and empty as she stumbled across the cobbles in her high heels and turned down towards the main road, already busy with evening traffic.

The hotel was situated on a narrow side street in Summertown. She hesitated on the threshold, not sure what to say if anyone asked what she was doing there. But she need not have worried. The hotel was posh enough for the bored-looking receptionist to raise her eyebrows at Beth's appearance but not so grand that the woman actually bothered to question her arrival. Far from having to account for herself, she walked up two flights of stairs unchallenged and found her way to room 27 without too much difficulty. Perhaps they were used to men asking for escorts at this hotel, she thought uneasily, checking her lipstick as she passed the mirrored surface of the lift door.

Upstairs, away from the well-kept public rooms, the hotel decor seemed far less impressive. She could not help noticing that paint had started to peel above the doorframes and the pale-blue carpet in the corridor was threadbare in places. Her heart was racing as she began to wonder what she might have let herself in for; coming here alone in such a dangerous outfit.

The door to room 27 opened and Beth stared in shock, recognising the man in the doorway. Bare-chested and with what appeared to be a glass of whisky in his hand, he stood there without speaking for a few seconds, his eyes narrowed on her face.

She took a step backwards in disbelief. 'Dr Milton?'

'Good evening, Beth,' her personal tutor said, a hard amusement in his voice. 'Won't you come in?'

Two

Beth did not know what to say, staring blankly at Dr Milton. She felt as though someone had punched her in the stomach. In a dazed silence, she allowed her tutor to steer her into the hotel room and heard the door close behind them with a soft click.

'I thought you might be surprised to see me,' he said coolly, lifting the whisky bottle and offering it to her. When she shook her head, he shrugged and took a sip of his own drink. 'That's why I made old Withenshawe keep his mouth shut and arranged for us to meet here. My rooms in college might have been a bit of a giveaway.'

'I think there's been a mistake.'

'No mistake,' Milton assured her with a sharp smile. 'And you can stop looking so worried. Nobody else need know about this. I booked the room in a false name and it's all paid for in cash.'

She glanced towards the bed, covers drawn back and the sheets already creased. 'I can't do this. Not with you. You're my –'

'Personal tutor,' he finished for her, nodding. 'I know. It's a disgusting world. But I understand you need the money and you don't much care how you earn it. Is that correct?'

Beth sat down on the bed and stared up at him, unsure how to reply. Her mouth was dry and she felt curiously light-headed, as though she were about to faint. Her personal tutor from St Nectan's College was the last person she had expected to see when the door opened, and she was still finding it hard to adjust to his presence. She even found herself dragging down the hem of her short leather skirt, painfully aware of his eyes on her legs.

'Professor Withenshawe had no right to tell you about that,' she said stiffly. 'We had a private arrangement. It was nothing to do with the college.'

Dr Milton took a slow sip of his whisky, watching her over the top of his glass with an ironic expression. 'My dear Beth, there's no such thing as a private arrangement in Oxford. These things have a tendency to come out into the public domain eventually, whether we like it or not. Better to admit your sins straight away than risk looking like a complete amateur by continuing to deny them.'

'But I am an amateur,' she pointed out bitterly.

'Perhaps.' Dr Milton regarded her steadily for a moment before putting down his glass. 'Then again, perhaps not. That's one thing I would like to ascertain tonight.'

Her tutor smiled, pulling her towards him. The well-used hotel mattress sagged under their combined weights and Beth felt herself shift slightly in his direction, flushing as their bodies made contact.

'Now, Professor Withenshawe is a confirmed amateur,' he carried on without emphasis, apparently oblivious to her embarrassment. 'Far too ready to be caught with his pants down. Old school; thinks he's above the law. But at least he did the decent thing this time and passed the information on to me before it went beyond his control.'

She was confused. 'Beyond his control?'

'Before the college authorities heard what was happening and sent you down for disreputable conduct.'

'Down where?'

Milton laughed at her bewildered expression. 'Threw you out of the university, you little fool.'

'Oh.'

'Oh, indeed.' He laid his hand on her thigh. 'But as it stands, Beth, this is your lucky day. I'm willing to make sure you're protected from any unpleasant consequences like that. And all I ask in return is a little friendly co-operation.'

'You mean sex?'

His eyes narrowed on her face. 'If you must be so tiresomely pedantic, then yes. That's precisely what I mean.'

The hand on her thigh stroked its way up her stocking until it reached naked flesh, warm and concealed beneath the short leather skirt. Beth shivered but did not try to stop him.

'Though I'm not sure I approve of these stockings,' he added, frowning. 'Is that what Withenshawe told you I wanted? Some cheap whore, straight off the streets?'

'He didn't tell me anything about you.'

'Good.'

She hesitated. 'Except that you wouldn't want to jeopardise your position at the college.'

'Which is why I was so interested to hear about your little sideline. You've always struck me as such a discreet girl, Beth. Discreet and well behaved.' He smiled dryly. 'The perfect combination for my needs, in fact.'

'Which are?'

Milton expertly unhooked one of her stockings from the black lace suspender belt, watching her face as his fingers played across the exposed skin of her thigh. She had never noticed before how dark his eyes were. This close, they seemed almost black, heavy brows drawn above them in a frown of concentration. 'Explanations later. For now, I want you to remove these ridiculous stockings and let me see what I'm paying for.'

She tried to sit up, her refusal automatic. 'Sorry, I don't do full sex. Professor Withenshawe should have told you. I thought you only wanted a blow job tonight.'

'Wrong again.'

He began to unroll her stockings, pushing her forcibly back against the sheets and clamping her hands above her head as she put up a brief flurry of resistance. When she tried to free herself, meaning to slap his face and make a break for the door, the dark eyes rose from their task and met hers. The smile in them had gone.

'Don't be stupid, Beth. We both know why you're here.'

'I never –'

'To sell yourself to me,' he finished curtly.

Before she could manage to stammer a denial, his hands pushed between her thighs again, pressing them further apart without the slightest pretence at gentleness. The short leather skirt rode up to her lace panties as he pushed her deeper into the mattress, ignoring her cry of alarm. If she had looked like a common whore before, she thought wildly, that image must be complete now. Her thighs had been spread wide for his inspection, her stockings puddling ignominiously around her ankles, rolled down but not quite removed, and she was helpless, flat on her back.

Dr Milton paused and let his gaze sweep over her prostrate body, lingering for a moment on the slender legs he had uncovered. 'Has anyone ever spanked you?' he asked coolly, slipping one long finger beneath the tight elastic of her panties. Her humiliated groan made no impact on him. 'Tied you up and caned you? Hit you with a belt, perhaps?'

'Of course not!'

'What a sheltered life you've led,' he murmured.

'I just haven't dated any perverts like you,' she said, loathing the knowledge that her sex was beginning to moisten as his finger probed deeper beneath her panties. 'My boyfriends have all been completely normal.'

'Trust me, there's nothing perverted about the human desire to be punished,' Milton corrected her. 'Or to punish.'

'I'm not into those games.'

'Are you experienced enough to be sure of that?'

Beth controlled her temper with difficulty, wishing she could slap the arrogant bastard but suspicious that he might slap her back. 'It's not a question of experience. I know my own tastes, thank you.'

'Really?'

His smile seemed to mock her as he pushed aside the thin lace of her panties and cruelly pinched her sex lips. She gasped at the pain and then squealed as he did it again, this time much harder. Dispassionate, his dark eyes surveyed her expression for a moment without comment. Then his fingers slipped between her bruised and aching lips – now pouting out from the dark wisps of pubic hair and embarrassingly slick with her juices – and located the hidden bud of her clitoris. He circled it expertly with his thumb until it betrayed her by growing tense and erect.

'Sometimes pain can act as the gateway to a new self, an identity you did not even know you possessed. Though it might be better described as a key. A key which serves to liberate a repressed mind and body, unlocking the pleasure within.'

'I'm not repressed!'

'Aren't you?'

'And this isn't about pleasure,' she continued unsteadily, avoiding his intent gaze. 'You were closer to the truth when you said I was here to sell myself. It's a business transaction. Nothing more.'

'You can lie to yourself if you wish, Beth. But your cunt seems to be experiencing things differently.'

She recoiled in horror as he pulled his juice-streaked fingers out of her sex and touched them to her lips. The pungent aroma of her arousal was unmistakeable.

'That's a physiological reaction,' she insisted, flushing to the hairline. 'It doesn't mean I'm enjoying any of this.'

'Liar.'

Milton pinched her vulnerable sex lips again, as if to demonstrate her inability to resist him. This time, though, he dug his nails in to make it more painful, and her gasp of protest only seemed to amuse him. Laughing under his breath, her tutor unbuttoned the see-through blouse and pushed up the black lace bra to free her breasts. His fingers pinched the delicate skin, rolling and squeezing it with casual brutality. She did not want to respond, hating the man for the way he was handling her, but it was impossible to hide such a powerful reaction. Beth felt her nipples stiffen to tiny hard peaks, her usually pale breasts beginning to flush with excitement at his treatment, and heard herself groan in a mixture of shame and anticipation.

He had seen what was happening to her body, his eyes narrowing on her breasts. 'You learn quickly,' he remarked. 'Perhaps you're more open to pain than you thought?'

'No!'

His dark frown was impatient. 'For God's sake, Beth. Take a look at yourself. Why don't you just relax and allow me to demonstrate how enjoyable this arrangement could be?'

'Enjoyable for you, perhaps.'

'For both of us.'

'You want to hurt me, Dr Milton,' she reminded him, a bitter irony in her voice. 'Tie me up, you said. Hit me with a belt. How could that ever be an enjoyable experience for me? Unless you're offering to let me hit you back.'

He smiled. 'Now you're being ludicrous.'

'I rest my case.'

'There's far more to this game than hitting and hurting,' Dr Milton murmured, watching her. 'I've taught you so much since you came up to Oxford. Why not let me teach you this?'

'And if I refuse?'

He shrugged, still playing with her exposed breasts. 'That would be a great pity. Let me put it like this, I'm not the only one interested in your services. It would be a wise financial decision to say yes.'

'I don't understand.'

'There's a special club I belong to, Beth. A highly exclusive gentlemen's club, which can be very generous to discreet young ladies like yourself who agree to become involved in our activities.'

'What sort of activities?'

He raised his eyebrows. 'Do I really need to spell it out?'

'Sex?'

'With your consent, yes.'

'Pain?'

He looked down at her, unsmiling. 'In my experience, the two have a tendency to go hand in hand.'

Beth felt a sudden moisture creeping between her

20

thighs and knew that she was aroused by what he was suggesting. She did not know whether to be angry at herself or give in to this insidious sensation of excitement. From the look in his eyes, her tutor was only too aware of her indecision, and she guessed it would not be long before he used that knowledge to his advantage.

'I'm not sure.'

'You don't have to make up your mind immediately,' he said, his tone less demanding. 'That would be a little unfair, after all. All our girls begin with a probationary period; some time in which to decide whether or not you want to be involved full time.'

She hesitated, still uncertain. It sounded like one hell of a leap into the sexual unknown, and perhaps too far for someone of her limited experience. It would be so embarrassing to accept and then have to change her mind, unable to cope with their demands. 'Perhaps you should be more specific about what would be expected of me,' she murmured, flushing slightly. 'I presume it's more than just the missionary position?'

His tone was dry. 'It's every position you can imagine, Beth, and some that you can't.'

'Anal?'

'That's an old favourite,' he said, narrowing his eyes at the distaste in her voice. 'I take it you're not keen?'

'How did you guess?'

'There's no negotiating on that, I'm afraid. It's an essential skill for a submissive.' Seeing her horrified expression, he shrugged. 'But I suppose we could agree to leave it until after the probationary period.'

'Thank God.'

'Have you ever actually tried anal sex?'

'Ugh, no way.'

Milton fixed her with his dark gaze for a long moment. 'My dear Beth, it might be wise to curb that unfortunate tendency to speak your mind,' he warned her softly. 'It won't go down well with certain members of the Club and I would hate to see you suffer unnecessarily.'

'OK,' she agreed shakily.

'So, no anal sex for the time being. But, if you do decide to stay on after the trial period, you will need to be initiated into its undoubted pleasures. Is that understood?'

'Yes.'

'Good.' He nodded firmly. 'Now take off those ridiculous little panties and bend over.'

Nothing Withenshawe or any of her former boyfriends had ever done could have prepared her for Dr Milton's decadence. Beth was hopelessly out of her depth with this man, but equally she felt unable to go back on her agreement without looking foolish.

Once he had insisted she remove her panties and bend over the bed for him, sheer black stockings still pooled obscenely about her ankles, his language had become crude and brutal. It was just as she feared, her tutor pushing her further and further into a role she had never played before, where none of her old rules and familiar safeguards could apply. She was desperate to refuse his commands, to grab at the cool sheets and cover herself from his eyes. But something inside thrilled at the humiliating poses Milton forced her to strike: supporting herself on the mattress, buttocks spread and exposed, or touching her toes while he inspected the moist inner lips of her sex.

'You look unspeakably cheap in those stockings,' he commented, making her step out of them at last, his hands rough on her skin. 'What possessed you to wear them? Because you hoped to get fucked to-night?'

'I thought –'

'That all men find women in stockings sexy?'

'Yes.'

The uncompromising slap across her buttocks came as a shock. She cried out and her muscles tensed for a second blow. But it never fell. Instead, Dr Milton changed his tactics and caressed the sore area with the tips of his fingers, his voice deepening. 'Some of us are rather less predictable than that, Beth. A woman in stockings is too commonplace, a poor tired image of sexuality. There can be little genuine arousal in such things. Whereas a girl like yourself, charmingly deshabille and a little breathless, her bottom nicely reddened by a man's hand . . .'

Her courage deserted her; a cold sweat had broken out on her palms and along her spine, leaving her shivering. 'Are you going to hurt me?'

His tone was calm. 'Would you like me to hurt you?'

'I don't know.'

'There's only one way to find out,' he murmured, and pulled her arms together behind her back. 'The hard way.'

Half-standing, half-bending, she swayed precariously above the bed as he bound her wrists together with one of her own stockings. The sheer black nylon bit cruelly into her flesh and Beth could not help wincing, a little scared now, suddenly aware that she did not even know the rules of this game.

'What's the matter?' He paused for an instant, those sharp eyes having caught her involuntary movement. 'Too tight?'

'No,' she whispered, not wanting him to think her a coward.

'Bravo.'

His praise brought an unexpected flush to her cheeks. Why was it so important what he thought of her?

She allowed him to bend her forwards again, arms tied awkwardly behind her back now, until her face and chest were pressed into the mattress. The danger she might be in belatedly occurred to Beth. They were alone in this hotel room and she had been restrained; there would be no chance to call for help if Milton became violent or pushed her further than she wanted to go. Yet Beth felt no fear, somehow trusting him to respect her limits. At least she already knew he intended to hurt her and that it would be done with her consent.

There was no sense of coercion as she felt his hands position her legs further apart, fingers moving between her thighs to check how wet she was. His laughter was damning. The flush in her cheeks deepened. Her tutor had done little besides strip and bind her, yet already she was moist and eager for him to be inside her.

'The idea of pain clearly excites you,' he said, laughing softly. 'I hadn't expected such a rapid response. Though you always have been one of my more promising students, Beth.'

'Thank you.'

Dr Milton's hand collided sharply with her buttocks again, the unprovoked attack leaving her shocked and breathless. 'You will address me as "sir" outside our tutorials unless I instruct you otherwise. Is that understood?'

'Yes, sir.'

'In fact, this evening would be a good time to run through some basic rules with you,' he said, idly stroking the skin he had just stung with his slap. The tenderness of his touch surprised her and made her tense in anticipation, wondering where he might strike next. 'Firstly, you must obey me without question and trust my judgement implicitly. I will not tolerate disobedience or any show of wilfulness. My girls are expected to submit themselves one hundred per cent to their training. And, if I suspect that you've failed to reach my standards in any respect, you will be punished.'

He began to spank her buttocks as he spoke, using a firm steady rhythm, each blow landing in a slightly different place so that her bottom was soon warm and painfully glowing.

'That punishment may take various differing forms, according to the extent of your failure. I do like a certain spiritedness in my girls, but I am not accustomed to insubordination and you will quickly regret it if I'm forced to punish you. Am I making myself clear?'

'Yes, sir,' she managed to gasp.

The clumsiness of her position, face down on the rumpled sheets and hands tied behind her back, added considerably to her sense of vulnerability and Beth found herself sweating into the mattress as the pace and force of his slaps increased, her breathing laboured. She had not expected a spanking to hurt quite so much. It had always seemed quite a gentle form of chastisement when compared to a belt or wooden ruler, implements she had never felt against her skin but whose use filled her with dread.

Dr Milton seemed to be an expert at spanking, though, his hand continually rising and falling without giving her a chance to recover her breath before the next blow arrived, and it was not long before Beth was squirming beneath him like a schoolgirl in the headmaster's office, frantically praying for him to finish before her stifled cries turned to sobs of despair.

His hand grew even harder against the tender aching skin of her buttocks. Tears sprang into her eyes. She tried not to shed them, though, turning her face into the pillows. He would not be impressed by such a display of weakness. She had agreed to submit to this and it would be cowardly to back out now, especially over nothing more rigorous than a spanking. Indeed, she had fantasised about precisely this sort of scenario many times before. Her hands bound while she was beaten, cries muffled by a mattress or the rough material of a man's trousers, the pain increasing until it was almost too much for her to bear.

Her tutor seemed to sense the change in her breathing, a cold note entering his voice as he paused. 'So is this what you came here for, Beth? To be punished like the eager little slut that you are?'

'Yes,' she moaned.

But that hurried answer failed to please her tutor. His next harsh slap caught her directly across the top of her thigh, an unexpected change that made her stiffen in pain. 'What was that? Did you forget to call me "sir"?'

'Yes, sir,' she managed to gasp. 'I'm sorry, sir.'

'You came here to be spanked?'

'Yes, sir.'

Beth felt the rigidity of an erect cock prodding against her sex. Her whole body froze as she realised his intention. Shock rose in her like a wave. Without her being aware of it, Milton must have positioned himself between her thighs while he was spanking her.

'And to be fucked,' he continued, a harsh note of contempt in his voice. 'Let's not forget that. That's why you wore such a short skirt and those cheap black stockings. Because you came here tonight begging for cock. In your mouth, in your cunt. Maybe even up your arse.'

She struggled as his fingers parted the cheeks of her buttocks, the heat of his body closing against hers. For one wild moment, Beth feared that he meant every word he was saying. That her tutor intended to take her anally, regardless of what they had agreed beforehand. To push himself into her unused back passage and come there, shooting spunk into her bowels while she fought uselessly to prevent him. The brutality of that image filled her with a wild heat, her skin burning even as she tried to drag herself free from the vice of his hands.

She was saved from such appalling indignity, though. Instead, he dropped his aim an inch or so and drove into the wet slit below her exposed anus, stretching the muscular walls and almost knocking the air from her lungs with the force of his entry.

'Have you done this with that old fool Withenshawe?' His voice taunted her with its crude indifference. 'Played the whore for him? Bent over in the lecture hall to take his cock?'

'No,' she gasped in shock.

'But you want to, don't you?'

Beth shook her head, moaning with despair as he gripped her by the hips and began to thrust. This was not how she had intended to behave this evening. It had all been a terrible mistake. She should have walked away as soon as she saw him in the doorway, refused to play his filthy little games. Now she had gone too far to pull back, shaken like a rag doll between his hands.

He grew demanding. 'And if I ordered you to have sex with him? Would you obey me?'

'Yes, sir,' she whispered, deeply flushed.

The tingling sensation inside her body grew and intensified as she struggled with that image of herself and Professor Withenshawe, bent over a desk in the

27

lecture hall, skirt bunched up around her waist, accepting the older man's cock inside her sex. It was too horrible to consider, yet she could not help imagining how it might feel . . . the pressure of his cock pushing inside her at last; skin reddened and sore from his tweed jacket rubbing against her buttocks with rhythmic accuracy; those pale hands on either side of her body, supporting his weight on the desk, veins blue and enlarged as the professor thrust determinedly towards a climax; all that spunk trickling like warm porridge down the inside of her thighs; his satisfied grunt, as he tucked a wilting cock back into corduroy trousers.

'That's good. Because you will be expected to fuck on command,' Milton reminded her, breaking sharply into her fantasy, his breath hot on her neck. 'We don't take personal tastes into account, I'm afraid. You'll be there to service the needs of the gentlemen members, regardless of how you may feel about them. Those are the rules.'

He parted her buttocks with both hands as he rode her from behind, one thumb pushing inside the tight hole of her anus and rotating until she squealed with discomfort. The thin skin of her rectal passage stretched to accommodate a finger as well, nerve endings jumping in a series of tiny electric shocks.

'What's the matter, Beth? Does it hurt?' he taunted her, his words deliberately crude. 'Soon you'll be forced to take a man up there. To bend and take his full length up your bumhole. Now that would be a sight worth paying for. It's about time you learned what else that hole's used for beside a good –'

'No!' she cried, twisting in hot-faced shame as her climax approached, desperate not to be reminded of her humiliating position.

Seconds later, Beth heard herself scream with agonised pleasure as her muscles went into spasm around his cock. She pushed back against him instinctively, her tortured bottom still smarting from the repeated spanking he had administered. Groaning somewhere above her, Dr Milton ploughed on towards his own climax with ever harder thrusts. One of his hands pushed her face further into the suffocating depths of the mattress; the other yanked at the black stocking which bound her wrists as though it were the reins of some pony he was riding.

He was about to come, she realised, the blood throbbing between her legs as she experienced wave after wave of intense pleasure. How could she find pain and degradation so exciting? This was her personal tutor, she reminded herself: a selfish and demanding tyrant, using her body without any sign of remorse or compunction. The thought made her reach a second climax, panting and red faced by the time he pulled himself free and forced her on to her back.

With a grunt, his hand jerked painfully on her hair. 'Change of plan,' he said suddenly.

Beth felt herself dragged forwards across the sheets until she was half-kneeling on the floor, leaning back against the bed with her face level with his groin. Her bound arms ached intolerably, still pinioned behind her back. Two or three brief tugs and his cock began to spurt, discharging a hot sticky load directly into her face.

Spunk was dripping like treacle down her flushed cheeks and chin, some of it even finding its way between her breasts. Her sex tingled with a not unpleasant aftershock as she opened her mouth, unprompted, to take his shaft inside and clean it with her tongue. His groan spurred her on to lick harder, even dipping her head to trace a circle around his damp scrotum. She told herself the job was over; she could stop now and ask him to untie her hands. Yet for some reason she was strangely unwilling to bring their game to an end. Beth shivered, aware of his gaze on her face as she licked. This was new and dangerous territory for her, she realised, acting the submissive and enjoying it rather too much.

Eventually he stepped away, indicating that he had finished, and she shifted uncomfortably, unable to raise herself from the bed or wipe his trickling spunk from her face. 'Dr Milton,' she managed to say, still a little breathless. 'My hands –'

He bent at once and turned her, releasing the tight black stocking which had been cutting into her flesh.

'Forgetful of me. But these little props make all the difference, as I'm sure you'll come to appreciate in time.' Dr Milton unfolded his wallet and threw a handful of notes on to the mattress before reaching for his unfinished glass of whisky. 'Buy something less vulgar to wear for our next meeting, and don't worry about the cost. You should find me considerably more generous than Withenshawe.'

Beth felt like a child dismissed from the headmaster's office, as though she had taken her punishment and no longer mattered. Head bent, she slipped back into her bra and fastened her blouse with trembling fingers.

'I have a tutorial with you on Tuesday afternoon,' he reminded her coolly, sipping his whisky as he watched Beth struggle back into her clothes. 'How's the essay going? Did you find those books I lent you useful?'

She nodded mutely, turning to fetch some tissues from the en suite bathroom to wipe the last traces of spunk from her face. Her heart was thudding with an irregular beat as she bent over the bed in her high heels, raked together the banknotes and put them away in her handbag without bothering to count them.

'There's to be a small gathering in a few weeks' time at a country estate on the way to Swindon. Some special friends of mine will be there, members of the Club.' He looked at her over the rim of his whisky glass. 'Would you be willing to accompany me to the meeting?'

'What would I be expected to do?'

'Nothing you can't handle.'

'Spanking?'

'I imagine so.'

She bit her lip. 'You mentioned caning before.'

'Yes, you'll probably face the cane at some point. But nothing would be done without your consent. We're not savages.'

Dr Milton finished his whisky and began to tidy his own clothes in an unhurried fashion, shrugging back into his shirt and tucking it into his trousers with neat careful gestures.

'So you'll come then, Beth?'

Three

'And can I have a new leather harness, too?' Charlotte asked her master, eyes shining with pleasure as she turned to admire her own reflection in the fitting-room mirror. 'To match the hoof boots?'

Milton smiled at his pony girl indulgently. 'That depends on how well you suck Fargher's cock when he returns.'

High above their heads, the ceiling creaked, reminding them that business continued as normal in the hushed and exclusive atmosphere of Fargher's, the men's outfitters on the floor above. Little did the tourists and customers know that beneath the polished floorboards lay a hidden room, accessible only to those wishing to purchase specialist equipment like the hoof boots they had come to collect today. It amused Milton to think that the majority of the staff knew nothing about this private fitting room. Only Fargher himself and a few of his senior sales assistants ever came down to the basement or were allowed access to its storeroom of pony accessories.

She tossed her thick blonde plait in disdain. 'Oh, not again. One of these days I'll give that creepy old bastard a heart attack.'

'Watch your tongue,' he told her lazily. 'You really should be grateful I allow you to speak at all. Other trainers aren't so lenient with their ponies. One more disrespectful comment like that and you'll be nursing a very sore bottom indeed.'

'Promises, promises!'

Milton fixed his pony girl with a stern eye, raising the crop by his side in a threatening manner, and saw that mischievous grin fade to a more submissive expression.

'Perhaps I should have brought the bit gag to keep you quiet,' he commented dryly. 'Now stop bitching and let's see how you handle a trot in those boots. They're rather steeper than your last pair. We wouldn't want you to take a spill at the races, would we?'

It was quite true: he ought to have brought the bit gag today and silenced the little minx. But it amused him to let her rattle on in that impertinent way, even if it did make his hand itch to punish her. Charlotte was the sort of naughty outspoken blonde it was difficult not to spank or beat at every opportunity. Keeping her gagged like a dumb pony would spoil his fun.

Milton surveyed her from his seat as she trotted neatly round the fitting room in nothing but plain white underwear and hoof boots. Public school to the hilt, front teeth still delightfully restrained by a brace, Charlotte was in her final year at university and looking forward to a highly paid job in the City. In spite of his often-stated belief that a trainer should never get too involved with his ponies, he was going to miss Charlotte when she left Oxford. For nearly three years now, she had kneeled or bent or trotted on command, gradually transformed before his eyes from an inexperienced fresher to this charmingly rude young woman, and it was hard to imagine anybody replacing Charlotte's firm mouth and fleshy rump. However, Beth had shown genuine signs of potential the other night, however much the younger student had tried to hide it. His partial erection twitched as he remembered spunking into her face; that startled expression giving way to a pleasing blend of distaste and excitement. Yes, Beth might make an excellent pleasure pony and possibly a useful racer, too. But how would she react when she encountered the more stringent members of the Club?

'Have I ever mentioned a student called Beth?' he asked idly, eyes narrowing on the pony girl's taut calves as she passed, then rising to check that her back was erect and her head held high. 'I'm thinking of training her up as a racer.'

Charlotte glanced at him in the floor-to-ceiling mirror but did not reply for a moment, her pale muscular flanks working steadily. 'I don't think so. Any good?'

'Perhaps. Given a firm enough hand on the reins.'

'Which college is she at?'

'St Nectan's.'

The pony girl paused, giving him an odd look. 'You're going to recruit one of your own students?'

'You sound as though you disapprove. But what better way to keep an eye on her progress than as her personal tutor? It need not compromise my position at the college.'

'Assuming that she's discreet.'

He gave his pony girl an irritable flick with the crop as she trotted past to complete another circuit, her thighs glistening with sweat in the overheated basement room. 'Are you questioning my judgement?' he demanded.

'Of course not.'

'But?'

Charlotte slowed to a walk, her hands falling to her well-rounded hips. He loved to watch the easy roll of

34

her body in motion, breasts bouncing playfully and her sturdy thighs made almost graceful by the high hoof boots. His pony was shrugging now, avoiding his gaze, plainly reluctant to say anything which might anger or offend him. But they had known each other long enough for the mere hesitation in her voice to let him know how she felt.

'But it could be dangerous if she finds the pony play too much of a challenge,' she admitted, then shot him a sideways glance. 'Perhaps I ought to have a word with this girl. Make sure she knows exactly what's involved before you waste any time training her.'

Milton was taken aback by the suggestion, but then grinned as he recognised the feminine bite behind her words. His number-one pony girl was bristling at the thought of relinquishing her master to another submissive. Her status as his favourite had been hard won, of course, he reminded himself. It was only natural she should be a little proprietorial towards him now that her time at Oxford was nearly over and he was searching for a new protégée to replace her.

'You're jealous, aren't you?'

Charlotte tossed her blonde plait over one shoulder, not bothering to respond, though the pout on her face was confirmation enough.

'You've absolutely no reason to be,' he told her, smiling. 'Though I am rather touched. I had no idea you were so attached to me, Charlotte. I ought to punish you for it, of course. It's quite against Club rules for a submissive to display jealousy.'

'Whatever pleases you,' she muttered, turning to present him with her firm behind, cheeks straining at the plain white panties.

His cock stiffened automatically. It was a sight he found hard to resist, as his pony knew only too well.

The sound of footsteps descending slowly from the shop above interrupted them, followed by a creak as the basement door opened. Milton lowered the crop warily, his eyes on the door, but it was only Fargher returning, a small leather case tucked under one arm. Milton decided to postpone Charlotte's punishment for the moment and motioned her to relinquish her submissive pose, bending to present her bottom so invitingly to the crop. It was a shame but he did not have time today for such delights.

Perhaps guessing that he had interrupted something, the thin-lipped tailor looked across at them with an apologetic smile. 'Terribly sorry for the delay, sir,' Fargher remarked, locking the basement door behind him. 'One of my colleagues had mistakenly stored the box in the sporting goods section. But I'm sure there will be something here to suit your particular need.'

Fargher placed the leather case on the floor beside Milton's chair, unlocking it with a reverent touch. His air of discreet professionalism remained unaltered as he removed an assortment of butt plugs specially designed to resemble horses' tails, displaying a selection of them along his sleeve as though they were silk ties.

'Do any of these take your fancy, sir? They are all made of genuine horsehair, of course. And we can have them altered if the fit is imperfect, at no extra charge.'

Milton frowned, tapping a particularly luxuriant-looking tail. 'This one, perhaps. Though the length seems a little extravagant.'

'I'm afraid so, sir. I have it on the very best authority that ponies are wearing their tails long this season. We are honoured to supply five counties from this shop, as you probably know, including some of the foremost riders in the land.'

'I bow to your superior knowledge,' Milton said and shrugged, slapping the crop against the side of his chair. 'Bend over for the gentleman, Charlotte, and allow him to check the fit. I have a two o'clock tutorial which I can't miss.'

The pony girl stepped out of her panties and adopted the correct position, hands placed on her knees as she bent forwards from the waist, back straight and her feet wide apart. Fargher greased the butt plug with a little pot of transparent lubricant and approached her, manoeuvring it between her cheeks. The plug was evidently on the large side, for the man paused in his task and gave a discreet cough. Charlotte raised her bottom even higher to facilitate its insertion, a choked gasp her only reaction as the tail slid snugly into position.

'A fine specimen, sir. In her last year here?'

'Unfortunately, yes.'

The tailor sighed and straightened, taking a few steps back to gaze appreciatively at Charlotte's hind quarters. 'Such a pity to lose her. But no doubt you have another filly in training for next season?'

Milton raised his eyebrows at the question and remained silent, not sure he wished to satisfy the man's curiosity. Training was strictly a personal matter, to be kept between master and pony wherever possible. Besides which, it was a well-known fact that Fargher had several other clients within the university who might benefit from learning their rivals' plans in advance.

Wisely, the tailor decided not to pursue the matter, producing a handkerchief to clean the grease from his fingers. 'If I could ask you to trot the pony about the fitting room? We'll have a better idea of the tail's suitability once she's in motion.'

Milton gave the command and watched his pony girl move into a brisk trot, horsehair tail protruding from her anus and swishing proudly against her buttocks and thighs at every step. The tailor might be an impudent bastard but he was right about one thing: Charlotte was indeed a magnificent specimen, well-developed leg muscles moving in harmony as she paraded about the room, that elaborate blonde plait bouncing rhythmically between her shoulder blades. It was pointless to mourn the end of her tenure as his pony girl. If everything went according to plan, he would soon be trotting another student about this fitting room in her place, and it was always a pleasure to train a young pony, especially one as shy and inexperienced as Beth. Though that did not mean he should waste any of these last precious weeks with such an exemplary submissive.

'Enough,' he said sharply. 'We'll take it, Fargher. And perhaps a new harness, too, on the usual terms?'

The tailor looked up at once from his task of returning ponytails to their leather case, a smile playing on those thin lips. 'That would be most satisfactory, sir.'

Fargher fetched a new leather harness from the storeroom, slipping it expertly around Charlotte's ample hips and breasts. After adjusting the straps until they fitted perfectly, the tailor suggested that the pony girl should perform a few basic show steps so he could check the harness for potential areas of chafing. Charlotte's eyes lit up at the idea. She loved to show off her skill to anyone who would watch and slipped into a professional routine straight away, stepping high and long with her customary grace.

The stiff black leather shone beneath her breasts, cupping them but leaving the nipples exposed, a strap running down the back which linked the bodice to a thick band circling her hips. Her sex too was inviting-

38

ly accessible, full shaven lips jiggling as she broke into a complex sideways trot. It was a beautifully designed piece of equipment, Milton thought, relieved that he would not have to pay full price for it. There was even a pair of blinkers and a bit gag to match the body harness, both items connected by long sturdy chains to a training rein, but Milton shook his head when Fargher attempted to fit them, too. It would be a shame to overload his pony with too many chains just at the moment. That sort of discipline could come later.

There was nothing subtle about Charlotte's pussy, Milton thought, smiling to himself. He was experiencing a strong urge to part those lips and bury several of his fingers between them. Most girls seemed much tighter-lipped down there, neatly built with their cunts hidden discreetly from view. Charlotte's sex always looked so swollen, gaping slightly and flushed a dark pink as though she had just taken several men up inside her. It was a provocative mental image.

Milton unzipped his trousers to relieve the growing pressure of his erection and motioned Fargher to do the same, aware that the tailor was also looking distinctly uncomfortable in the groin area. Unlike many of the other trainers, he did not mind sharing his pony with other men. Indeed, it gave him a keen sense of pleasure to watch his girls at work, their mouths bulging with cock while he himself mounted them from behind.

The tailor did not waste any time in coming forwards, his cock already in his hand, eager to claim his reward for that steep price reduction on the harness. A tall man with lanky greying hair slicked across his temples to conceal a receding hairline, his long fingers tilted Charlotte's head back as she knelt before him.

'Most satisfactory, sir,' he repeated, his eyes beginning to glaze as she opened her mouth to receive him.

Positioning himself at the other end, Milton lifted her buttocks to a more accessible height and drew the horsehair butt plug from her anus. It slid out easily enough, still greased with lubricant and smelling deliciously of her own darker juices. His shaft ached to replace it, rigid with anticipation, but he had no intention of spoiling this moment by hurrying. The loosened star of her anus flexed as he used several fingers and a thumb to separate her buttocks, nudging the head of his cock into that cleft until he felt her anus twitch against him.

Her tightness never failed to amaze him, considering how often the girl had been used there. It was only an act of sheer will that held back his orgasm, clamping down on that impulse in spite of her sucking Fargher's cock right in front of him, greedy lips wrapped about that purplish length and her pale skin flushed with arousal. The tailor was groaning now, a look of apprehensive excitement on his face. Milton knew how he felt. It was always an act of faith, feeding the cock gingerly into the depths of her throat and hoping it did not catch against that vicious-looking brace on its way.

Taking a firm purchase on the harness, he began to thrust into her anal passage with slow control, determined not to come before the older man. Charlotte gave a muffled whinny of pleasure as he pushed inside, her whole body arching back against his. She might be more outspoken than the average submissive but that impertinence soon disappeared once she had clicked into the role of pony girl.

Milton settled into a steady unhurried rhythm, relishing the drag of her muscular passage at each withdrawal. Looking down, he saw a familiar stain muddying the base of his shaft and felt her lovely bottom clench hard around him.

'You love it up your arse, don't you?' he taunted her, pushing back inside right up to his balls. 'You're such a greedy slut.'

That answering groan let him know how excited she had become, blonde head still bobbing up and down on Fargher's cock.

He reached down between her thighs, unceremoniously shoving two fingers into her sodden pussy. The full puffy lips enveloped his skin, warm and wet, her soft interior walls sucking him in like a mouth. Charlotte arched gratefully beneath him, making those little strangled noises in the back of her throat that indicated her readiness to come. Milton started to withdraw his fingers, teasing her into thinking he had finished with her. Then he pushed them back inside her pussy as far as they would reach, amused by the way she instantly began writhing and mewling like a cat on heat.

'What's the matter?' he demanded cruelly. 'Can't you speak with a cock in your mouth? Charlotte the Harlot. That's what men should call you, sweetheart. Because that's what you are. A whore with a sticky mouth and a well-used arse.'

The tailor grunted his assent, clamping her head with both hands and holding her still while she sucked.

Milton's fingers drove deeper into the moist heat between her legs, speeding up to match the rhythm of her hips. Realising it would not take much to tip her over the edge, he eased his fingers from her sex and found the swollen hooded bud of her clitoris instead. Rubbing and pinching that taut flesh the way she had shown him, he soon felt Charlotte tense beneath him and guessed that she was about to come. As the orgasm swept through her entire body, he pushed his fingers back inside and smiled at her deep muffled cries.

'I'm going to spunk up inside your arse,' he told her succinctly. 'No holding back, just the way you like it. I hope you brought something to clean yourself with. This is going to be messy.'

But it was the tailor who lost control first, his face clenched in uncharacteristic emotion as he came into the pony girl's throat. It was obvious that the brace on her teeth had not impeded her ability to suck cock. Fargher wrenched his cock free only to spill the remainder of his load over her face and neck, a deep grunt signalling to Milton that he too could finally come.

It gave Milton immense satisfaction to close his eyes and relax into his imminent orgasm. Seconds later, he shot his spunk deep into the girl's bowels and heard Charlotte's piercing cry as she climaxed for a second time, her fleshy bottom backing to meet him.

'Splendidly done,' he muttered afterwards, glancing down as he disengaged himself from that dark puckered entrance. Her skin glistened with the creamy flecks of his come, a sticky trail which had already begun trickling down to her exposed labia. It was a glorious sight which he would not be able to enjoy for very much longer.

Milton raised the crop and slashed her across the buttocks with its thin leather, unmoved by her squeal of surprised pain. A sharp red line with a white halo instantly burst under the skin, the colours growing more intense by the second.

'That was for your impertinent remarks earlier. Or did you think I'd forgotten?'

She was breathless, still recovering. 'No, sir.'

'Perhaps you ought to speak to Beth after all. It would be a pity to waste so much experience,' he conceded, throwing the crop to the floor and casually wiping himself on her discarded panties. 'I'm taking Beth with me to the gathering next week. If she still wants to play the game after that, I'll introduce you to her.'

Charlotte turned to smile up at him, trembling slightly from her exertions, her neck and chin still damp and milky from the other man's spunk. The crop mark across her buttocks was a shocking scarlet weal, weeping at one end where the thickened tip had made contact, yet she did not seem bothered by the pain.

'Sounds like fun,' she purred.

Four

Beth stared out of the car window in an uncomfortable silence. It was raining. Countryside flashed past in the dusk, a patchwork of unfamiliar lanes and fields. Dr Milton was driving beside her, his face preoccupied, listening to some mellow jazz number he had stumbled across on the radio. Beth watched his hands on the wheel, not having a clue where he was taking her and strangely reluctant to ask. She was not even certain yet whether she liked or loathed it, this feeling of helplessness whenever she was in his company, but it prickled constantly at her nerves.

'Is it much further?' she asked.

Dr Milton glanced across at her, his dark eyes secretive. She could not read the expression in them, though he sounded amused. 'What's the matter? Nervous?'

Beth did not reply, fixing her gaze on the road ahead, and heard him laugh under his breath.

Moments later, they turned off the main road through a pair of wrought-iron gates and down a narrow track bordered by thickly planted trees and shrubs. Beth could see a house in the distance now, catching glimpses of its lit windows through gaps in the trees. As they drew closer, she realised that it was a stately Victorian building, a thin smoke rising from one of its many chimneys, the front door standing open as if their arrival had been expected.

Dr Milton pulled up near the side of the house, the tyres grating over the gravel. He switched off the engine and turned to look at her. The car ticked gently as it cooled and she listened to it, averting her gaze. Her tutor's eyes moved over her in silence, examining every detail of the little black dress, neat heels and discreetly muted make-up she had chosen to wear that evening. 'You look very fetching,' he murmured at last. 'It's certainly better than your last outfit. Did you shave yourself according to my instructions?'

'Of course.'

He waited in silence, raising his eyebrows when she did not move. 'Show me, then.'

Trying to appear indifferent, she drew the hem of her dress right up until the shaven lips of her pussy were exposed. Her soft denuded skin felt cool, tingling beneath his gaze. She shivered, relieved to cover herself again when he nodded his approval. There was something disturbing about the way he treated her, as if she were nothing but an object to him, another one of his possessions; and yet she could not deny that she also found it deeply exciting. Sensing a sudden familiar rush of warmth between her legs, she shifted uncomfortably on the leather seats and pressed her bare thighs together. It was no use trying to hide her physical response, though. Milton guessed what was happening and raised one hand to stroke her cheek, smiling dryly.

'There's no reason to feel ashamed of your sexuality,' he told her, and leant across to open the car door as though she were incapable of doing so herself. 'We are all sexual creatures, after all. It's only natural to become aroused when reminded of that fact.'

She began to protest but he laid a finger on her lips. 'No more words tonight, Beth,' he said coolly. 'You are about to enter a world where you are no longer my student but my slave. From now on, you will obey every order and not give me any reason to be embarrassed by your behaviour. Is that clear?'

Her heart thumping, Beth stared at him for a few defiant seconds, tempted to refuse, then gave a brief nod. She was relieved when he leant back, releasing her so that she could escape.

A sombre butler stood in the doorway to the house, waiting for them without comment. He inclined his head when Milton gave his name, silently gesturing them to follow him. The long entrance hall was carpeted in a rich dark red with oil paintings of scantily clad women on the walls and chandeliers burning overhead at intervals. Beth kept her head lowered and walked several steps behind her tutor as they were led down the hall and into a comfortable book-lined room where several other people were already gathered. There was a fire in the hearth, logs cracking quietly and giving out a welcome warmth.

An elderly gentleman rose from a deep leather armchair as they entered the room, a smile on his face. 'My dear Milton,' he said, extending his hand. 'I'm so glad you could make it. Dreadful weather for May.'

'It was a pleasure to be invited, as always.'

The old gentleman nodded and glanced past him at Beth, his smile broadening. 'But I see you have not come here tonight empty-handed. Please do introduce me to this charming young lady.'

Milton ushered her forwards at once, his eyes on her face. 'This is Beth, one of my second years at St Nectan's. She's rather shy, so I've promised her we won't go too fast tonight.'

'Excellent, excellent.'

Taking her hand, the elderly gentleman drew Beth gently towards the fire. She glanced at him, then looked away hurriedly in case he was offended by her scrutiny. This must be the owner of the house whom Milton had mentioned in the car; the retired Dean of her college.

She guessed the man to be in his seventies or early eighties, his face deeply lined and the narrow blue eyes watering slightly as he examined her body in the elegant black dress. He turned his head towards Milton, while continuing to pat her hand as though she were some wild animal he wished to reassure. 'With your permission, might I . . .?'

Her tutor nodded, smiling easily. 'Consider my girls as your own, Thomas. Use them however you wish.'

With a quiet word and a gesture, the elderly gentleman asked her to turn around and Beth obeyed, staring in silence at the wall opposite as his hands lifted her dress. She felt cool air on her buttocks, then the dry touch of his fingers exploring her bottom. In spite of her determination not to betray any emotion, she could not prevent a sharp intake of breath as the old man reached even lower, finding and stroking the shaven lips of her sex.

'Smooth as velvet,' Thomas murmured, his fingers still moving between her thighs. 'I must congratulate you once again, Milton. She's exquisite, another impressive find. And one of your own students, too. Rather daring of you, I must say.'

One of the other men present laughed angrily; facing away from them, Beth could not tell which one.

'Teetering on the edge of the acceptable again, Milton?'

'Not at all, Hughes.'

47

Her tutor's reply seemed bland enough but she sensed irritation behind the polite words. Whoever had spoken, she thought carefully, Milton did not like him very much. There was a tense silence in the room, broken only by the crackling of logs in the fireplace. Before the situation could escalate, however, the old gentleman intervened in a mild voice. 'There's nothing in the rule book to forbid it, Hughes. If Milton considers it safe to recruit from among his own students, then we have to accept his judgement without question. You know the rules.'

Beth trembled, lifting her arms as the former Dean pulled the little black dress up over her neck and removed it. She stood there naked, still facing the wall with her skin cooling, wondering what would happen next. There had been an oddly inflexible note in the old man's voice and for a moment she had thought he was going to punish her straight away, perhaps to prove a point to the unseen Hughes. But she need not have worried. The old gentleman turned her back to face him with a gentle enough hand.

'I would like to show you something, my dear. Go to the bottom drawer of that cabinet and take out the photograph album you'll find there. That's right. Now bring it to me.' He turned irritably to the butler, who was still hovering in the doorway. 'Don't just stand there, Haddon. Fetch drinks for our guests. Some wine for Dr Milton and a glass of chilled lemonade for the young lady.'

She knelt beside the old gentleman, holding out the old Victorian photograph album. Its cover was a burgundy leather, heavily embossed and decorated with a fine silver crest, beneath which was a short phrase in Latin which she could not translate.

Thomas took the album from her and turned the first few pages, careful not to damage the gossamer-

thin protective paper covering each set of photographs. 'This lady was my grandmother,' he murmured, tapping one of the larger photographs. It was
a portrait, cracking at the edges now and printed in
fading sepia, but the gentle eyes and beautiful face
staring out of the photograph at them were clear
enough. 'She reminds me a little of you, my dear.
Such grace and charm; a magnificently submissive
creature.'

The elderly gentleman turned over another few
pages, smiling as he browsed through the photograph
album. 'And here she is again, posing naked for my
grandfather . . . before they were married, too, quite
a shocking thing in those days.'

Beth glanced down at the photographs and her
eyes widened in surprised disbelief. Had they really
done things like that in Victorian times? In one
photograph, his grandmother was completely nude
except for a pair of knee-length boots, smiling into
the camera as she lay back in a large wicker chair
with her legs spread wide. The photograph opposite
showed the same woman bending from the waist in
flagrant invitation, an ornamental fan sticking out of
her fleshy bottom. A few pages further into the
album, she was kneeling on a bed with her head
buried in the crotch of a middle-aged man in military
uniform while another plump-bottomed woman fin-
gered her from behind.

Thomas nodded dryly, watching her face. 'Astonishing what those Victorians got up to behind closed
doors, isn't it? That, I believe, is my great-uncle
Bertram. And his second wife, Eugenie. Just look at
those Rubenesque thighs, that skin. White and flaw-
less as alabaster.'

Milton seemed amused by her discomfort, his voice
ironic. 'Better not show her any more of your

infamous collection, Thomas. You're in danger of scaring the horses.'

'Surely not.'

'Though my adorable little Charlotte wouldn't look out of place in one of your albums.'

The old man's face lit up as he closed the album. 'Oh absolutely, my dear fellow. Do you think she would agree to pose for me before she leaves? Now that would be delightful.'

'Perhaps, perhaps not.' Her tutor lit a cigarette, slipping the lighter back into his pocket with a careless shrug. 'I wish I could say yes. But the girl's a law unto herself, as you know.'

One of the other men stood up, throwing open a window to let the smoke from Milton's cigarette drift from the room. His face seemed tight, possibly even angry, though Beth was not sure why. He was younger than the other men present, possibly in his late twenties, with a neat goatee beard and a single earring. When he finally came forwards into the light, she guessed from his voice that it must be Hughes, the man who had spoken so sharply before. 'Do you know what your problem is, Milton?' There was a sneer in the young man's voice and she suspected that he had been drinking. 'You're far too free with your ponies. Give Charlotte to me for a few weeks and you won't recognise her again. A girl like that needs to be whipped whenever she opens her mouth.'

'Is that so?' Milton smiled dryly. 'No wonder you have such a poor track record for holding on to your ponies.'

'At least I train them to respect their masters.'

'You think mine need to be disciplined?'

'Yes, actually.' Taking Beth's arm in a steel-fingered grip, the younger man dragged her towards him. There was a dangerous light in his eyes and she did not resist, assuming that Milton would step in if the young man hurt her. 'Down on all fours for me, slut. That's right ... head up, arse out, and play the pony.'

He swung his leg across her back and she cried out, feeling his weight come down on her without warning. There was an agonising pain as the young man leant forwards and yanked at her breasts, jerking them back like a pair of reins, his fingers squeezing her nipples. She found herself slapped into motion, her knees scraping the floorboards, her hands scrabbling frantically across the polished wood.

'Giddy-up!' he urged her with cruel slaps. 'Come on, round and round the room we go.'

Milton stubbed out his cigarette, barely looking in their direction. His voice was cold, though, an icy threat behind his words. 'Get off her, Hughes. I don't recall giving you permission to ride my pony.'

'Yes, that's bad form.' The old gentleman had half-risen from his armchair, a look of frowning displeasure on his face. It was obvious that he was shocked rather than impressed by the younger man's behaviour. 'Have you forgotten the rules yourself, Hughes? You heard him; the girl's not ready to be ridden yet. She hasn't even been broken in.'

There were a few tense moments when Beth feared the young man would refuse to get off her back, forcing a confrontation between himself and Milton. She was surprised by her own newfound subservience as she tried to suffer his weight in silence. The hard polished floorboards were hurting her knees; her nipples were smarting from his cruel pinches. Then her tormentor shifted, untangling his fingers from her hair.

'I'm sick of this Club,' Hughes muttered, giving her buttocks a final slap before climbing reluctantly off her back. 'Too many rules and not enough fucking.'

The old gentleman made a noise under his breath. She could not be sure whether it was anger or amusement. Then he rang a small silver hand bell on his side table and waited in silence, only turning his head when a full-breasted blonde appeared in the doorway. 'Ah, Charlotte,' he said pleasantly. 'Do come in. There's a young man here who would like to be entertained.'

The girl entered the room slowly and deliberately, lifting her feet high with every step. She was wearing a complicated-looking black leather outfit in the style of a horse's harness, and nothing else, her pale skin gleaming in the firelight. The harness ran between her thighs and around her breasts, a thin silver chain attached to the neck-band and looped over her arm like a dog lead. The outer lips of her vagina were noticeably shaven, the flesh down there dark pink and gaping, rather like a permanently pouting mouth. And, though she tried hard not to look, Beth could not help noticing how flushed and erect her nipples seemed, both breasts displayed through a cradling gap in the harness.

But it was the boots she was wearing that really caught Beth's attention, each thick wedge heel fashioned in the shape of a hoof. They looked so painfully high it was astonishing the girl could even walk in them. Somebody had gone to a great deal of trouble and expense, she thought, to turn this girl into a pony.

Reaching Hughes's side, the girl lowered herself silently into a kneeling position and offered him the silver chain. The young man did not move at first, looking the blonde pony girl over with grudging admiration. There was a distinct glint in his eye when he finally took the silver chain from her outstretched hand and jerked her forwards. Taken by surprise, the girl overbalanced, nearly hitting her head on the floor. She recovered her composure immediately, though, returning to a kneeling position without even a hint of expression on that calm face. Hughes jerked her forwards again but this time she was ready for him, her blonde head raised proudly, shuffling towards him on her knees.

Hughes looked down at the kneeling girl, his eyes narrowed on her face. 'Tell me, pony. What do you think of your master? Are you satisfied with Dr Milton's training methods? Do you think he disciplines his ponies enough? Feel free to speak.'

There was an angry murmur from some of the other men in the room, but Thomas silenced them with a look. 'We are all agreed that it is highly unorthodox to ask such a question of any pony. But, on this occasion, the pony may answer if she wishes.'

The blonde girl did not alter her gaze, still staring at a fixed point on the far wall as she replied softly, 'Dr Milton is a good master and trainer. We win many events together.'

Clearly infuriated by that reply, Hughes wrenched hard at the silver chain, yanking the girl to her feet. He turned irascibly to one of the men near the fire and demanded a leather belt. Wrapping the broad leather firmly about his wrist, he then struck the pony girl on the thigh with the loose flailing end of the belt and began to drag her around him in a circular motion.

Charlotte appeared to understand what was required of her, only a brief and quickly hidden flicker of pain disturbing her face each time the leather belt snapped across her thighs. She raised her legs high on every step, breaking into a graceful trot as he commanded her to move faster.

As far as Beth could tell, she moved around the room in perfect rhythm and did not make a single mistake. Yet Hughes still seemed dissatisfied with her performance, catching her smartly across the buttocks and thighs every few steps. 'Is that the best your pony can do?' he taunted Milton. 'Perhaps we should organise a private race. Your ponies against mine.'

'I should remind you that private racing is dangerous and against the rules,' the old gentleman said quickly before Milton could answer, shaking his head in a disapproving manner.

'Everything is against the rules according to you,' Hughes muttered irritably. He threw back his head to stare challengingly at Milton. 'If you don't like the idea of risking them in a race, then how about a head-to-head contest? As far as these fancy steps are concerned, my Lizzie could match your Charlotte any day of the week.'

Milton looked on, unmoved. 'She sounds like an excellent filly. You have my congratulations.'

'Coward,' the young man said deliberately, watching him.

Lurching to his feet, Thomas clapped his hands and the blonde stopped dead as if at some previously arranged signal, her chest heaving and her full buttocks shiny with perspiration. The old gentleman lifted the polished stick he had been leaning on and pointed unequivocally towards the door. 'I think both you and young Charlotte should adjourn to the playroom,' he said sternly to the young man. 'Try to release some of your aggression, Hughes, before it gets you into trouble.'

Hughes looked back at him, his mouth tight. But he did not argue, using his leather belt to drive the pony girl towards the door. There was already a cruel bulge in the front of his trousers and Beth shivered as she imagined what he might do to the blonde once he was alone with her. Hughes was aroused by forcing girls to submit, she thought, even though it was not always necessary in a place like this. Charlotte, for instance, seemed content enough to submit without being prompted to do so. Hughes, however, was the sort of man who would probably not be happy until he had made her cry.

If the blonde girl belonged to Dr Milton, why was he allowing a man like that to take her away? Beth glanced up at her tutor and was surprised to see a look of controlled rage on his face. Milton was not at all happy with the situation. But he did not protest or argue, those heavy lids drooping down to hide the expression in his eyes as he watched Hughes lash the blonde pony from the room.

'Now where has little Beth gone?' Thomas asked as the door closed behind them, turning his head to look for her.

Beth rose from the floor, where she had been crouching ever since Hughes attacked her, and approached the old gentleman with a shy smile on her face. She was beginning to quite like the former Dean. He might not be as sexy and attractive as Dr Milton, but at least he had not been cruel to her.

'So now you know how it feels to be a pony girl. Was that your first time on your hands and knees?' He stroked her hair, his tone coaxing and gentle. 'Come, don't be afraid to tell old Thomas the truth. Did you enjoy being ridden like that, carrying a man bareback?'

These were not the sort of questions she had expected from him. Beth swallowed and shook her head, staring down at the floor in sudden acute embarrassment. The old gentleman put his fingers between her naked thighs and brought them out slick from her arousal. His voice became harder, almost frightening. 'Don't lie to me, Beth. It's insulting.'

'I'm sorry, sir.'

He slapped her face lightly, using only the tips of his fingers. She could smell her own arousal on them. It did not really hurt but the shock made her gasp.

'Silly, silly girl. You are not permitted to speak except to answer a direct question. Had you forgotten?'

Beth opened her mouth, then shut it again in confusion, unsure whether she would be slapped again if she answered or whether a simple yes was permitted.

'I shall have to punish you now,' the old gentleman sighed. 'Go to the cabinet and open the top drawer this time. Inside, you'll find a long red case. Bring it to me.'

When she'd obeyed, having hurried in case she offended him any further, Thomas opened the case and removed an old-fashioned wooden ruler and a cane. Much to her relief, he laid the wicked-looking cane on the desk behind him without giving it a second glance.

'Would you mind holding out your right hand, my dear? Palm upwards, with your arm bent at the elbow.'

Innocently, she held out her hand as though demonstrating that it was clean and could hardly believe it when he raised the wooden ruler and brought it down with a resounding slap across her palm. Yelping and hopping with pain, Beth snatched back her hand and rubbed it against her side. Her skin stung like mad where the ruler had landed, though she was not sure which was worse, the pain itself or the shock of the unexpected blow. Still wincing, she gave the old gentleman a look of hurt betrayal but dared not say anything aloud. Dr Milton was watching too closely and she might face an even greater punishment if she angered him by speaking out of turn again.

'Now the other hand, please.'

Her face must have been scarlet, she was breathing so hard as she held out her left hand and felt Thomas bring the wooden ruler smartly down across her palm.

Hissing wordlessly, her eyes brimming with tears, Beth tucked both hands under her arms in an instinctive attempt to relieve the pain. Her skin was on fire, both palms throbbing right through from the tips of her fingers to the fleshy mound above her wrist. Yet, within seconds of that initial shock receding, she felt an odd tingling sensation between her legs and was horrified to realise that she was aroused, the tops of her thighs rapidly becoming damp as her sex began to leak warm fluid.

'I know it hurts,' he said mildly and turned to pick up the cane, flexing it between his hands. 'But you must learn your place. Now bend over the desk for me, with your legs slightly apart and your bottom raised. Come along, don't make me wait.'

As if in a trance, Beth found herself complying automatically. She bent over the desk as he had instructed her, hands gripping the sides for support, breasts squashed against the polished walnut surface. Seconds later, she heard Milton cross the room, placing her legs further apart. There was something oddly reassuring about the touch of his hands and she relaxed a little, less apprehensive about the pain to come. She wondered how long it would take before she became as compliant and submissive as Charlotte. The other girl had looked so impressive in her black leather harness and hoof boots that Beth had felt almost envious watching her perform for the men.

'According to the rules of our Club, a submissive may not speak in the presence of her masters without

57

permission.' The old gentleman positioned himself behind her, his voice growing stern. 'Taking into account that this is your first offence, I shall administer only three strokes of the cane today. Another time, I will not be so lenient.'

She had begun to tremble at his words, her eyes fixed on shadows thrown by the firelight. Then Milton spoke, somewhere close behind her. 'Since she is not permitted to cry out, perhaps a gag would be appropriate?'

There was a muted consultation among the men, then one of the other members came forwards and lifted her chin, pushing a length of some velvety material into her mouth. She caught a brief glimpse of his face, bearded and impassive, a man in his late fifties. Then he turned away and she was alone again, staring ahead.

She did not hear the first stroke coming and jerked in pure shock, her cry muffled by the velvet gag.

'One,' the old gentleman intoned, no hint of remorse in his voice as she writhed helplessly against the desk.

The second stroke came almost immediately, exploding across her bottom with terrible accuracy. This time she was more prepared for it, biting down on the gag and raising herself on tiptoe as if that might help her escape the pain. Through a blur of tears, Beth stared at the men's shadows on the wall and heard the old gentleman count the second stroke aloud. The men in the room had fallen silent, no doubt watching the weals beginning to form on her white skin.

As the third stroke of the cane cracked across her buttocks, far harder than the two preceding ones; a seductive heat stirred between her thighs, taking Beth's mind off the pain and driving a hot embarrassed colour into her face.

'Three,' Thomas concluded, moving round to stand in front of her. He removed the gag and held out the cane, his tone unequivocal. 'Now demonstrate your consent by kissing the cane.'

Dry mouthed, she touched her lips to the thin wood, too ashamed to lift her head any further to look at him.

Milton raised her from the desk with a gentle hand, wiping the tears from her cheeks and unclenching her tight fists. He stared down into her face for a few minutes, as though assessing her state of mind, then gave an abrupt nod. 'That was well handled, considering it was your first time under the cane. I'm proud of you.'

Such praise was unexpected and she flushed with pleasure, looking away before he guessed how much it meant to her. Her legs were shaking so hard now she could barely stand.

He led her across to the leather armchair but advised her not to sit down, because of the painful streaks across her bottom, telling her to lean on it instead. Beth laid her face against the smooth antique leather back and closed her eyes, incredibly aware of the other men watching every movement of her nude body, that air of tense arousal in the room. She was on display, placed here by her tutor for the others to admire and covet, like some slave up for auction. Curiously enough, it was not an unpleasant thought.

After a pause, she felt Milton tread silently behind her. Before she realised what was happening, something soft and heavy had been placed over her head, drawn down to cover her face and throat.

The firelight and the book-lined room disappeared, to be replaced by a glimmering darkness broken only by the occasional glimpse of moving shadows. It was a hood, she realised, as she turned her head from one side to the other in an effort to see. There was no constriction, as the thick black material hung loosely enough, yet she still found herself panicking.

'Don't upset yourself,' her tutor murmured soothingly, his fingers stroking down her spine in an unexpected caress. 'You will soon adjust to the hood.'

'I'm scared,' she whispered.

'That's perfectly normal. Deep breaths, Beth, don't tense up. If you are relaxed enough, the hood will enhance your pleasure.'

To Beth's surprise, he seemed to be right. As Milton continued to stroke her skin, her body gradually became limp under his fingers and she felt her jaw slacken, the panic beginning to recede as her breathing slowed.

'That's better,' Milton said, raising her with firm hands. There was a curious note in his voice as he stepped away, leaving Beth alone in the centre of the room, nude and hooded. 'Hooded, perhaps you'll be more prepared to shed your inhibitions.'

Five

'Raise your arms above your head.'

Beth obeyed, not recognising the deep voice, but guessing it must belong to one of the two men who had led her through the labyrinthine corridors of the mansion to this room. She could not see anything, still hooded and in darkness. These men who had taken her away from Milton must be able to see every bare inch of her body, she thought, blushing fiercely. Although it was May and only a little chilly, there was no warming fire in this room and she shivered, wishing that she could cover her nudity.

It had not really occurred to her, when she first agreed to become a member of Milton's Club, that she would find herself alone with other men at any point. For some reason, she had always assumed that Milton would be with her, either joining in or watching from a distance. It was disturbing, standing here naked with two anonymous men whose faces she could not even see because of the hood.

Male hands snapped a pair of cold metal restraints on her wrists, securing her in that position, arms high above her head and her breasts lifted into prominence by the arch of her shoulder blades. This man's voice seemed rougher than the other, as though he were a smoker. 'Now spread your legs and let the bar take your weight.'

She must have been secured to some kind of bar above her head, she realised, racked up precariously on to tiptoe as they adjusted its height. Beth heard the dull clank of metal against metal, her arms beginning to ache almost immediately. Discomfort made her panicky. How long would she be left hanging there? All evening? All night?

One of the men kicked her feet further apart and the bar above her head danced violently, presumably attached to the ceiling by the chains she could hear rattling. Beth gave a high worried cry, struggling to keep her balance, and was rewarded with a slap across her buttocks.

'Stop being a drama queen and settle down.' The man with the smoker's voice sounded impatient as he adjusted the restraints on her wrists. 'Thomas may believe in going slow with new recruits but I don't see any point in that crap. Why pretend it's easy when it's not? Better to show you straight off what's expected. Then you can decide whether to stay or drop the whole thing before you get in too deep.'

Her feet almost slithered on the polished wooden floor as the bar danced sideways yet again. This time she tensed her calves and buttocks, managing to maintain her balance until the swaying stopped.

'That's it,' the other man murmured approvingly, close by her ear. His hands moved over the clenched muscles of her bottom with long smooth strokes, making it hard for her to concentrate. 'Go with the restraints, not against them. Make them your friend.'

Beth tried to do what he suggested and found that it did actually help. His hands were warm against her cool skin, surprisingly gentle as he traced the outline of her hips and buttocks. Becoming aroused, she fought against the mental image of what he might be planning to do with her. It was one thing to perform sexually for her lecturers, but quite another to allow herself to be treated like a plaything by strangers. She felt horribly vulnerable in this position, held captive in an unseen room by these two men, hooded and dangling from a metal bar in front of them like a piece of meat.

Dr Milton was her personal tutor, though, she reminded herself sternly, and would never do anything to put her in danger. He had told her to expect some frightening moments tonight. This was just one of them and she would have to bear it until it was over.

The warm hands dropped away and for a few moments Beth hung there in silent anticipation, her skin rising in goose pimples. Hooded, she could not see what they were doing and had to strain her ears instead. There was a swift muttered conference between the two men, followed by heavy footsteps crossing the floor, the creak of a wooden drawer as it was opened and shut, and then an odd leathery sound like dust being shaken off a piece of thick material.

She frowned as the one with the rough voice came back to her side, still making that odd rustling noise. What on earth was he doing?

'Do you know what a tawse is?'

Beth stiffened at his words, suddenly remembering an old black-and-white film she had seen where a gipsy girl was stripped to the waist and held between two men while a third flogged her back. That had been a tawse in his hand, she seemed to recall, a terrifying instrument with split ends rather like a snake's tongue. She had watched that scene as a young girl with a sense of horrified fascination, trying to imagine how it would feel to face such a cruel punishment herself and never dreaming that one day she might genuinely have to.

'A sort of whip?'

'Yeah, sort of,' the man said grudgingly, though there was a jeer in his voice. Something was brushed back and forth across her bottom, feeling thicker and more solid than she had expected, more like a broad leather belt than a whip. 'It's a bit of an old-fashioned punishment, getting the tawse. I remember they used to have it in secondary schools, quite a regular thing for the smokers and the kids who missed lessons. Did you ever get the tawse, Simon?'

Simon, the younger man, sounded amused. 'Before my time, I'm afraid. Though I would have liked to see that at my school, especially with some of the girls.'

'They didn't tend to give it to girls ... not the tawse, anyway.'

Simon had cupped her breasts in his hands and was now pinching and squeezing them, standing so close she could smell his aftershave. 'What a pity. It's such a delicious sight, watching girls dance and cry out as it lands. Those little hands, clutching their bottoms –'

'You're getting me worked up now,' the other man said thickly. 'Stand clear, I'm going to give her a couple of whacks.'

'You carry on. I'll be fine where I am.' His long clever fingers caught her nipples and twisted them, bringing the dusky-pink centres to an embarrassing erection. His voice dropped lower and he spoke to her alone. 'Let your body hang limp; don't waste your energy fighting the pain. It will only detract from your pleasure.'

Not daring to speak, even if only to beg them not to hurt her, Beth pressed her lips tightly together under the black hood. He need not worry that she was too scared to enjoy herself. She had been warned this might happen if she joined the Club, being touched and punished by complete strangers. It had all seemed cold and rather perfunctory in her imagination. But now that she was hanging here naked, unable to see a thing, one man pinching her nipples and another preparing to beat her with a leather strap, her sexual excitement was only too real.

She felt fluid oozing like tears from her pussy and blushed a fiery red, wondering if they could see her shame, had already guessed how those damp shaven lips longed to be parted and filled. Dr Milton had not exaggerated, she thought dizzily. This was a far cry from sucking off elderly lecturers in return for pocket money.

As if sensing her thoughts, Simon slipped a few exploratory fingers between her legs and exclaimed at what he found there. 'Jesus, she's soaking down there,' he told the other man over her shoulder, wiping stained fingers on her inner thigh. 'This little slut is absolutely soaking. I think she deserves more than a couple of strokes for that, don't you?'

'Filthy bitch,' the other man croaked, laughing in agreement. 'I was only going to give her three, but since she's enjoying the idea so much –'

Beth had not expected the man to strike at that exact moment, foolishly imagining there would be some additional warning beforehand, a word or maybe a gesture, something to indicate she should ready herself for the pain. But there was no warning at all. The tawse slammed into her bottom with an enormous crack like someone banging the Bible shut and she jerked violently against her restraints, giving such a shriek of agonised shock it must have echoed all over the mansion house. The fingers pinching her nipples were torn away as she danced on tiptoe, rattling the metal bar and chains above her raised arms and gasping at the air like a landed fish.

'Steady,' Simon said reassuringly, catching her and turning her back to face him. 'Don't panic.'

She trembled uncontrollably under his hands, suddenly wishing Milton were there to rescue her. Her mouth opened to beg them not to continue, then she realised that would only mean she received further punishment for speaking without permission, and shut it again. Her bottom throbbed terribly. She clenched the muscles, trying to shake the pain away by jiggling her thighs and stepping rhythmically up and down on the spot, but it was no use.

'Hurts, doesn't it?' It was the rough-voiced one who had spoken. She heard him flicking the tawse lightly against his palm. There was a hint of a cruel smile in his voice. 'It's a pity you can't see yourself. That first mark's coming up a treat, a lovely deep cherry red right across the fleshy part of your arse.'

She yelped as the tawse slapped into her soft flesh again, wincing and wriggling as she tried desperately to recall how many strokes there would be. What had the man said? Three strokes? Or was it to be more, to punish her for getting so excited?

It must have been more than three, Beth quickly realised, as the third stroke landed forcefully on her backside and a fourth followed it almost immediately. There were real tears in her eyes now. She swayed like a sapling in the wind as the next few blows landed, and she was flushed and breathless under her hood, glad these men could not witness the humiliation on her face.

'Hold on,' Simon muttered after about the sixth stroke. 'I'd better check how she's coming along down there.'

He reached between her parted thighs and stroked the sodden flesh with an adept finger. That finger knew what it was doing, Beth thought grimly, trying not to react as it flicked deliberately at her clitoris a few times, then burrowed deeper between her lips, rooting for the tight little entrance to her pussy. After finding it without any trouble at all, the finger pushed its way inside. Judging by the ease with which Simon's finger entered her, she was even looser and wetter than before the beating started. The flush in her cheeks deepened and she let a little moan escape, her hips moving against him of their own accord as if she was begging for sex. It was so embarrassing, she wished she could die.

'I don't know what to do now,' Simon said, laughing as he withdrew his finger and wiped it along her heaving belly this time. 'Paste her a bit longer and see how much wetter she can get, or cut the trollop down now and give her a good fucking.'

The tawse thwacked against her aching skin again, harder than ever before, and she cried aloud.

'I say keep beating her,' the older man said, a little out of breath. 'It won't do her any harm to learn her place.'

'Shall we toss a coin to decide?'

'Yeah, why not?'

There was a brief silence, followed by a rustling sound behind her, then the unmistakable sound of loose change clinking in somebody's pocket.

Simon dropped his hands from her tingling flesh and stepped round her, his voice brisk. 'Heads we carry on with the tawse, tails we fuck her, OK?'

'Sounds right to me.'

With her heart thudding against her ribs, Beth listened as they tossed the coin in the air, hearing it slapped down on the back of someone's hand. Simon gave an abrupt laugh, close to her ear. 'Sorry, darling. Heads it is,' he said dryly, turning to flick her nipple with one cruel fingertip. 'Looks like the gods have decided not to reward us for all this hard work.'

'And heads was . . .?'

'The tawse.'

'Oh fuck it.' The man with the rough voice ran his hands less than gently over her stinging buttocks, making her wince. 'OK, why don't we swap ends then? You give her the pasting and I'll stop her jumping all over the shop. Dirty little bitch can't keep still to save her life. Who brought her in?'

'Dr Milton.'

'Trust him to pick the difficult ones. Charlotte was just the same on her first night, kept begging us to hit her harder.'

There was a smile in the younger man's voice. 'I remember.'

'She was a peach.'

'Yeah, she knew how to take it.'

'Eager little bitch.'

'Such a sweet mouth, too,' Simon reminisced, walking around Beth's helpless suspended body. 'Hot as an oven. It was impossible to choose which to use first that night . . . cunt or mouth.'

'I had her arse.'

'You always were a dirty bastard!'

Beth shivered, listening to them talk as they swapped positions, the younger man testing the tawse against something hard nearby, the seat of a chair, or perhaps a table top? The noisy thwack made her jerk in her restraints, tensed in anticipation of the next blow colliding with her flesh. The older man was by her side in an instant. Rough callused hands steadied her body as she swayed uneasily from side to side, the high arch of her feet burning as she attempted to correct her position, straining on tiptoe for balance.

So Charlotte had suffered this punishment, too? And had actually begged them to hit her harder, in spite of the Club ban on girls speaking without permission? Beth could not imagine behaving like that, and certainly not wanting to be hit any harder. Her respect for the blonde grew immeasurably.

Simon had a harder hand than the older man. Oddly enough, she had not expected that. His first blow knocked her sideways, the air expelled violently from her lungs. Before she had time to recover, he struck again, contacting the soft tender flesh just below her buttocks and sending an electric shock through her body.

She yelped unashamedly, twisting against the restraints in a desperate effort to escape the next blow, and felt the older man's hand part her shaven lips and locate her clitoris. The hot fleshy bud was erect with excitement. He pinched it between forefinger and thumb, laughing out loud, as she cried and whimpered with a sudden painful desire, her neck too weak to support her head any more so that she was actually leaning against her own upstretched arm.

'Once more,' the older man urged Simon, joking as he squeezed her imprisoned clitoris. 'With feeling.'

The tawse made a scary whooshing noise as it came flying down towards her through the pitch black of the hood, so that she could hear even if not actually see it coming. Her buttocks clenched tight against the impact, her body trembling, her sex embarrassingly slippery and aching with the need to be filled.

Then it struck and the pain scorched across her skin in a rippling heat trail that reached right down to the balls of her feet. Her clitoris contracted with fierce pleasure as the older man pinched down hard on it at the same time. The cry in the back of her throat shot out like a shriek in the night, a thin cat's shriek as somebody treads on its tail, making both men laugh. She hated their callous laughter, imagining how she must look to them, her poor tortured bottom on show, each red strip of the tawse gradually merging with the others to leave her skin glowing and on fire.

The beating continued for some time, even the men losing track of the number of strokes she had taken, only pausing at one point when a door somewhere behind her opened and she heard a rustling sound and murmuring voices as several others entered the room.

Beth was shaking and panting like a racehorse by the time she was eventually released from the metal restraints above her head. She slumped forwards on to the floor, tearful and with her shoulders and upper back aching from holding the same position for so long. Yet, in spite of the dreadful discomfort she had suffered, she was still oddly frustrated, her physical needs unsatisfied.

On her hands and knees on the wooden floor-boards, she felt a firm pair of hands lift her head. The hood was dragged off without warning and she blinked, her eyes taking a few seconds to adjust to the low lighting. There was a table lamp directly ahead of her, even its soft glow intrusive after the uniform darkness of the hood. The man who had released her crouched down and put a glass to her lips.

Unthinking, her mouth like dust, she took an eager gulp. The taste of it made her gag and recoil, pushing the hateful stuff away as brandy dribbled from the corners of her mouth.

'Drink it,' he insisted, holding her chin between harsh fingers and tilting the glass against her lips.

Dazed, Beth recognised the voice and turned slowly towards him, forgetting the rule about not speaking without permission. 'Dr Milton?' she said hoarsely. 'Does this mean it's over? Are you going to take me home now?'

'Not yet.' Milton sounded as uncompromising as ever, though his smile reassured her a little. 'You're doing beautifully, Beth. There's no reason to take you home. Do I take it you aren't enjoying our little initiation ceremony?'

'No ... yes ... I mean –' She accepted another sip of the revolting brandy, letting it warm her throat with its fiery liquid. The heat seemed to give her new courage and she thanked him, her voice husky. 'I mean I'm not sure.'

Her tutor watched her, a sardonic gleam in the dark eyes as he noted her trembling limbs and flushed cheeks. 'Confusing, isn't it? You hate it and yet it releases you.'

'Yes,' she breathed, knowing exactly what he meant.

Milton stood up, nodding to the two men who had strung her up from the ceiling and beaten her. 'Thanks for your help,' he said casually. 'You can go now. We'll take it from here.'

The two men gathered their things and left the room, barely even bothering to glance at her on their way out. Simon, the younger one, was blond and slim hipped, not much older than a graduate student; and the rough-voiced one looked about thirty, swarthy and with colourful tattoos on his arms and the backs of his hands. She suspected the older one must work at one of the colleges, probably as a groundsman or an odd-job man. They had done their job here tonight and were leaving. She wondered whether they ever got frustrated, knowing she would happily have taken either of them in her mouth or pussy after they had finished beating her. But perhaps they would get their reward in another room, perhaps with the full-breasted Charlotte or one of the other girls she had seen that evening.

There was a movement behind her and Beth saw a pair of highly polished black shoes step round in front of her. It was Thomas. Looking up, she met the old gentleman's serious gaze.

'This must have been a long evening for our new initiate,' Thomas murmured, watching her thoughtfully. 'We don't want to tire the poor girl out on her first visit here. How do you feel, my dear? Are you able to continue?'

Beth nodded silently, grateful for Milton's firm grip on her waist as she stumbled to her feet.

'Very well,' Thomas said calmly. 'Then I think it's about time you were penetrated.'

With careful hands, the old gentleman turned her to face the wall and drew in his breath, a note of admiration in his voice. 'Well, young lady, I'm looking at your bottom and I must say the tawse has marked you quite magnificently. Such brilliant ruby speckling. Its red stripes complement the thinner strokes of the cane superbly.'

She flushed, heat stirring between her thighs as she met Milton's eyes and saw the expression of lazy desire on his face.

'In my experience,' Thomas continued cheerfully, 'this sort of pain gives females an appetite for sex which they would otherwise not enjoy. Don't you agree, Milton?'

Her tutor smiled dryly. 'These days, the majority of females seem to enjoy an appetite for sex however you treat them. But I'm sure you're right, sir. There is a sense of extremity which accompanies physical pain, and we do tend to want sex more when *in extremis*.'

'Well, I'm certainly of the opinion that such needs should always be assuaged. It would be churlish to leave a young girl like this empty and frustrated.'

The old gentleman's hands moved purposefully to his crotch and Beth watched in stunned silence as he extracted a long pale-skinned cock from a cluster of white hairs, before using both hands to massage it to a semi-erection. He smiled at her encouragingly, nodding to the space in front of his feet. 'I'm going to need a little help with this, I'm afraid,' Thomas murmured, his eyes moving over her nudity. 'If you wouldn't mind taking this old bone in your mouth and giving it the kiss of life.'

Aching from the tawse but still prepared to be obedient, Beth kneeled and accepted the old gentleman's cock between her lips. Sliding her mouth back and forth on his shaft, she was surprised by the unexpected smoothness of his skin, so wrinkled elsewhere on his ageing body. His cock lay firm and heavy on her tongue, patches of discoloured skin stretching as it grew even larger under her licking and sucking.

The excitement she had been suppressing all evening began to flicker into life again. A warm familiar moisture dampened her pussy lips and the tops of her inner thighs; it would not be long before she needed sex, the satisfaction of being spread and entered. It had been exciting to perform fellatio on Professor Withenshawe in the public lecture hall, and to let Milton use her in the hotel room, his casual brutality like nothing she had ever experienced before. But she had never had sex with a man of Thomas's age, a man in his late seventies, and the idea filled her with sudden heated arousal.

Her eyes began to close, her mouth still working diligently on his cock, and she allowed herself to imagine how it would feel to have the old gentleman inside her. Would she need to be on top, crouching over his body so that he did not become tired? Or would Thomas have enough stamina to fuck her in the missionary position, or perhaps even from behind, pushing inside with the ease of a man half his age? His rapidly thickening member would certainly have no trouble penetrating her, Beth thought, flushed with desire.

Thomas was clearly thinking along the same lines, pulling her away by her hair. 'That's enough now, don't want to jump the gun,' he muttered, slightly breathless. The old gentleman clutched at the descending waistband on his trousers, shuffling across towards a large leather sofa. 'Better hop up on this sofa for me. On your hands and knees at the far end, facing the mantelpiece. Good girl, that's the way. Now spread your legs nice and wide so I can fit between them.'

The leather sofa creaked under their combined weight, its cushions shifting slightly, and Beth had to adjust her position to give him the best possible chance of mounting her. Out of the corner of her eye, she saw Milton moving quietly behind them and felt the heat flare in her face with sensual longing, suddenly wishing her tutor would join them for a threesome.

The old gentleman was not as timid with her as she had expected. If anything, he seemed to be in a hurry. His hands stung like crazy, fondling her striped and burning bottom before reaching down to find the entrance to her pussy. With any other man, she might have been tempted to reach back and guide him into her. But she suspected that Thomas would not welcome her help.

The fat tip of his cock prodded against her lips urgently, and her mouth opened in a soft moan as she leant forwards on her elbows to allow him better access. She had been waiting to be entered all evening. The old gentleman's hands shook as he gripped her hips, then with a grunt and a good hard shove he was right up inside her, the withered thighs pressing against her bottom as he began to thrust.

She felt a hand under her chin and looked up into Milton's dark mocking gaze. Her personal tutor raised his eyebrows, presumably noting her flushed cheeks and moist parted lips. 'You never cease to amaze me, Beth. How foolish to assume that to-night's beatings would reduce you to a quivering mess. Are you always this eager to get fucked?'

By way of reply, Beth kept her eyes on his face and let her tongue run slowly around her lips. It was a blatant invitation to sex and they both knew it. The sofa creaked rhythmically beneath her hands and knees as she swayed back and forth, her breasts continuously brushing the cool leather. She saw Milton's face darken, a hard flush coming into his cheeks, and knew that he had become abruptly excited.

Dropping her eyes deliberately to his crotch, she watched the material strain as his cock stiffened under her glance. Milton unzipped his trousers and pulled free his cock, its purplish head shiny and tense. His eyes glittered down at her: strange, dark, hypnotic. Without a word, she let her lower jaw drop open and raised her head for his cock.

Milton stepped forwards and she felt the thick head push against her lips. Staring into the firmness of his lower abdomen, she allowed her muscles to go slack and suddenly he was in there, filling her mouth, the taste of his skin smooth and hot and salty.

His hands framed her face as though they were lovers, stroking back the loose chestnut hair and tucking it behind her ears. One hand settled at the back of her head, nudging her into a faster rhythm. She did not resist, accepting the change of pace; her tutor could be cruel as well as kind if she did not obey quickly enough.

Her eyes flickered up to his face, thinking of all the times she had sat opposite Dr Milton in his college study, reading her essay aloud to him or discussing the merits of Victorian women poets, and never once guessing at his darker side. She had always found him sexually attractive, of course. There was such a dangerous edge to those eyes, the way he would go still when she made a mistake, an unspoken threat in the tense lines of his body. It had excited her in ways she had not understood until now. Perhaps she had been secretly wishing her tutor would bend her over his desk and hurt her, punish his student for some poor phrasing in her essay, the clumsy development of an idea.

Milton looked down at her, his expression unreadable, and pushed her face back into his groin.

She could smell fresh sweat, listening to the unsteady slap-slap of the former Dean's thighs against her body. He was gripping her buttocks now, heaving himself forwards in great awkward jerks. Her groan of pain was lost, muffled by the swollen shaft filling her mouth, the marks of cane and tawse smarting as the old man's fingers pinched and scrabbled at her flesh. Yet her sex responded traitorously, tightening around his organ as he pushed deeper inside, her muscles contracting on a wave of sharp pleasure.

The old gentleman broke the silence first, his voice hoarse. 'Damn tight, this new girl of yours.'

'Isn't she?' Milton replied smoothly, as unruffled as though he were reading a newspaper rather than being fellated by one of his own students.

'An excellent mount.'

'Thank you, sir. I'm glad you approve.'

Thomas dragged her closer, his narrow haunches working hard as he ploughed her with faster and faster strokes. His breathing was shallow, the occasional fit of wheezing momentarily disturbing his rhythm while he coughed and spluttered over her buttocks. Yet the old man did not stop, clearly determined to finish inside her. 'How are you getting on at St Nectan's these days?' he asked Milton between thrusts.

'Not too badly, I'm happy to say. I'm hoping to be made a Fellow of the college this year.'

'So I should think.'

Milton sounded almost amused. 'Yes, sir.'

She sensed a touch of unsteadiness in her tutor's voice and sucked a little harder. She worked her tongue forcefully along his shaft as he withdrew, welcoming it back into the depths of her throat with hot pulsating suction. The hand on her head tightened its grip, urging her on, and for the first time she felt his body begin to tremble. So Dr Milton was not as cool as he liked to pretend, she thought, a fierce excitement answering his own as her sex contracted again. She began to move her hips rhythmically against the old man's thrusts, her belly undulating like a dancer's, unable to help herself. Her eyes shut tight, blocking out reality. A tense fiery heat was building in her groin, pulling her inexorably towards orgasm.

'I can put in a good word for you, if you like,' Thomas grunted, thrusting harder as he clawed at her buttocks. 'I may be retired, but my recommendation still carries some weight at the college.'

Milton sounded near the end. Somehow, though, he managed to formulate a coherent reply, forcing himself deeper into her throat, rigid with the need for release. 'That . . . would be most . . . kind.'

'Not at all. Least I can do for a man of your talents.'

'I'm flattered, sir.'

Expertly licking the underside of his shaft, she heard Milton groan under his breath and eagerly accepted his next forward thrust. Beth held him there in her mouth as his cock began to throb and spurt, shooting his come rapidly down her throat. Milton muttered something, possibly an expletive, but she did not quite catch it. He held her head still while he came, the warm salty taste of his come deliciously filthy. Beth drank his spunk without hesitation, slipping a hand between her thighs and finally allowing herself to climb towards a tense and long suppressed orgasm.

Writhing with glorious uninhibited pleasure as she climaxed, still sucking and swallowing hard, Beth raised her bottom for the old man's last thrusts. Thomas came mere seconds later, moaning in a breathless voice and falling forwards over her back like a dying man.

Her face milky with spunk and their mingled perspiration, Beth gazed up at her tutor through misty eyes as he pulled away. She had never seen him like this before and she found it exciting to see what effect her mouth alone had managed to achieve. There was a hard colour in her tutor's face, his breathing rough, an unsteady little smile on his lips.

'Now that was a virtuoso performance,' Milton murmured, tucking his damp cock back into his trousers. 'I knew you would not disappoint me tonight, Beth.'

With a little more difficulty, the old gentleman raised himself from his slumped position on her back, collapsing back on to the leather cushions and reaching into one of his trouser pockets for a handkerchief, first to wipe his forehead and then his wilting cock.

Seeing her tutor's impatient gesture, Beth dropped her trembling legs to the floor and stood up from the sofa, feeling the old man's spunk begin to dribble from her pussy. She tried to clasp her thighs together to prevent its embarrassing leakage as she moved. The swollen lips still gaped from his intrusion, though, and there was no way to stop his come escaping. So she stood there like a statue, head bent and hands clasped respectfully before her, her pale skin marked by the cane and tawse, her inner thighs soaked with spunk.

'Yes, indeed.' The former Dean pushed the handkerchief back into his pocket, looking her over with a nod of satisfaction. 'You're bound to achieve a First at this rate, my dear girl. Most impressive, most impressive.'

Six

Beth woke up in a bedroom bathed with light, turning her head on the white pillows and struggling against a sense of disorientation. Slowly, she remembered dear old Thomas suggesting she stayed in the mansion overnight, then being shown to one of the bedrooms by a discreet-looking man in a dark suit before tumbling into a fathomless sleep almost as soon as she slid beneath the duvet. Beth was not even sure whether she had slept alone or with Milton. She did seem to recall a hard thigh pressing against hers during the night but, if her tutor had shared the bed with her, there was no sign of him now.

She was still nude, the duvet falling away to reveal bare breasts as she sat up and stared about her. Her nipples tingled and her body ached all over, a flush on her cheeks as she remembered the outrageous things she had consented to; the way she had behaved with all those different men.

Laid out at the foot of her bed was a neat pale blue linen skirt and a white blouse, next to a pair of low-heeled shoes which looked as though they had never been worn. Beth had been wondering how on earth she would manage to get downstairs without any clothes on; suspecting her nudity might not be as acceptable in broad daylight as it had been the night before. Clearly, though, somebody in that household had already anticipated her needs.

She slipped out of bed and padded across to the en suite bathroom for a quick wee to discover that someone had also placed a new toothbrush, hairbrush and freshly laundered towels by the sink for her. Beth turned to examine herself in the bathroom mirror, staring aghast at the criss-cross of marks and weals decorating her lower half. Her bottom and upper thighs were a complete mess. The lines might already be fading to a purplish-red, more like bruising from a bad fall than the marks of a cane and tawse, but she was even more relieved now that she did not have to go downstairs in the nude.

After a hurried shower, Beth slipped into the new clothes that had been provided for her. The blue linen skirt came down to her ankles, and the white blouse with its row of tiny buttons right up to the neck – like something a Victorian girl might have worn – lent her a demure, almost childlike air. She perched on the edge of the bed, feeling like an extra from *The Railway Children*, and tried on the low-heeled shoes. To her surprise, they fitted perfectly.

She wandered down the main staircase into the sunlit hall and glanced about at door after door, uncertain which one to choose. There was a dark-skinned woman in a short black dress and white apron arranging flowers near the front door. Beth approached her with a smile and asked where she could find the kitchen.

'I am the housekeeper. You would like some breakfast, miss?' When Beth nodded, the woman pointed down to the furthest door, her eyes friendly. From the heavy accent, Beth guessed she must be Spanish or at least Spanish speaking. 'The breakfast room is through that door. You should find scrambled eggs and fresh rolls already laid out for you. Would you like anything else? Bacon, perhaps, or sausages?'

'No, just some coffee will be fine.'

The housekeeper put aside the flowers she had been arranging and wiped her hands on her apron. 'I shall put on some fresh coffee at once and bring it through to you.'

'Thank you.'

'Not at all, miss.' The housekeeper looked down at her clothes and smiled shyly. 'I'm glad they fit so well.'

Beth stared at her, her face flushed. 'So it was you who left the clothes on my bed?'

The master told me you needed something to wear,' she explained discreetly, not meeting her eyes. 'Those belonged to his late mother. They are a little old-fashioned but –'

'Better than nothing,' Beth finished dryly.

The phone began to ring at that moment and the dark-skinned woman pushed hurriedly through a swing door into what looked like the kitchen, her English careful and precise as she said, 'I'm sorry, miss, I must answer that. I will bring you some coffee in the breakfast room, if you care to go through.'

The breakfast room was spacious and sunlit, looking out over the gardens; the French windows stood open and outside she could see Milton and Thomas on the lawn, gently putting golf balls across a miniature green. Just as the housekeeper had said, there were rolls on the table and scrambled eggs being kept warm on a hotplate.

Beth ignored the eggs, helping herself to a croissant from the breadbasket instead. She sat down at the long dark-wood table and spread the croissant with a little butter, devouring it hungrily. It tasted delicious and she soon reached for another.

The former Dean saw her through the windows and raised his golf putter in a cheerful gesture, calling her name. 'Do you play, dear girl? My eye seems to be out today; I keep missing the damned putts.'

She smiled and shook her head, raising her voice so that he could hear her. 'Sorry, I don't know a thing about golf.'

'Pity, pity.'

Raising his head briefly from a putt, Milton glanced across at her and their eyes met for a moment. Then he struck his ball, rolling it smoothly and confidently into a hole at the far side of the miniature green. The former Dean let out a strangled cry of despair, throwing his own putter to the ground, and Milton gave him a wry smile. 'Don't worry, sir, you can always take your revenge next time.'

'Perhaps I should take my revenge right now,' the old gentleman said, though he was also smiling. 'By enjoying myself again with your newest little protégée.'

Milton looked at her and snapped his fingers, summoning her to his side as though she were a servant or a trained dog. Her skin prickled at his arrogance but she chose to comply on this occasion, smoothing down the creases in her linen skirt and walking slowly towards them across the sunlit grass.

'Very nice, most suitable,' the old gentleman muttered, gesturing her to turn around for him and examining her with careful eyes. 'Those were my mother's clothes, Milton. They hang a little loose on your girl in places; I fear my mother was somewhat bigger in the chest. But you still look very fetching in them, my dear.'

She smiled at the old gentleman, hurriedly lowering her eyes to the ground as she became aware of Milton's scrutiny.

'Now face the breakfast room and raise your skirt to your waist,' the old gentleman told her rather more sternly.

Silently, Beth obeyed and heard them both draw in their breath as she hoisted the blue linen skirt high above her buttocks, displaying the mess of bruises and weals inflicted on her skin the night before. In spite of a light breeze that morning, the sunshine felt soothingly warm on her skin, the fragrance of freshly cut grass drifting past as she waited for his next command. It must provide an incongruous little scene for any observer, she thought with sudden amusement: a demure-looking girl showing her bottom to an elderly gentleman in this beautiful garden.

In a deliberately expressionless voice, Milton ordered her to bend forwards from the waist and grab her ankles. Beth followed his command with a slight flush in her cheeks, hoping the housekeeper did not come back at that moment to witness her degradation, bending over like this to display her buttocks and the tight puckered star of her anus. Though that was not her only source of embarrassment, she thought grimly, spreading her legs for balance. She had not been given any panties to wear and the swollen hairless lips of her pussy would also be clearly visible in that position.

Thomas retrieved his putter from the grass and approached her, swinging it in a jaunty fashion. Hanging upside down, clutching at her ankles with her bare rump exposed for all the world to chastise, Beth felt decidedly apprehensive about the sight of that sturdy iron golf club in the hands of the old gentleman.

'Such impressive markings!' Thomas muttered, standing right behind her so she could only see his black shoes and a pair of tweed trousers. 'You bruise easily.'

Beth tensed herself for a whack from that golf putter which never came. She heard someone saying, 'Excuse me, sir,' in a polite voice and she straightened up, breathless and red in the face, hurriedly dropping her skirt over her abused bottom and tidying her hair.

The housekeeper had appeared at the French windows, clutching a pot of freshly made filter coffee and smiling discreetly. 'I'm sorry to interrupt, sir, but that was your wife on the phone. She wanted you to know that her flight is due to land in an hour and she wondered if you would be picking her up at Heathrow as arranged.' Her mild gaze turned to Beth. 'Would you like your coffee out there, miss, or should I leave it on the table for you?'

'On the table will be fine,' Beth managed to say huskily. 'Thank you.'

The housekeeper nodded and disappeared into the cool interior of the house, taking the coffee pot with her.

'Damn it to hell,' Thomas said peevishly, frowning down at his watch. 'I'd completely forgotten about that. Amelia's been in Paris all weekend, shopping with our daughter. I'm meant to be picking them both up from Heathrow ... and all their blasted shopping bags, I expect. No time for lengthy farewells, I'm afraid.'

Milton shook his hand, polite as ever. 'Please don't worry about it, Thomas, we can see ourselves out. And thank you for your hospitality. I really enjoyed last night.'

Once the old gentleman had driven away, Beth poured herself a cup of coffee and drank it under Milton's ironic gaze. He wanted her to hurry up and leave so the housekeeper could clear away all signs of their presence in the house. Beth, however, was not so keen on the idea of being alone with him for the next hour or so.

Oddly enough, Beth felt awkward and rather uncertain how to behave in these old-fashioned clothes. With Thomas, it had been easy. The old gentleman had treated her with an almost Victorian courtesy from the start and Beth had automatically responded in kind. Her tutor was a different proposition, though. Milton had a hard hand and an even harder heart; she had seen that close up last night and this morning. And she disliked the way these deliberately restrictive clothes made her feel weak, vulnerable, perhaps even a little ridiculous.

Her tutor scooped up her discarded dress and heels from the night before and led her firmly to his car. 'Time to go,' he insisted, the dark eyes flicking over her face. 'And do stop looking so frightened. I'm going to take you back to Oxford ... eventually. First, I want to get my camera out of the boot and take you for a lovely walk along the river. The weather's perfect for it and I know just the spot for some interesting pictures.'

'Oh no,' she said fiercely. 'No photography.'

It was cooler in the woods, a dappled sunlight filtering down through gaps in the leafy branches. The grass was marshy in spite of the summer heat and choked with reeds as it sloped away towards the river in a kind of ditch, making every step precarious. She had already managed to slip several times on the way down, her linen skirt and white blouse covered with ugly little smears of mud by the time Dr Milton ordered her to strip naked. Somewhere nearby, out of sight beyond the trees, there was a dog barking and the sound of children playing, their high excited voices echoing across the woods.

'Towards me again,' Milton muttered, sounding absorbed. 'Can you tense your bum, make the muscles look tighter?'

Flushed and irritable, Beth obeyed with reluctance, staring blindly into sunlight as she raised her head from between her legs, a position she had been holding for several minutes. Every muscle in her body was protesting and the weals from last night stretched uncomfortably on her bottom and thighs whenever she moved. 'How much longer?'

'Stop chattering.' His voice was stern, adamant. 'If I don't capture your markings on film today, the bruises will start to change colour and then they won't be worth photographing.'

She blinked away a few angry tears, exhausted now and wishing she were back in her safe little room at college. Milton had taken her for a walk beside the river and then pulled her into this secluded area of woodland, telling her to strip off. Too tired to argue initially, Beth had found herself being forced to adopt a series of ridiculously contorted positions: aslant a rotting tree trunk; down on her hands and knees among the reeds; plastering thick smelly mud over her belly and erect nipples; sprawling in the undergrowth, legs held up and apart to expose her shaven pussy and the darker hole beneath.

Now her temper was beginning to boil and she could no longer contain it. 'I've got that essay to research, remember?'

'Which one?'

'The Shakespeare Apocrypha.'

His voice was impatient and dismissive. 'Oh, don't waste your energy worrying about that. There are plenty of secondary texts in the college library to help you with the Apocrypha. It's not due in for another week, anyway.'

She straightened and glared at him, her hands falling to her hips, her back hurting badly. 'Look, Dr Milton, I really do need more time for my college work. I mean, what about my extended essay towards Finals? I can hardly expect any extra time for that and I'm way behind with my note taking.'

'OK, five more minutes. Then we'll stop.'

Her mouth tight with determination, Beth reached for the blue linen skirt which was lying in a crumpled heap in the bushes. 'No, we're stopping right now. I'm tired and I need to get back to college.'

Milton moved swiftly; she caught the flash of something in his hand, then jerked in shocked agony, dropping the skirt and clutching her bottom with both hands instead. She looked round at him, her lip trembling with pain and fury. He had grabbed a fallen branch from the undergrowth and sliced at her buttocks with its thin spiny wood, showing no regard at all for her already bruised skin.

He sounded mildly irritated, throwing the branch aside. 'Now shut up and bend over that log there. We'll stay here another ten minutes to teach you a lesson in obedience.'

Tearful and smarting with resentment, Beth shuffled back under the trees and bent over the ivy-thick log he had indicated. Spreading her legs wide, she gasped in unexpected pain, realising too late that she was standing in a patch of tall dusty-headed nettles. Not daring to move again in case she received another lashing, Beth muttered an expletive beneath her breath, forced to grit her teeth as her skin itched and stung under the cruel kiss of nettles.

'Don't move, that's perfect,' he said, observing her discomfort with an expression of amused satisfaction. 'And no more little outbursts or I'll make you lie face down in those nettles.'

'Get lost,' she hissed.

'Actually, that could make quite a kinky picture –'

'Don't even think about it!' Beth snapped, raising her buttocks into the sunlight so the marks on her skin would be more clearly visible to his camera lens. 'There are limits to the amount of punishment I'll take, Dr Milton. So just take your sodding photographs and let's get out of here, OK?'

He laughed but thankfully did not pursue the matter, and Beth soon heard the now familiar sound of his camera shutter clicking steadily away as her hamstrings ached and her nipples stiffened inexorably in the breeze. The pain of this position was bad enough, she thought. What made her situation worse was the sneaking awareness that, in spite of the stinging nettles and against all logic, she was excited by his ruthless treatment. Her pussy had begun leaking the warm traitorous fluid, her shaven lips swelling with undeniable arousal as she saw herself though his eyes: firm buttocks bruised and invitingly presented, her sex gaping between spread thighs, and that tight little hole – where she had not yet been used – staring back at him like a challenge he would one day take up.

Dr Milton eventually finished taking his pictures and began packing away his camera. Beth gathered her muddy clothes and was preparing to get dressed when her tutor plucked them away from her hands. She stared up at him in stupefied silence, wondering what on earth he could be planning now.

After shaking out a black leather coat from his holdall, Milton threw it across to her with a glint in his dark eyes. 'Put this coat on instead. If you button it right up and don't walk too fast, no one will know you're not wearing anything underneath.' He pulled a pair of knee-length soft leather boots from the bag. 'And these, too.'

'You've got to be kidding!'

Milton gave her a hard look. 'Hurry up and do what you're told. You can't wear that muddy skirt. I'm taking you for a pub lunch, Beth, and I expect you to be suitably attired for the occasion.'

'A pub lunch?'

'That is correct,' he agreed dryly. 'Please lower your eyebrows. It's a long-respected Oxford tradition. Tutor and student, lunching together in a civilised fashion, discussing the vagaries of English literature over a pint of real ale and a cheddar ploughman's. It's a lovely afternoon for it, don't you agree?'

Beth buttoned up the black leather coat as he had suggested, the material oddly cool against her nude body, and then pulled on the knee-length boots. The coat finished a few inches above the boots, leaving quite a gap of bare flesh and the definite suggestion that more might lie hidden above. Milton watched in silence as she stood up again, a sardonic look in those dark eyes as he took in her mutinous expression and sulky pout. He led her back along the river towards the pub, holding her arm firmly as though half expecting her to run away.

It was a pleasantly warm Sunday afternoon and there were plenty of people about, walking their dogs or cycling and walking along the dry riverside paths. Several men glanced sideways at her as they passed, interested desire in their eyes, and she felt her cheeks flare with colour, only too aware what they must be thinking. She probably looked like a prostitute to them, her chestnut hair dishevelled and the tight leather fitting her body like a lewd second skin.

'Why exactly do we have to do this today? Couldn't we have a pub lunch tomorrow?' she muttered.

Milton tightened his grip on her arm, giving her a dry smile. 'I'm afraid not. Tomorrow is a weekday and I'm all booked up. Tutorials, lectures, seminars, department meetings ... it never seems to end. No wonder your visits lift my spirits, Beth.'

The pub he had chosen was absolutely packed and they had to look outside in the garden for somewhere to sit, before finally spotting a bench which had just been vacated by another couple. A little apart from the rest, it faced the waterfront and one other bench, where a group of rowdy young men were drinking. As she sat down opposite the young men, struggling not to let the leather coat ride up to expose her nudity beneath, she felt their eyes sliding first over her and then over her tutor. Luckily for both of them, although Milton was not particularly brutal looking, he was over six foot tall and visibly muscular; so, apart from the odd wolf-whistle and suggestive remark thrown across the grass, the young men opposite did not disturb their lunch.

Milton went inside the pub to order their meals and came back with a half-pint of real ale which Beth sipped cautiously, not really sure that she liked beer.

He grinned at her expression. 'No good?'

'It's OK,' she said grudgingly. 'But not really my thing. To be honest, I prefer white wine or vodka.'

He nodded slowly, picking up his own pint and taking several long swallows of ale. 'Interesting you should say that, Beth, because it highlights one of the key elements of this game we're playing. There will always be times when I ask you to do something you don't want to do, or don't really fancy. But you'll have to do it anyway, simply because someone has ordered you to and you're a submissive.'

'I hate that bit,' she admitted.

'Yes, but you must learn to get round your natural aversions; relax a little bit more into the persona you've adopted.'

'What persona?'

He smiled. 'It's a pity you couldn't see yourself last night, twisting under the tawse with the juice running down your thighs. The pain was excruciating, yet you loved it. Why?'

'I don't know.' She could not meet his eyes. 'I felt like someone else last night, like it wasn't happening to me.'

'Exactly.'

Their meals arrived and they ate in a thoughtful silence. Beth was still turning over what he had said in her mind, not entirely certain that she understood. Part of her was deeply ashamed of the way she had behaved at the old gentleman's house and wanted to tell Milton that he could go to hell and that she'd never go to any of those sordid meetings again. Another part of her kept remembering the sting of the tawse across her buttocks and the sweet release of orgasm, one inextricably linked to the other. It was a far more complex business than she had realised when she first agreed to join his Club.

Milton's eyes kept flicking to her face as they finished their meal, his gaze watchful. 'So are you ready to take the game to the next level? See how far you can sustain that sort of submission?'

'I suppose so.'

He wiped his mouth with a napkin, nodding over her shoulder at the students sitting behind her. 'Turn around and unbutton your coat for those lads, then. Show me how serious you are.'

Beth stared. 'What?'

'You heard me, don't act coy. Unbutton your coat and show them what's underneath.'

She leant forwards furiously, her voice almost a hiss. 'That's not a fair challenge. You know perfectly well I can't do that, Dr Milton. We're in a public place and I'm naked under this.'

'You refuse?'

Beth saw the raised eyebrow and heard the steely note in his voice, her confidence faltering. 'We'll get arrested!'

'I doubt that somehow,' Milton said dryly. 'You think any one of those hormonally challenged young men is going to dash off and find a policeman because some beautiful young woman in a leather coat and boots showed him her cunt? He's more likely to ask how much you're charging.'

Her cheeks were burning. 'And what would I reply?'

'Oh, I think you can leave those sorts of negotiations to me,' her tutor said, a deliberately lazy smile on his face as he lifted the pint glass to his lips and downed it. 'This is another test of your submission, Beth. Now turn around to face those young men, start unbuttoning your coat, and let me deal with the consequences.'

Her cheeks flushed with a wild colour, her body trembling, Beth turned on the bench and slid her legs round so that she was facing the lads opposite. They had been talking loudly among themselves, rowdy and a little bit drunk, but now the group fell silent, watching her with undisguised lust. She started to unbutton the coat, her fingers slipping awkwardly on the smooth black leather.

One of the lads shouted something crude and gave a high cat-call; another whistled in disbelief, and then, as she unbuttoned the coat lower and lower, revealing more of her nakedness beneath, several of them began a slow appreciative clap.

They must be able to see her breasts now, she thought, the leather falling open across her pale skin and the dusky-pink buds of her nipples. Reaching the bare curve of her belly, burningly aware that only three buttons remained to be unfastened, Beth faltered in her task. There were tears in her eyes as she turned back towards Milton. 'I can't do this,' she whispered through numb lips, shaking her head. 'Not here, not in public.'

Milton looked back at her with a dark intent gaze, sitting perfectly still on the other side of the bench. He made no attempt to rescue her or even indicate that she could cover herself again, clearly unmoved by her distress. 'Your feelings are irrelevant. Obedience is everything.'

'Please . . .'

'This is not a democracy. Finish it, Beth.'

Shutting her eyes against the fascinated desire in the lads' faces, Beth slowly unfastened the last three buttons and let the leather coat fall away from her body. Sunlight caressed the shaven lips of her pussy, squeezed tight by her thighs, her curved belly and breasts above, nipples stiffening to erection as she heard the lads shout and howl, one boy whistling so loudly that every head in the beer garden must have turned in her direction.

Even though her cheeks were damp with tears of shame, she felt a dizzying heat begin to stir between her thighs. Her head spun with filthy images: these rowdy lads fingering her intimately, their thick dirty thumbs pushing into every orifice, sliding the coat from her shoulders and bending her over the bench, forcing their cocks into her mouth and pussy, taking turns to come over her body until she was coated in hot creamy spunk. Her pulse racing, Beth longed to be able to touch herself, to slip a hand between her thighs and masturbate openly in front of them while the lads howled and stamped, a pack of slavering dogs eager for the bitch. If she had the nerve, she would even spread her legs wide and let them watch the pink shaven lips enclosing her pussy peel back to reveal her moist heat, only too willing to be entered and fucked by every single one of them.

An outraged shriek cut across her fantasies, making Beth jerk upright in shock. Her eyes flew open to see one of the pub barmaids staring down at her, arms full of dirty pint glasses, her disgusted gaze moving over Beth's nakedness. 'You dirty little slut!' the girl spat at her, her large chest heaving with indignation, a look of loathing on her face. 'Cover yourself up this instant or I'm calling the police.'

Snatching at the leather coat, Beth dragged it tight around her body and stumbled from the bench, moaning in humiliated horror as she ran into the pub. Behind her, she heard the lads hooting after her with a mixture of derision and disappointment. Not daring to meet any of the curious eyes trained on her fleeing figure, she made straight for the ladies' toilets and locked herself into a cubicle while she fastened the buttons again until her nudity was completely hidden. She did not know what to do; her heart was hammering in panic, her whole body shaking uncontrollably. What would Dr Milton expect her to do? Had he left the pub or was he out there, waiting for her?

She cried bitterly for a few terrible minutes, then let herself out of the cubicle and stared into the mirror above the sinks. Her eyes were wide and scared, her cheeks deeply flushed. Beth ran the cold tap and hurriedly splashed her face, not caring that her hair was also getting wet, trying to restore a look of composure before she went back out to face those people.

When the door into the toilets opened, she turned at once, tensed for a confrontation. Just as she had feared, Beth saw the barmaid standing there in the doorway with an older woman behind her, presumably the landlady of the pub. Both women glared at her in stark accusation.

'I think you'd better leave,' the older woman said bluntly, looking her up and down with an expression of repulsion, her lips pursed and her eyes narrowed. 'And don't come back. If I ever see you in my pub again, I'll have you arrested. You're lucky I haven't called the police this time. This is a respectable public house, not a brothel.'

'Yeah,' the barmaid sneered, standing squarely in the doorway so Beth had to squeeze past her in order to leave. 'Stick to street corners in future. That's where sluts like you belong.'

Beth pushed past them both without a word and ran through the cool interior of the pub, blinded by sunlight as she escaped into the car park. Much to her surprise and relief, Dr Milton was waiting for her outside, leaning against the wall by the main entrance. He straightened up as she appeared, catching her by the shoulders and steadying her wild flight. His voice seemed deep, surprisingly calm. 'Shhh, it's OK,' he murmured, pulling her close, his warm lips brushing her throat as he drew her into his body.

'I'm never going to do that again.'

He stroked her damp chestnut hair. 'Don't worry, Beth, I won't ask you to,' he reassured her.

'I hated it!'

'Of course you did.' His gaze was hypnotic; he was holding her face between his hands now, thumbs touching her trembling mouth. 'But you obeyed me and that's what counts. You were magnificent.'

'I thought they were going to –'

Milton shook his head angrily, looking down into her wide shamed eyes, as she broke off. 'I would never let anyone hurt you. You're worth far more than that. I want you to remember that in future. Whatever you do when you're in my company is about submission, Beth, not degradation. You were not offering yourself to those boys; you were displaying yourself. And you did it because I ordered you to. It was an act of obedience, pure and simple.'

Beth nodded, trying to compose herself as he released her. She dried her damp cheeks on the back of her hand. 'I'm OK now,' she said huskily.

He offered her a cigarette from his packet and, although she did not normally smoke, Beth accepted it with a shaky smile. As she bent her head to the cupped flame of his lighter, she heard a contemptuous shout from behind and turned to see one of the lads from the beer garden watching her with a grin on his face, about to unlock his car.

'Ignore him,' Milton advised her.

Some devilry must have been in her heart at that moment, though, because Beth simply could not bring herself to look away. Spurred on by the memory of their taunts and whistles, she turned more fully towards the young man and met his frank gaze. Dragging flirtatiously on her cigarette, she raised the leather coat in one smooth movement, once again displaying her pale thighs and the soft shaven mound of her sex. Fuck me then, her eyes were daring him. Take me and use me.

The young man stared, his eyes flicking from her nudity to Milton and back again. Then, a dark colour in his face, he slid behind the wheel of his car and drove away.

Milton laughed beneath his breath. 'What a fool,' he said dismissively. 'Cover yourself, Beth. There's no point wasting your talents on a boy like that.'

Her tutor picked up the holdall and tightened his grip on her arm, leading her away from the pub towards the shady river path. 'Come on,' he murmured in her ear. 'Let's walk back to where I parked the car. If that's the sort of mood you're in, I can think of a much better way to finish the weekend.'

Seven

Milton pulled down a side road off the A34, heading for a secluded lay-by he often frequented on afternoons like this, and parked up there in the shade. The road itself was a cul-de-sac, only a smattering of industrial units and warehouses situated beyond the bend in the road, and few people ever seemed to come this way on a Sunday. He knew it was a little early in their relationship to be taking things to a more personal level, but Beth had surprised him today. She was progressing rather more swiftly than he had expected from shy inexperienced student to willing submissive. It was a progression he knew well, and usually took some months to achieve. Beth was different, though. She had incredible potential, that innocent face at odds with her reaction to domination, so inviting and sexually excited under the tawse.

She was looking about herself nervously, a pulse leaping in the side of her throat. 'Why have we stopped here?'

'Use your imagination, Beth. Why do you think?'

The girl's eyes fell before his and he smiled to himself. He liked the way she could not always hold his gaze; her natural timidity was charming and demonstrated how malleable she was, in spite of these sudden flares of independence she kept surprising him with. Even her tone was submissive, tinged with excited apprehension.

'So you can fuck me.'

Milton raised his eyebrows. 'Is that what you want me to do?'

'No,' she replied automatically, then blushed, biting her lip at his quick look of derision. 'I mean, yes. I think so.'

'Well, that's not why I've parked here. If all I wanted from you was sex, life would be much simpler for both of us. And far less interesting.'

Milton paused to light a cigarette, opening his window so the smoke could escape into the warm afternoon air. He could hear a bird in full song high above the car, possibly a thrush, hidden somewhere up there among the thick leafy branches of a horse chestnut.

'When I look at you, Beth,' he continued, 'I see the raw material for personal transformation. Sex is one way of getting there. It's not the most important one, though. You're a beautiful and sensual girl, there's no denying that. But you could be so much more if you allow me to take your training to the next level.'

'I'm not sure I know what you mean.'

'OK,' said Milton, nodding, dragging enjoyably on his cigarette. 'In terms you might find easier to understand, I see you as a sort of modern-day Sleeping Beauty.'

'Oh,' she said, her mouth round with surprise.

He smiled at her naive response, choosing his words carefully so that he could monitor her reaction. 'Except that my Sleeping Beauty is different from the one in the fairy story. This girl needs to be woken with a whip, a slap, a hard word . . . not with a kiss.'

The brunette shivered delicately, not meeting his eyes. Milton looked down at her in that tight leather coat, remembering how she had bared herself in front of the boys in the beer garden, so totally unaware of her own sexuality, and experienced an urge to show her what he meant; words were often useless compared to a physical demonstration. Had Beth progressed far enough to obey him, though? It was one thing to expect a new girl to behave lewdly in a private house and quite another to command her obedience in a place like this, parked up at the side of a public road for all the world to see. Whether she was ready or not, his cock was twitching. It felt like a good time to put her to the test.

His voice hardened. 'Pull your coat up to your waist,' he said curtly. He watched her hurry to obey, noting with satisfaction how the girl's hands trembled as she hitched the smooth black leather above her buttocks and thighs. 'Now kneel up in the middle here and straddle the gear stick.'

'The gear stick?'

'Come on, Beth, don't make me angry with you. It's time you got what you've been begging for all day.'

Ignoring her instinctive protest, Milton threw his cigarette out of the window and lifted her into position above the gear stick. He reached down between her trembling thighs and parted her sex lips with one ruthless hand, forcing the knob end of the gear stick inside her. There was a brief moment of resistance, her warm muscular channel rebelling against the intruder, before its thick knob slid home with satisfying ease. Her anguished cries of humiliation as her sex stretched to accommodate its girth only made the situation more amusing; from the heightened colour in her cheeks, Beth was actually enjoying what she had been forced to take. That surprised him. Most of his other girls had found the gear-stick exercise difficult to perform. Her sex must be extraordinarily pliable, Milton thought to himself, aroused by the possibilities behind that idea.

She had not yet completed the exercise to his satisfaction, though. He tightened his grip and pulled Beth down until she was kneeling there with her mouth open, knees trapped between the front seats, impaled on his gear stick like a butterfly pinned to a board. 'Fits like a glove, doesn't it?'

Beth could not reply, staring back at him in speechless paralysis. The shock on her face was perfect. Milton felt himself stiffening to a workman-like erection. He released her, then unzipped his trousers and began to masturbate with firm even strokes.

'Now fuck yourself with it,' he ordered her in a rough voice, his choice of words deliberately crude. 'Don't just sit there staring at me like a frightened schoolgirl. This is what you need, isn't it? Something thick and hard up inside you? Fuck yourself with the gear stick, Beth. Show me how much you want it.'

'Please, Dr Milton, I can't.' Her eyes pleaded with him, wide and tearful. 'It's too big; it hurts.'

'Shut up and fuck the gear stick,' he insisted. 'Now!'

The girl fell silent at once, closing her eyes. He guessed she was not going to argue with him any more, triumph in his heart as he realised how far under his spell she was falling.

Painfully, with little gasps and whimpers, his young protégée began to push herself up and away from the gear stick until its knob end could be seen stretching the moist entrance to her sex. Milton watched in aroused fascination as the girl leaned forwards, gripping both front seats for support, and lowered herself again in slow tentative stages, about three-quarters of the gear stick disappearing inside her now without too much difficulty. She repeated the same move several more times, her cheeks deeply flushed, her body shuddering in helpless response. Each time the gear stick emerged slicker and slicker with pussy juice, fluids dribbling down its leather-enclosed column to pool around the black plastic base.

It was probably the thickest implement she had ever taken up inside herself, Milton realised with amusement, to judge by the stunned expression on her face. He was still not satisfied, brutally slapping her buttocks and ordering her to move faster up and down, to build up a rhythm which would bring her to orgasm.

Just as she was approaching her climax, a red truck drove slowly past the lay-by where they were parked and hooted loudly. The balding middle-aged driver leaned out towards them, shouting some encouraging expletive that Milton did not quite catch. Beth turned to stare at the man through the car window, her face scarlet with shame and excitement, her sex fully impaled on the gear stick.

'Oh, God,' she moaned, kneeling up and desperately trying to pull herself off the slippery shaft.

'Stay where you are,' he said firmly. 'He won't stop.'

'But he can see my face –'

'That truck driver doesn't know who you are and he doesn't care. All he's thinking about right now is having witnessed a dirty young girl masturbating on a gear stick.'

'What if he turns round and comes back?'

'Don't be ridiculous.' Milton shook his head, a thin sardonic smile on his lips as he watched the red truck lumbering heavily past and tried to imagine what must be going through the truck driver's mind. 'He saw me in the car, so he knows you aren't alone. I expect his primary concern will be looking for somewhere private to park up and have a good wank. Now just shut up and keep fucking yourself.'

Although the girl groaned and hissed with discomfort, she settled back above the gears without even needing to be slapped. Her hands supported her weight on the front seats and her thighs pumped with a steady pistonlike motion as she began to slide up and down once more on the knob-ended gear stick.

Milton continued to jerk at his own cock, watching the large red truck disappear up the slip road ahead and on to the swift-moving A34. Secretly, he had been worried for a few moments there. It was not part of his plan to be caught in such a compromising position, and find himself not only dismissed from the university but very possibly arrested, too. Luckily, the truck driver had not bothered to stop. Nor did Milton think it likely that his number plate could be visible from the road in this shady spot, deliberately hidden away from onlookers among the undergrowth and overhanging foliage. The game felt a little dangerous now. But Milton had no desire to break off without finishing properly. It was important his little protégée learned to pleasure herself even under difficult circumstances – and even more vital that Milton relieved his own sexual tension before his testicles exploded.

'That's enough,' he said, abruptly ordering the girl to climb off the gear stick and bury her face in his lap. 'Suck me until I come.'

To his delight, Beth did as she was told without a single protest. She pulled her sex free from the slick creamy shaft of the gear stick and clambered back on to the passenger seat, sticking her face deep in his lap and her bottom high in the air. Milton pushed the leather coat aside and exposed her buttocks, slapping her for a few minutes until the skin felt hot and flushed beneath his hand. Then he forced his thumb and forefinger into her tight anal opening, amused to hear the girl begin to moan in the back of her throat as she sucked, a deep humming sound that resonated through his cock and balls.

'Good girl.' He drew her head deeper into his groin, deliberately pulling the loose chestnut hair and smiling at the girl's muffled yelp. 'Yes, that's a good girl.'

His thumb and forefinger worked further into her anus, ruthlessly pushing and probing. The girl seemed highly aroused now, her body twisting beneath him as though she were on the verge of orgasm herself, lips clamped tightly around his shaft. Thick musky juices flowed freely from her sex, soaking her inner thighs and probably the passenger seat of his car, too. That thought irritated him but he let it pass. Beth was jiggling against him, sucking and slurping at his cock and balls, her mouth eager though not entirely expert. He could probably have brought her off with a single flick across her clitoris, but his head was somewhere else; he had no time for the girl now.

Milton shut his eyes against the sunlight and felt his facial muscles clench into a tight mask, his climax approaching fast. Why had the truck driver hooted? What had he actually seen as he drove past? Perhaps the car had been shaking to the rhythm of her fucking, the girl's semi-clothed body shuddering up and down on the gear stick. Perhaps he had even been able to see Milton's cock squeezed in his fist as he masturbated, thick veined and almost ready to burst, transparent beads of pre-come oozing from the slit and down his fingers, leaving the foreskin slick and easy to manipulate.

'Blow me, you slut!'

Her mouth tightened dutifully on his cock and a pressure valve blew somewhere deep inside him. Milton threw his head back and groaned aloud, pumping what felt like the entire contents of his balls down her sweet willing throat.

'Swallow it,' he said thickly, holding her head in both hands as he came. 'I want to watch you drink my spunk.'

Milton heard the girl's muffled cries in counterpoint and realised those feverish little movements he had felt against his arm had been her free hand, rubbing and pressing between her legs, masturbating in secret like a naughty little schoolgirl while she sucked his cock. He could scarcely believe it. Had she learned nothing about her role as a submissive? Horny little bitch!

Milton emptied himself pleasurably into her mouth and kept on pushing. He felt the girl struggle against the invasion, his hand clamped on her head as she moaned and tried to escape. Go on, sweetheart, choke on my cock for a few more minutes, Milton thought with grim amusement, then perhaps it will occur to you not to fight it. Though it might seem cruel, it was best for her to learn about self-control the painful way. That was a necessary stage in her development if she was to join his stable. Beth needed some serious lessons in submission and he had never been one to sidestep a challenge, however daunting it might appear at first glance.

Eight

Charlotte put down her pen, stretched her tired wrist muscles and took a few minutes to check through her examination papers for the last time. It had been such an exhausting term, first all those interminable revisions, and then exam after exam, testing her knowledge of everything she had studied over the past few years at Oxford. If it had not been for the odd pony-girl session with Dr Milton, kitted out exquisitely in her harness and hoof boots, she would probably have gone mad.

The moderator finally dismissed the students, and Charlotte was only too happy to make her way out of that elegant high-ceilinged hall where the examinations were held and downstairs into the back lane. The crowd of students struggled through the narrow entrance and she was carried with them, hearing a shout go up from the waiting crowds outside.

Emerging into bright sunlight, she began to tear at her subfusc, the sober and archaic uniform that was obligatory for all examination candidates. She released the ridiculous bow at her neck, dragged the black gown from her shoulders and tossed her mortar board to the floor, leaving her in just tight black trousers, the material straining over her full buttocks, and a white blouse with no bra underneath. Someone in the crowd directly ahead of her had brought a bottle of champagne for the celebrations. The cork was popped violently above their heads and Charlotte shrieked wildly, covering her face as she was showered in warm sticky champagne. She pushed through the massed students to where her friends were waiting for her, uncaring that her large breasts were bouncing freely with each step, nipples proudly erect under the sodden white blouse. Those boys in the crowd could stare all they liked, she thought defiantly, thrusting her shoulders even further back. She was not ashamed to let anyone see her body.

'So that was your last exam, Charlotte,' one of the lads shouted to her above the roar of the crowd. 'How does it feel?'

'Fantastic!'

Robert kissed her, his lips warm and wet on her face, enthusiastic as a puppy. Ever hopeful for more than just a kiss, he slipped an arm around her waist and drew her near. 'I didn't know you were having your brace removed. Your teeth look great . . . and it's much easier to kiss you now.'

'Yes, it came out last week.' She assumed a sinister tone, flashing her beautifully straight teeth at him. 'All the better to eat you with, my dear.'

'Scary!' He laughed, gazing down at her mouth. 'We'd better go. Everyone's meeting down at the Turf. No more revision! You can really let your hair down at last, get pissed –'

'I can't, Robert. I've got to work later on,' she reminded him, though she knew that had never stopped her from enjoying herself in the past.

'But it's party time. You can't work tonight.'

'Sorry, sweetie.' Charlotte smiled at him apologetically, ducking under his arm and collecting her damp gown and mortar from the cobbled street. It was tempting simply to abandon them in the street, but they were incredibly expensive and she would probably need to wear the bloody things again at the graduation ceremony. 'I'm saving for that deposit on my flat in London,' she pointed out, a little irritated by his attitude. 'I'm still several thousand pounds short. Your parents may be planning to help you out when you leave Oxford this summer, but mine don't give a toss. They'd rather book a world cruise and have me living on the streets.'

He looked at her sulkily. 'Is this escort work again?'

'It's good money.'

With a quick glance at her nipples, now stiff and perfectly visible through the thin wet material of her blouse, Robert gave a little shrug. 'I suppose we all have to make a living. So long as you don't let those sleazy bastards actually touch you.'

She laughed, patting his cheek as they wandered back into town together, arm in arm. Robert was not really her boyfriend, though he was always interested in taking up that position. 'They're not all sleazy, you know. Some of them are quite nice.'

'Charlotte, you wouldn't –' He stared at her, frowning. 'I mean, after these blokes have taken you to dinner or whatever, you don't –'

'Fuck them?'

Robert looked away, an embarrassed colour on his face. 'Now you're making fun of me. I'm just worried about you, that's all.'

'I know, sweetie.'

'Don't call me that,' he said stiffly.

'Sorry.'

They turned down the narrow cobbled alleyway near New College leading to the Turf Tavern. It was darker out of the sunlight and most of the other students had already reached the pub, shouts of laughter rising above the ancient buildings in the quiet afternoon.

After drawing a sharp breath, as if telling himself not to blow it, Robert pushed her up against the wall and kissed her. The stone felt cool on her back through the wet blouse. Charlotte stared up at the cloudless blue sky above the alley walls, unmoved by his mouth pressing against hers. He kissed her throat and slipped a hand between them to squeeze her breast, awkward and tentative, groping for the nipple.

'Look, I'm dead serious. Don't bother with the escort work tonight,' he whispered unsteadily. 'Come back to my place instead.'

'I thought you'd been invited to a party.'

'Who cares about that? It's just something Crawford's arranged, a sort of lads' night out. Besides, it's all the way out in Abingdon and most of the posh lot are going, probably all champers and caviar.' He stroked her breast again daringly. 'I'd rather be with you.'

'I'm flattered,' she murmured, gently removing his hand. Robert was such a sweet boy, if a little ineffectual, that she hated to hurt his feelings by refusing yet again to go on a date with him. 'But there's no way I can wriggle out of this job tonight. I can't just pull a sickie. I'm meant to be training a new girl, the one who's going to replace me when I leave. You know how it is.'

'No, I don't know how it is,' he told her angrily, his eyes narrowed on her face. 'Training a new girl to do what, exactly?'

'Oh, come on. Use your imagination.'

His face flared with sudden dark colour. 'You don't have sex with them, do you? Tell me you're joking, Charlotte.'

'Why shouldn't I have sex with them?'

Robert sounded almost desperate. 'You know why.'

'Yeah, I know why.'

Tossing her thick blonde ponytail over one shoulder, Charlotte stared up at the boy with a challenging look in her eyes, irritated by the way he was making her feel. She was no grubby slut, bending over for some stranger in a bus shelter. Dr Milton had seen her potential, and he had spent years training her; she was one of the best in town. So why on earth should a little innocent like Robert tell her how to live when he had no idea what the real world was like out there? Even if he knew the sort of things she got up to at night, she thought angrily, he would never believe it. What he knew about sex could be written on a postage stamp. Robert was probably still a virgin and there was no way she was letting someone like that make her feel guilty.

'Because you want to fuck me yourself and you don't like the idea of some other man shooting his load up me first.'

Robert slapped her face so hard that she rocked back on her heels, his eyes blazing with fury. 'That's a foul thing to say! Go on, then, piss off to your escort work. Fuck as many men as you like, Charlotte the Harlot. I'm going to this party in Abingdon and I'm going to have a good time without you.'

Charlotte watched him stride back along the alley, disappearing round the corner towards the town centre without a single backward glance in her direction. She rubbed her burning cheek with a surprised and slightly rueful expression. Ouch. That slap had really stung. She had been laying it on pretty thick but then she had not expected mild-mannered Robert to be quite so forceful with her. Perhaps he might be worth dating, after all.

111

Her party mood had sort of fizzled out after their argument, so she swung on her heel and hurried back to college. There would not be much time for celebrating anyway; she had to take a quick shower and drive straight across town to collect Beth from St Nectan's. It was fortunate she had brought her car to Oxford that term. Though the parking costs were high, at least it meant she could take on the more lucrative jobs outside the town centre.

The porter leaned out of the window as she passed the college lodge, calling her back. 'Parcel for you, miss.'

It must be the costumes for tonight's job, she thought, wondering what she would be expected to wear this time. Not just the usual mask and black sequinned thong, by the look of it. It was a large bulky parcel, discreetly wrapped in brown paper and string, with Milton's distinctive black scrawl on the address label.

Charlotte bent over the lodge counter and signed for the parcel, glancing up to see the heavy-set porter staring at her with a suspicious look in his eyes. 'What's the matter?' she asked.

He pointed to her face. 'Nasty bruise coming up there, miss. How did that happen?'

'My boyfriend hit me.'

The porter straightened, frowning. 'Is he a student? You'd better report him to the university police, miss. I can give them a call right now; it won't take a minute –'

She smiled, shaking her head. 'Sorry, I was just kidding. I slipped in the loo and banged my face on the sink.'

The porter was still frowning as Charlotte, carrying the heavy parcel in her arms, made her way jauntily across the quad, free to walk on the grass now it was summer and students were outside sunbathing. Some people have no sense of humour, she thought wryly, heading for her room at the northern end of the quad. She had been lucky to get a place in college for her final year, rather than having to live out. It was much easier to pull someone down in the college bar and go straight up to her room for sex than stagger across town and freeze her arse off screwing him in some dingy bedsit.

In the privacy of her small college room, Charlotte cut the strings, tore off the brown paper and gave an incredulous laugh as she stared down at the contents of the parcel. This had to be another of Milton's little jokes, she thought wildly, wondering how the new girl would react to his sense of humour. Inside the parcel were two brown furry dog costumes with a stud-fastening flap at the groin, studded collars made of thick black leather, heavy-duty chain leads, even a thick black kohl pencil for drawing on whiskers. He wanted her and Beth to dress as dogs at the party tonight, and Charlotte could already imagine the sort of tricks they might be expected to perform in outfits like these. Her shrug was eloquent; it did not matter to her what she wore or how ridiculous she looked, as long as she enjoyed herself in the end.

She showered and threw on some faded hipster jeans with a white top, slicked on a little lipstick and eyeshadow, and hunted the room for her car keys. By the time she eventually found them, it was getting quite late. The two girls were meant to be at the party by ten o'clock and, from the look of the darkening sky outside her window, the long summer evening had to be heading towards that time.

Leaving the room, Charlotte glanced down at the address that Milton had scribbled on a loose sheet of paper and slipped between the dog costumes for her.

It was a private house on a road just outside Abingdon and belonged to one of Milton's old college buddies; she seemed to recall having driven past it once or twice in the past. Her mind flashed back to what Robert had been saying earlier. Something about a party in Abingdon that night, some sort of posh do for the lads, all champers and caviar. God, what if Robert was going to the same party tonight? That possibility nearly turned her stomach. She hoped desperately that she was wrong. If he managed to recognise her, even disguised in this furry dog costume, he might be tempted to tell the world exactly what she had been doing to earn money in her spare time. That could ruin her chances of landing a good job now that she had finished her exams. That sort of bad news would spread fast across the university, no matter how hard she tried to stop it.

She collected her rather battered-looking car and drove hurriedly towards St Nectan's to pick up Beth outside the college entrance. The slim brunette climbed into the passenger seat beside her with an awkward smile. She looked almost like a schoolgirl, wearing no make-up and with her hair tied back in an untidy ponytail. Charlotte had not managed to get a proper look at Beth while they were at Thomas's place together – she had been too busy entertaining that oaf Hughes – but she had noticed how gauche and unpolished the new girl seemed in comparison with the regular party-goers.

'So you're Beth. It was a pity we didn't get a chance to chat when I saw you the other week,' Charlotte said, giving Beth a quick glance up and down as she shut the car door. 'No offence, but you don't look much like a pony girl ... or even a submissive, come to that. Are you sure you're ready for this tonight?'

The other girl shrugged and pulled on her seatbelt as Charlotte accelerated into the dusk in the direction of Abingdon. 'Dr Milton seems to think so.'

Charlotte shot the brunette an ironic little smile. So this new girl of Milton's was naive as well as inexperienced. She was still bathed in the warm glow of initiation and had not seen beyond it to the reality of her situation. It would be amusing to see how Beth reacted once she realised exactly what her tutor expected of her tonight.

'Darling Milton, he's a fabulous master but he thinks with his dick a little too often. Any pony girl worth her oats will tell you becoming a good submissive requires months of rigorous training. How long is it since he recruited you?'

'I'm not sure. Just over a month?'

'Oh, for God's sake, is that all?' Charlotte shook her head, cursing Milton silently. How on earth did he expect her to cope, having a novice dumped on her like this at the last minute? 'You can't possibly be ready to work publicly yet. Tonight is going to be an utter disaster.'

'I'm a quick learner,' Beth said, her tone defensive.

'You'll bloody well have to be, darling. Because the sort of men we cater for have no patience with beginners. All I can suggest is you try not to speak and just copy whatever I do, even if you find it really difficult or embarrassing. Do you understand?'

'Uh-huh.'

'Oh, and Milton's given us some dog costumes to wear tonight. So I hope you don't mind a bit of fancy-dress work.'

'Dog –?'

'That's right, darling. As in woof, woof.'

'What kind of dog?'

Charlotte smiled dryly. 'The kind who does what she's told.'

115

It was almost dark as she turned down a familiar leafy avenue on the southern side of Abingdon and parked a few hundred yards away from a large modern house on their left. From the loud rock music pumping out of the windows and the number of expensive-looking cars on the drive, she guessed it must be the right place. After silently handing Beth her costume, she kneeled up on the driver's seat and struggled out of her jeans and white top, pulling on the brown furry outfit instead. They dressed hurriedly and in semi-darkness, drawing uneven whiskers on each other's face and little rounded blobs on the ends of their noses, suddenly giggling at their appearance as they finished.

'We look absolutely ridiculous,' Charlotte muttered, adjusting her costume so that her breasts were not quite so cramped.

Beth nodded. 'Funny, isn't it?'

'Funny? Just wait until we get inside. Then I bet you won't think it's quite so amusing, darling.'

'What do you think they'll –?'

'Do to us?'

The slim brunette nodded, her face apprehensive.

Charlotte gave a cynical laugh, as she climbed out of the car and locked it behind her. She looped the heavy dog chain over one arm, then stood there for a moment, pinching her nipples between thumb and forefinger until they came pleasingly erect under the thick brown fur. 'Fuck us until we leak, I should imagine. But not before thoroughly humiliating us first. That's what these costumes are about. To make us feel like idiots before they start treating us like dogs.'

'I thought it was a disguise.'

'Well, yeah, it's that as well. So, if you don't want to be recognised, keep the costume on at all times and

116

make sure you alter your voice. I think I've guessed who's going to be at this party tonight. If I'm right, it's going to be a bit rough and ready. Don't expect any gentle treatment, OK?'

Beth nodded without comment, following her obediently up the garden path to the front door. After ringing the bell, Charlotte heard a series of shouts from inside and then the door was flung open. She did not even have time to speak. The lad who had opened the door, a great broad-shouldered hulk who looked like a champion rower, gave a whoop of drunken delight and dragged her into the house. She tripped over his boots, landing on the carpet, and hurriedly scampered forwards so Beth would not bump into her, then rearranged her tail and the brown furry hood which had fallen over her eyes.

Some of the other party guests spilled out of the living room to stare at them both. They were all lads in their late teens and early twenties; Charlotte recognised a few of them and lowered her face to the carpet, dying to laugh at their shocked and fascinated expressions. She was used to entertaining older and much more experienced men than these. These were just kids by comparison. In fact, the mere sight of her curvaceous body in the furry dog costume appeared to have struck most of them dumb.

'How much is that doggy in the window?'

As if to demonstrate how wrong she was in her assumptions, one of the lads broke into song at that moment, yanking at her studded dog collar and pulling Charlotte up off her knees until she was level with his groin. His hand slapped her bottom rather more smartly than she had expected, making her yelp in surprise.

'The one with the waggly tail.'

'Ouch!'

His hand caught her hard across the back of her thighs. 'I beg your pardon, bitch? That didn't sound very doglike.'

The sudden pain cut across her thoughts and reminded her why they were there tonight. To arouse and entertain, on behalf of the Club to which some of these older students might be admitted if they stayed on at Oxford as postgraduate tutors.

'Woof?' Charlotte corrected herself, her eyes fixed on his raised hand, half-laughing, half in earnest. 'Woof, woof, woof.'

A warm glow began to spread throughout her body as he smacked her a few more times, pressing her face into the crotch of his jeans. He might be a little drunk but it was obvious what duties he intended her to perform next. She wriggled and hissed with pleasure each time his hand descended, enjoying the discomfort, her sex chafing against the furry flap between her legs. Slapping and sucking were one of her favourite combinations, she thought. Perhaps this evening would not be so dreary after all. The college boys did not appear to be as inexperienced and predictable in their sexual tastes as they had seemed at first sight.

The boy's crotch smelled muskily of sweat and possibly even a hint of urine; he had probably not washed these jeans in weeks. Charlotte did not care about his lack of hygiene; if anything, the smell aroused her even more. She nudged her face in deeper, sniffing at the faded blue creases running through the denim, turning her cheek to rub against the growing erection beneath, her mouth obediently wide as the boy stopped slapping her and reached down to unzip his flies. He held her head still and unceremoniously stuffed his cock into her mouth, a warm live piece of flesh that hardened to instant

118

rigidity as she accepted it eagerly between her lips and started to suck.

Behind her, she heard Beth cry out in protest and guessed that something similar must have happened to the other girl when silence descended, followed by the humiliated slurps of a woman reluctantly sucking cock. Even though it might be a little unfair of her to gloat, a small spark of triumph flared inside Charlotte as she tried to imagine what was going through the other girl's mind. It was always exciting to witness a complete novice like Beth being pushed to her knees, she thought, and made to perform fellatio. Especially in a situation like this, where the men she had to satisfy were not her elders and betters, but students her own age. Her lips curved into a smile around the thick saliva-slicked shaft bloating her cheeks. Beth was slimmer and prettier than she was, and that knowledge rankled.

The boy started humping her face, gripping the furry hood of her dog costume, pulling her right into his pelvis until she could hardly breathe. Charlotte struggled to take his full length as it slammed repeatedly into the back of her throat, the massive well-oiled wedge of meat growing harder by the second. It was not long before the boy came, shooting his full load into her mouth with a hoarse cry of satisfaction. Still on her knees before him, like a supplicant receiving communion, she swallowed as much as she could before the excess spilled from the corners of her mouth, unable to prevent the precious white fluid rolling down her chin. Abruptly he released her and she slumped backwards into the arms of a waiting student.

Turning her head as the new lad dragged her towards his crotch, a heavy purple-headed cock dangling there like ripe fruit, Charlotte suddenly caught a glimpse of Beth on her hands and knees a little further along the hallway. One boy was fumbling with the stud fastenings between Beth's legs, his erect cock exposed as he tried in vain to get into her furry dog costume; at the other end, a second boy, pale and slim hipped, kneeled by her head and slid himself delicately into her throat. Judging by Beth's stifled moan of pleasure and the way her limbs began to tremble at his increasing thrusts, she was not quite as reluctant to perform for these students as she had been when they first entered the house.

Charlotte was surprised and perhaps even a little envious, taking the purple-headed cock into her mouth and beginning to suck hard. She had never seen a girl change her mind so quickly before. Was it part of some clever tongue-in-cheek act, designed to excite men into thinking she needed to be forced? Or could the girl be so inexperienced that she was genuinely unaware of her own sexual desires?

The new boy in Charlotte's mouth grunted and came unexpectedly, jerking himself free at the last second and pumping several thick white streamers of spunk into her face. With an approving shudder, Charlotte licked at the warm traces of fluid coating her lips, her vision obscured as a few stray gobbets dripped from the fur hood into her eyes and matted her eyelashes. She was such a slut, she told herself with mock severity. She loved that familiar salty taste in her mouth far too much, and as for the sheer wicked filthiness of having spunk sprayed in her face without any warning . . . mmm.

Her sex ached to be handled and prised open by these boys, her moist swollen lips rubbing against the furry crotch of her costume with increasing horniness. It was always lovely to give head, but when were they going to get down to the more serious business of fucking?

Someone reached down and snapped open the crotch on her dog costume, dragging her thighs wide apart. This is it, she thought hungrily, arching her body towards him. But, no, she was wrong. It was not sex he wanted, not here at least. The boy had clipped the chain lead on to her studded leather collar and was pulling her through to a brightly lit conservatory at the back of the house. Here, the white Roman blinds had all been pulled down firmly, shutting them off from the neighbours and the prying eyes of anyone passing in the street. She kneeled there, shivering at the change of temperature, listening to his harsh voice and wondering what was coming next. The cold tiles of the conservatory hurt her hands and knees. What did the bastard want from her? To pee on the floor like an untrained puppy?

She heard his command in disbelief, amazement giving way to an amused irritation. What on earth would they think of next to humiliate her, the little pricks? As if the boy could read her thoughts, he broke a thin stalk off the bamboo plant in the corner and whacked it across her buttocks.

'Piss right there on the floor for me and do it properly! No half-hearted little trickles, OK? I want to see a real gush.'

Smarting from the bamboo stalk, Charlotte hurried to obey the boy's order. She scuttled on all fours to the centre of the room, thighs spread wide to avoid splashing her costume with pee. At least she was not too concerned about having to pee on command like this; Milton had trained her how to urinate in public with the minimum of effort. But it still took a little concentration of will, biting her lip as she focused on relaxing her internal muscles and letting the whole pelvis hang loose and heavy. The other guests had followed them into the conservatory and the room was packed, boys standing on chairs in every corner, shouting and clapping their hands now as Charlotte gave a little sigh and obediently wet herself in front of them.

Glancing down as her muscles relaxed, it was with a real sense of satisfaction that she noted the puddle gradually expanding between her knees. Once the flow had started, there was no stopping it. The warm fluid poured out in a gush, just as he had insisted it should do, and she was glad to have spread her legs safely apart. The tiled floor was soon awash with piss, the strong acrid smell of it unmistakeable as she finished peeing and scrabbled to one side before the puddle touched her fur-covered leg. The dog costumes they had been given to wear were all-in-one bodysuits, with a flap opening at the crotch for ease of access, and she did not want the thick brown fur ruined.

'Now you!' The boy with the bamboo switch applied it to Beth's buttocks, still faintly laced with cane marks from her last training session, and used the tip of his boot to push her further into the centre of the conservatory. 'Hurry up, don't keep us waiting.'

It seemed to Charlotte that he had done this sort of thing before. Once Beth was in position, the boy hoisted the stick over his shoulder and stepped back to watch her performance. He might only be in his early twenties, but his voice seemed confident, uncompromising.

'Squat down there, legs wide apart so we can all see, and do exactly the same as your friend.'

Beth spread her thighs as ordered, obediently down on all fours in the middle of the tiled room, but after a minute or so it became clear that she could not produce a single drop. There was sweat on the girl's forehead, her body trembling and a glazed look in her eyes as she glanced towards Charlotte for help. She looked vaguely comical with those thick-drawn dog whiskers disguising her face and Charlotte wanted to laugh.

She did not laugh, though. It was a serious matter, disobeying a direct order, regardless of whether it had been done intentionally or not. There were no prizes here for 'doing your best', after all. Not at this level of the game and with these players, Charlotte thought cynically. These boys were not experienced enough to overlook the odd mistake and carry on with the fun. No, they would make poor Beth pay for her silly incompetence. Which was not too upsetting a thought. Charlotte smiled to herself, watching the proceedings with malicious anticipation. She was rather looking forward to seeing the other girl squirm under some terrible but fitting punishment.

With a muttered expletive, the boy stepped forwards to discipline her. The bamboo switch cut through the air with an ominous noise and Beth tried to escape it in fear. The audience of fascinated students prevented her from escaping her punishment, though, enclosing her too tightly, and the switch came down with punishing severity on her bare bottom. It left a sharp red line each time it made contact, the brunette continuing to cringe and duck away.

'When you're given an order, you must learn to obey it,' the boy instructed her, his switch driving Beth into the pool of pee until she was slipping all over the place, scrabbling across wet tiles and crying out loud, her cheeks burning with shame. 'That's it, you dirty bitch. I ought to rub your face right in it.'

Much to Charlotte's disgust, Beth's eyes were soon brimming with tears and she seemed on the verge of begging him to stop. How this girl had ever survived the terrors of the cane and tawse was beyond her, if she could not handle a simple beating with a bamboo switch. Perhaps she was finding the audience too humiliating, constantly reminded by their laughter and coarse jokes that these boys were from her own peer group. That was no excuse, though. If Beth was a member of the Club, she ought to have been prepared for this sort of activity before she agreed to work here tonight. Charlotte did not want to think any less of Milton, as he had made the last two years at Oxford so exciting for her. Perhaps he had finally lost the plot, though, recruiting someone with so little experience to the Club. She only hoped this girl would learn what was expected of her . . . and bloody soon!

Beth was biting her lip, shivering like a real dog under the threat of his stick, her eyes wide with entreaty as she looked at the ring of forbidding faces around her. 'I'm really sorry I couldn't wee when you told me . . . I didn't mean to make you angry. Please can I try again?'

The bamboo switch came down again. 'Is this what you girls call obedience? Don't speak without permission!'

One of the older lads dropped to his knees behind Beth and felt around between her legs. Seconds later, he had pushed aside the furry flap that covered her sex and was poised to mount her, his large cock already out and erect in his hand.

'Don't worry. I'll teach the little bitch not to disobey an order,' he told the others, driving inside the girl with a determined smile on his lips. His hands descended to her hips, confident and determined. 'I'll plug this end. Harris, why don't you take her mouth? I think this one's got far too much to say for herself and needs to be shown her place.'

Beth gasped and moaned beneath him, a wild flush in her cheeks as he began to thrust. Another boy, thicker set and with unruly blond hair above a freckled face, shuffled forwards until he was directly in front of the girl's face and unzipped his jeans.

From where she was crouching, Charlotte could see a thick and sturdy cock springing out from his nest of gingerish hairs and felt a little envious of the other girl. This must be Harris, she thought, her mouth suddenly dry as she imagined being forced to experience the same rough treatment: an energetic young man kneeling at each end, both lads driving strenuously into her body, throat and cunt filled with their firm meat and only too eager to receive their spunk, too.

The chain lead jerked at Charlotte's neck and she responded obediently, turning to follow the boy on all fours. 'Dinner time for good doggies!' he said, and the others laughed. A large metal dish filled with some dark gravy-covered meat was shoved in front of her face. The students stood above her, waiting for her to eat it. Charlotte almost recoiled, her face grimacing with immediate disgust, then she collected herself. If they wanted her to eat dog food, she had to eat dog food. If you choose to be a slave, she reminded herself, you could not then choose which orders to obey. Milton had talked her through this situation often enough. As a slave, you obey all orders that will not physically harm you, and consider yourself lucky if they are not too disgusting or cruel. She gave a mental shrug and plunged her head obediently into the bowl of dog food.

To her delight, though, it tasted great. Thick chunks of nicely cooked steak in a rich gravy; it was not dog food at all, but a meal specially prepared for them and served in a dog dish. How inventive of them, she thought with appreciative humour, impressed by such an attention to detail.

Suddenly rather peckish after missing her supper, Charlotte used her teeth and agile tongue to manoeuvre the larger chunks of meat into position. She chewed them up one at a time, swallowed them down and then bent her head to lick the bowl clean, ignoring the warm gravy that soon coated her mouth and chin.

'God, she's disgusting,' one of them was saying, and with a shock she recognised Robert's voice.

Staring up at their watching faces, her chin dripping with gravy and dried spunk still matting her eyelashes, she realised that her friend was standing only a few feet away among the other students.

Robert was gazing down at her, his eyes almost black with a look of fascinated contempt. 'Someone ought to take her outside and hose her down like the dirty bitch she is.'

Her heart leapt in shock and it took all her self-control not to scramble to her feet and run away. Had Robert recognised her?

'I've got a better idea,' one of his friends replied.

'Yeah,' another boy said, lust thick in his voice. 'I didn't come here tonight just to watch a dog eat her dinner.'

Someone grabbed Charlotte by the furry hood of her costume and dragged her back into the centre of the room. They pushed her down until her cheek was resting against the piss-soaked tiles and the musky scent of her own pee was strong in her nostrils. She felt her knees being kicked brutally apart and then a hard cock entered her without any preliminaries and began stretching the walls of her cunt. Within seconds, she was soaking wet with glorious anticipation. Yes, yes, yes. She was going to be fucked now, pushed face down into her own piss and fucked in front of Robert, and there was nothing she could do to prevent it. She writhed and groaned, flushed with humiliated pleasure. What would Milton say if he could see her now?

She could hear Beth somewhere close at hand, crying aloud as the boy pushed in and out of her mouth, suddenly tensed and came, right in her face. The note of excitement in the other girl's voice made Charlotte shiver with anticipation, hoping to suffer a similar fate herself. This could turn out to be quite a memorable evening. She was still sticky from the spunk that had been shot into her own face earlier, but there was plenty of time for more of the same, she thought eagerly. Half the boys in the conservatory had not yet come. All it ever took were a few quick jerks and . . .

The boy inside her gave a deep savage grunt and dug his fingers into the tender skin of her hips, no doubt leaving bruises which would show for weeks. Not wasting any time afterwards, he withdrew almost before he had finished coming and she felt warm trickles of spunk begin to decorate her inner thighs. The reason for his overhasty departure became clear; another student had been waiting impatiently to take his place, his hands clumsy and inexperienced as he fumbled for a minute between her thighs, trying to fit cock and pussy together. But her sex lips were too slick with spunk and the poor boy did not manage it in time, groaning and spasming in creamy jerks before he was even inside her.

'Shit, Butler,' one of his mates said, with a laugh, shoving him aside and manoeuvring himself behind her gaping cunt. Before penetrating her, he had to use the furry flap of her costume to wipe away the last boy's come. 'You're useless. Look at this mess. It's like trying to fuck a bowl of porridge.'

'Cold porridge at that,' someone else added.

'Oh, that's gross.'

'Shut up and give the dog a bone!'

To her horror, Robert had jostled his way to the front of the group and was now wanking as he awaited his own turn inside her. There were boys watching on all sides now, some of them clapping and jeering as Butler slunk out of the room with his soiled jeans round his ankles. The boy behind her was inside now, hammering himself in and out with noisy little grunts. She could only imagine what she must look like to Robert, down on all fours like a dog, her face slimy with spunk and gravy and piss, her legs wide apart and another boy mounted between them, pumping her hard.

Robert ignored the noise around him, fisting his cock with total focus, unable to take his eyes off her body. 'Hurry up and come, OK?' he said tensely. 'I can't wait much longer. I've got a stiffy like a piece of rock.'

'Make her suck it, then.'

He did not need much persuading, she thought wryly, as Robert hurried round to her mouth, lifted her chin and shoved his erection between her lips like a cigar. Charlotte sucked hard and lovingly, her tongue worshipping the full length of his cock. It was longer and thicker than she had expected, having judged him only by the bulge in his jeans whenever they had kissed in the past. Perhaps she should have let him fuck her after all. She had always thought of Robert as a little boy but he was almost a man tonight: a man that tasted of sweat and deodorant and stale piss, balls sticky with heat, his shaft growing ever more rigid between her lips.

Robert stroked her hair. 'That's good, that's so good.'

Not long now, she thought in a spunk-white daze, her mouth full of cock. Her sex was so hot and wet and open that the boy inside her kept slipping out every time he withdrew too far. Her nipples ticked with excitement, taut and painfully erect, rubbing against the furry dog costume. Her whole body felt like a bomb, just counting down the seconds, waiting to explode. She closed her eyes and let herself relax into the pleasure just as Milton had taught her, gagging a little on the excess of saliva that sucking cock always seemed to generate.

She was so aware of them watching. It was like being in the centre of a circus ring, the spotlights hot on her face. These boys did not care about her, not even Robert. This was sex, nothing more. She loved their rough hands on her body, so cruel, so dismissive, so casual. Someone had even tilted her head further back and was wanking into her face, his cock pressed against the vulnerable orifice of her nostril.

Charlotte paused to think about the implications of that, unable to move away, her legs trembling with desire. Was the bastard going to explode there, shoot his come up her nose and watch it erupt from her mouth and nostrils again, blind her with fear and pain and ecstasy as he took his selfish pleasure? Oh yes, she thought wildly, slipping a hand between her thighs to rub at her exposed clitoris. She could hear Beth moaning plaintively in the distance as her body began to tense towards a fierce uncontrollable orgasm. This was how to take several men at once. Not struggling, like poor inexperienced Beth, to accommodate two or more cocks at the same time; but absolutely revelling in the filthiness of it, giving herself completely and unashamedly to the group, allowing them to use her in any way they wanted.

She screamed against the thick shaft in her mouth, climaxing with high muffled cries of pleasure as Robert continued to work himself back and forth between her stretched lips. Her fingers pinched and squeezed her clitoris hard, hard, hard; cruel as any man, enjoying her own pain. The boy rapidly jerking against her nose came in an unexpected burst, perhaps triggered by her own excitement. Luckily, he missed the nostril opening and sprayed his sticky come all over her face instead.

Robert stiffened to orgasm a few seconds later. Rocking against her as though her face was a cradle, apparently oblivious to the spunk being mashed into his belly, he gave a deep hoarse cry and emptied himself into her throat. Her mouth tightened obediently around his shaft as she felt the first gush of come and he dragged her head even closer. 'Swallow my spunk,' he was muttering incoherently. 'Swallow it right down, I love your sweet filthy mouth, you slut, you whore. Have dinner with me; have babies with me.'

His enthusiastic little speech excited and alarmed her. Was it possible her friend had guessed who she was? That would be disastrous for both her and the Club. Her throat convulsing as she swallowed, Charlotte stared up at her friend in dismay. But his eyes were shut, his face clenched tight in a mask of pleasure as he let his balls empty fully and relax against her. He had not seen through her disguise, she realised, sagging back to the floor as he released her. Robert had no idea whose throat he had just spunked into so eagerly.

And it had to stay that way, for everyone's sake.

Nine

There was a knock at the door. Milton looked up from the pornographic magazine he had been reading and frowned. It was a little before ten in the morning and he was in his college study at the top of staircase III. His next tutorial was not until after lunch. He glanced down at the charming centrefold shot of nineteen-year-old Eleanor in white socks and gym skirt, bent over in breathless anticipation of her teacher's cane, and reluctantly closed the CP magazine. Another few minutes and he would have been there, poised to avail himself of the white tissues he kept for ever handy in a box by his computer. Sighing, Milton slid the magazine discreetly into the top drawer of his desk, locked it and pocketed the key. He tucked an uncomfortably stiff cock back into his trousers and reached for an authoritative critical text on nineteenth-century women's poetry. Opening it randomly to a point halfway through the third chapter, he tried to look as though he had been engaging deeply with *Emily Dickinson: A Lost Voice?* before that knock at his door had disturbed him.

'Come in,' he barked irritably, hoping the tone of his voice would be enough to send whoever it was back down the stairs.

It was Beth, clutching a piece of paper in her hand. The girl looked round the door at him with tentative eyes, chewing at a strand of chestnut brown hair which had come loose from her ponytail. 'Have I come at a bad time, Dr Milton?'

She behaved like such a child at times, he thought pensively, having to remind himself again that she was a second-year student and far from sexually inexperienced. Though she had to be at least twenty years old, Beth always looked as though butter wouldn't melt; the girl would not be out of place in the pages of the CP magazine he had just locked away in his top drawer, clad in tennis whites and a pair of lace-up pumps, perhaps innocently twirling a racquet as she stood by the net. His cock jerked in his trousers at the image, still pleasantly tense. 'What do you want, Beth?' he asked curtly.

'You asked to see me,' she stammered, showing him the crumpled piece of paper in her hand. 'I found this in my pigeonhole. It sounded urgent. Should I come back later?'

With only a moment's hesitation, Milton laid aside the book on nineteenth-century poetry and shook his head. 'No, come in and lock the door behind you,' he said firmly. 'I did leave you a note, I remember now. It was about that student party you attended last week.'

'At Abingdon?'

He nodded, amused by the sudden look of consternation on her face. 'That's right. Charlotte told me what happened. You were ordered to urinate in front of the boys and refused to obey.'

She was wearing a pair of hipster jeans with a tight black T-shirt, her breasts pert and quite clearly unfettered by a bra. He could see her nipples beneath the stretched material, stiffening in the breeze coming off the quad through his open window. Beth might be looking a little apprehensive right now but she was no longer the same shy girl she had been that first evening, when he enjoyed her body at that seedy hotel in Summertown. It was almost laughable how fast some of these students changed once you showed them the darker face of sex. It was as though their bodies were designed for submission even if their minds initially rebelled against it.

She stood before him, the note crumpled in her hand. 'I tried my best, Dr Milton. I just couldn't do it.'

'Charlotte also tried her best. She succeeded.'

'Yes, but –' Her eyes fell before his, her voice husky and low. 'She's much more experienced than me. Even she said it was hard, the first time she had to wee in front of other people.'

'Hard but not impossible.'

Beth bit her lip, nodding reluctantly. 'I'm really sorry, sir. I'll do better next time, I promise.'

'What you need is practice.'

'Yes, sir.'

He leaned back in his chair and crossed his legs. 'Starting right here and now, I think.'

'I beg your pardon?'

'Oh, you don't have to start begging yet. That will come later. Just for now, stop standing there like an idiot and sit down.'

Pointing at the old leather armchair opposite, Milton ordered her to take off her hipster jeans and T-shirt, and to make herself comfortable in nothing but her underwear. An embarrassed flush came into her face as she complied, her bare thighs squeaking against the leather. He watched her through narrowed eyes and barely noticed the church bells of Oxford pealing chaotically as they all began to strike the hour at once. He was too intent on his new protégée.

Milton tried to soften his tone, not wanting to scare the girl away. 'No, don't cross your legs like that. You have to keep them wide apart, so I can see your knickers.' He gave her a cool smile. 'How else am I supposed to know?'

'Know what?' she whispered, reluctantly opening her legs.

Between them he could see her prim little panties, white stretch cotton decorated with pink and mauve flowers, quite different from the skimpy lace underwear the majority of his 'girls' usually wore when they visited him. At either side of the elasticated edge, he could see the smooth flesh of her sex beginning to show, still shaven and just as tantalising as he remembered. She was no innocent. Did she wear such things just to tease him? His cock stiffened a little more.

'When you can't hold on for a moment longer and you're about to wet yourself, of course.'

Her lip trembled. 'Please, Dr Milton –'

'Sit straight. Hands flat on the arms of the chair, please.'

'But –'

'And do stop interrupting me. It's becoming rather an irritating habit of yours. Haven't you learned anything about obedience yet, you silly girl?' His eyes narrowed on Beth's face, willing her into a humbled silence. 'Unless you want another punishment like the one I had to give you the other day? Is that it?'

Her face paled. 'No, sir.'

'Then sit still and stop squirming about like that. When did you last go to the toilet?'

'Erm – about two hours ago, sir. When I got out of bed.'

'Do you need to wee again now?'

'Yes.' She was looking distinctly uncomfortable in that position, her nipples erect, her eyes flashing nervously every now and then to the windows which overlooked the quad. 'I'll need to go pretty soon.'

'Excellent.'

'Can anyone see us from here?'

It was extremely unlikely, his study was too high above the college quad, facing the blank chapel wall; and the only other rooms on this level belonged to graduate students and had skylights instead of normal windows. Beth was safe enough in that position, he thought, but did not tell her that. Let the girl sweat; it was more amusing that way. 'That's none of your concern.'

Beth flushed again at his cruelty but made no reply, holding her thighs obediently open for him, her small breasts and belly lit up by the sunshine streaming in through his windows.

Milton watched the girl as she settled into an uneasy silence, a smile playing on his lips as he tried to imagine what must be going through her head. The pale skin on her thighs showed fading marks from earlier punishments and he longed to trace his fingers along them, perhaps even adding a few fresh marks so he could watch her expression turn to pain. The girl was so marvellously untrained, as Thomas had remarked, everything about her raw and unpolished. Yet somehow she managed to convey a genuine sense of submission at the same time, as though her desire to curb that disobedient streak came naturally and needed very little prompting from anyone else.

They sat facing each other for some time, both listening to the ticking of the small gold carriage clock on his desk. Her hands gripped the sides of the armchair with unconcealed tension. Her knuckles were beginning to whiten under the pressure, he noticed, and felt amused by the rigidity of her body as she fought against nature. Her bladder must be uncomfortably full by now, prompting her to expel its contents as soon as possible. He had played this delightful game with other students in the past and recognised the warning signs. It would not take long for Beth to reach such a point of discomfort that the urge to relieve herself would override the desire not to disgrace herself in front of her tutor.

Milton crossed the room to the water dispenser, poured a large glass of chilled water and offered it to her with a solicitous smile. 'You look a little flushed,' he murmured. 'Better have some of this water. It's wonderfully cool and refreshing.'

'Thanks. But I'm not thirsty.'

He pressed the glass into her hand. 'My dear, I insist.'

'Honestly, I –'

His brows snapped together in a harsh frown, irritated by her unrelenting disobedience. 'Drink it!'

Silenced by his angry tone, Beth lifted the glass to her lips and took a few tentative sips, her eyes on his face.

'All of it,' he prompted her, his voice softening slightly, though it was no less insistent. It was important that his girls obeyed him when given a direct order, but there was no reason to behave like a tyrant. 'Water is excellent for your skin, Beth. You should drink several glasses every day.'

'Yes, sir,' she agreed in a muted fashion, and drained the entire glass in front of him with obvious reluctance.

He nodded his approval of the girl's obedience and took the glass from her hand. But, if she thought that would be an end to it, she was soon to be disappointed. After refilling the glass right to the brim, he carried it carefully back to her without spilling a single drop. Beth looked up at him from the armchair, her thighs still held wide apart for his scrutiny, her face ashen as she realised he meant her to drink a second glassful as well. Nevertheless, she accepted her fate without any further protests. She drained the glass with several noisy gulps and handed it back to him in a submissive silence. He refilled the glass for a third time and watched her struggle to drink so much water, her eyes hazy, her whole body tensing at intervals as though having to resist a strong urge to pee.

Milton was impressed by the capacity of her bladder. He was also pleasantly aroused again, his revived erection pressing a little too uncomfortably against his zipper as he imagined how she might clutch herself with embarrassment just seconds before the pee poured uncontrollably through those tight-crotched panties. He had seen such things on numerous occasions before today: first, a spasm of panic and excited humiliation, fingers desperately flying down to stem the flow; then that look of peace passing across their faces – beautifying them, leaving them almost angelic – as they finally realised it was too late and there was no point trying to hide their shame. Ah, the first time a girl peed in her panties was a moment of pure alchemical transformation. It was always worth waiting for.

'Comfortable?' he asked, settling back into his chair.

Unaware that she was increasing his excitement, the girl shook her head and grimaced, her bare thighs moving restlessly against the squeaky leather armchair, opening and closing as though she could not make up her mind which position was more uncomfortable. 'No, Dr Milton. Not particularly.'

'I'm sorry to hear that. I shall speak to the Domestic Bursar about the state of these old armchairs. They must be fifty years old or more, some of them, and in bad need of restoration. It's shocking what they expect students to put up with these days.'

She did not manage to speak again for several minutes. His eyes moved over her slowly, noting every tiny change in her expression, every twitch of her muscles. The game must be nearing its natural end, he thought coolly: she no longer seemed so willing to meet his eyes; her breathing had become unsteady; and there was even a fine sweat on her forehead as though the torture was physical was well as mental.

'God, I really need to –'

'To . . . what?'

'Pee.'

'Naturally you do,' he agreed smoothly. 'That's the whole idea of this exercise, my dear Beth. So tell me. Do you feel able to pee in front of me now or would you like another glass of water?'

'No more water.'

Milton tightened his jaw angrily at her sharp tone. Why did Beth always have to be so tiresome? Her training seemed to be a case of one step forwards, two steps back at the moment. Whenever he thought she was finally beginning to understand her role, she would ruin everything with some irritating remark or momentary flare of insurrection. His voice was heavy with irony. 'Look, you're not helping yourself much here. Would you prefer to be spanked before or after you've pissed yourself?'

'What?'

He leaned forwards and slapped her thighs apart again, dragging each one up and over the arms of the chair so he could see the stretched fabric at her crotch. The idea of spanking her was incredibly tempting. He was cross enough to give her a bloody good wallop on the backside right here and now; forget those complex accompanying rituals designed to heighten her awareness of his power. But he did not have enough time to indulge in the pleasures of corporal punishment.

'For God's sake, what the hell's the matter with you? I've never had so much difficulty breaking in a new girl for the Club. Why can't you just keep your mouth shut and do what you're told?'

There were tears in her eyes now, shining and threatening to spill. He had not handled her that roughly. Perhaps she thought she could manipulate him by crying.

'I'm sorry, Dr Milton,' she whispered, staring up at him as though she had never seen him before. 'I didn't mean to speak to you like that.'

Milton reached between her legs and pinched her sex lips through the moist tight fabric of her panties. 'Ready to pee yet?' he demanded.

'I don't . . . think so.'

'What do I have to do? Siphon it out of you?'

The girl closed her eyes and strained, biting her lower lip so hard he could see the skin breaking. But nothing happened. She shook her head, her voice shaking. 'I'm trying really hard, honestly. I just can't seem to relax enough for it to happen.'

'More water,' he insisted and fetched it for her, tilting the glass to her lips himself and forcing her to drink.

She could not seem to swallow it as fast as he wanted her to. The water splashed freely down her chin, trickling into the pale cleavage between her breasts, leaving her choking and pushing his hand away with a frantic shake of her head.

'Please –'

'What's the matter now?'

139

She clutched at herself, clamping her thighs shut in an instinctive gesture, suddenly desperate. 'I'm going to –'

'Excellent. But not on that leather armchair.' He frowned, gesturing her rapidly to stand. 'It would take far too long to clean up afterwards and the smell would linger for days. On your feet now, hurry up. I want you to fetch something from over there.'

Milton directed her to a corner of his study, his voice deliberately harsh, watching her stumble clumsily over the clutter of books and newspapers. It would not do to lessen the pressure. The girl was right there on the edge, wound up to an almost unbearable pitch. She would break soon. And, when that happened, and she stained those girlie cotton panties with piss, Milton would take great pleasure in ordering her to suck him into her throat until he came.

'You see that yucca plant? Take it out of the ceramic planter and stand it on the floor. Good. Now bring the ceramic planter back into the centre of the room and put it in front of me.'

'The planter?'

'Don't waste time questioning me; just do what you're told.' He snapped his fingers and almost laughed out loud, as she stumbled over the piles of books in her haste. Wishing to prolong the girl's discomfort for just a few moments longer, he deliberately shook his head when she brought the pot back into the centre of the room. 'A little further to the left. No, closer to me. That's too close. Pull it back about three inches. Perhaps another inch. Now to the right . . .'

Beth obeyed every instruction as quickly as she could, a contorted look of anguish on her face as she tried to clench her internal muscles until the ceramic planter was in position. It was almost too late; that

140

was clear from her body language. The poor girl was practically hopping up and down on one foot in her desperation as she tried to position the planter in exactly the right spot.

Finally, he was satisfied with its position. She straddled the planter with surprising alacrity, spreading her thighs as wide as they would go – presumably to avoid splashing herself – and squatted right down until her crotch was only a few inches above the rim of the pot. From his prime position, still seated in his tutor's chair, facing her as though waiting for her to deliver a four-thousand-word essay, Milton could see absolutely everything. That long and frequently tedious period of preparation was about to pay off.

His cock was rigid with excitement, hardening even more at what he saw and heard for the next forty or fifty seconds: her initial gasp of consternation, and then the first few pale spurts of piss as they pulsed through the thin fabric of her panties. The girl was steadying herself with one hand, crouched low down with her buttocks almost touching the pot, but her other hand had gone automatically to her crotch as the flow began; almost as though she was still trying to stop herself even when it was clearly too late. She groaned and the expression on her face was delightful, simply delightful. The stream of piss hit the side of the ceramic planter with an embarrassingly loud gush, the noise reminding him of sheep he had seen urinating in the fields. It changed gradually to a splattering and then a high-pitched tinkling as her pee began to pool in the bottom of the ceramic pot, a lovely strong golden colour.

He kept staring from her face to her groin, not sure which of them was more arousing; that look of sweet horrified relief in her eyes or the way she was trying to shield her disgrace from his gaze, spreading her fingers and pressing them against the yellowish-stained panties as the stream finally slowed to a trickle and then ceased altogether. It was almost a gesture of covert masturbation, those sticky fingers pressing harder into the soiled fabric, her face flushed with humiliation and pleasure, her mouth opening on a long moan. As she moved her head from side to side in appalled denial of her own actions, the chestnut ponytail swung and brushed against her bare shoulders.

The pungent smell rising from the ceramic planter nearly finished him but he managed to control himself with an effort. He had extricated his prick from his trousers and was now jerking the foreskin back and forth in a workmanlike fashion.

'That's enough, don't worry about the last few drips. Just get over here and take me in your mouth.'

It was with a genuine sense of relief that he watched the red-faced girl shuffle from the pot, beautifully nude except for her stained panties, firm breasts swaying as she kneeled before him and tilted back her head to accept his cock. He would not have been able to last much longer and it was always a shame to waste a good sacful on his study floor or in the folds of a handkerchief.

He fed his shaft into her willing mouth and groped for her breasts, not wanting the experience to be entirely unexciting for her. She had such charming little nipples, pert and almost virginal as they stiffened into peaks beneath his fingers. He could scarcely believe these breasts had been touched before, even though he knew the opposite to be true. They looked so pale and sweetly untouched. But he had squeezed and fondled them himself often enough over the past term, and even hard enough to leave bruises on more than one occasion.

She groaned under her breath and sucked with an urgent, almost manic pressure, pulled ever forwards by his hand on the back of her head. She was no professional fellatrice, he thought wryly, but that was not a cause for complaint. Her girlish eagerness to please him more than made up for her lack of expertise.

'Well done, Beth. Good strong sucks, further to the back of your throat. Yes, that's perfect.'

Milton rather liked the amateurish way Beth tended to drool from the corners of her mouth as she sucked. It reminded him of a Labrador dog he had once owned, whose favourite pastime had been lying out in the backyard chewing enthusiastically on a bone. Every now and then the girl even clutched at his trousers as if she would collapse without his support, pinning herself against him with tense little claws. Beth's incompetence was appealing at times, he thought, stroking her smooth chestnut hair. Unfortunately for her, it also made him want to be cruel, though he fought the urge to humiliate her further on this occasion. She was not yet ready to handle the sort of punishments he would normally mete out at this stage and, besides, there would be plenty of time for that in the future.

'Rub yourself,' Milton ordered her quickly, noting the wild flush in her cheeks as she squirmed on her knees before him.

Then it was too late to add anything else, because a deep groan was wrenched from his stomach and he felt the hot spunk shoot from his prick with only a few seconds' warning between sensation and sudden delicious expulsion. He was still recovering from that unexpected jolt of pleasure, his knees trembling slightly, both hands leaning on her head, when his cock was ejected from her mouth and she cried aloud, her lips stretched wide and white with spunk, deep in the throes of her own orgasm.

For a moment Milton was confused. Then he took a step back and saw her hand down there between her thighs, working feverishly under the damp fabric of her panties, rubbing hard just as he had told her to. The filthy little slut had not only peed herself like a professional in the end but had climaxed almost as uncontrollably as him. So much for being embarrassed by their little game. He had severely underestimated Beth, he thought, his brain ticking over as he tucked himself back into his trousers.

'I think you're ready, my dear,' he murmured.

Still on her knees, the girl stared up at him through misty brown eyes, her voice shaking and breathless. 'Ready for what?'

'The final hurdle.'

'I don't understand,' she said, her face perplexed.

'Anal.'

'Oh no,' she leaped up, grasping his sleeve. 'Not that.'

'Yes, that.'

'Please, Dr Milton. Give me another month.'

'I'm afraid there's no escape from it, my dear. It's a *fait accompli*. I've made up my mind.'

'But it's a mistake. I – I'm not ready.'

He shrugged, unmoved by her visible distress. 'Ready or not, you're going to take it up the arse. This Saturday at four o'clock, right here in Oxford. Put your clothes back on and I'll give you the address.'

She stood there without obeying, her eyes fixed on his face, the colour draining from her cheeks. 'You mean,' she stammered, 'it won't be you ... who –'

'I shall not be performing the deed, no. But you need have no fear. The gentleman in question is courteous and gentle. Especially with first-timers. That's why I am sending you to him.'

'But Dr Milton –'

'You'd prefer me to break you in myself?'

She nodded nervously, then dragged her wet panties down to her knees and bent to display herself. It felt as though the girl were offering her anal innocence to him there and then, head lowered submissively between her legs, hands gripping smooth ankles and that tiny puckered hole winking at him from its dark cleft.

'Please, sir. Don't make me go to someone else for this. I'd rather a stranger didn't touch me there. I always thought that, when the time came, it would be you who did it. Taught me how to ... well, you know. I think I'd be sick if another man –'

He listened to her voice tailing away into silence as she realised he was not planning to take her up on the offer. It rather amused him, though, the touching affection she had obviously developed for him, and for a moment Milton was tempted to change his mind and bugger the silly girl himself. He had rarely managed to take any of his other students in the arse for the first time, after all. There always seemed to be some other member of the Club who was owed a favour or needed to be appeased with precisely that sort of special gift. He had only ever been able to watch from a distance as they were initiated, or listen to their tearfully ecstatic accounts of it afterwards. However, he had promised the Reverend Smith-Holland that he would be the first to penetrate her delightful little bottom and it would be churlish indeed to deny an elderly cleric one of his few remaining pleasures in life.

'Look, I'm sorry,' he said, shrugging. 'The decision is out of my hands.'

Milton glanced a little impatiently at his watch. It was nearly time for lunch. They were serving bread and butter pudding for dessert today, one of his all-time favourites, and he did not want to be late getting to the Senior Common Room.

'I know you aren't comfortable with this, Beth,' he added more gently, seeing the fear on her face. 'But don't make me look bad. Submit to it with a good grace. Now here's his address. He's the Reverend Smith-Holland and he used to be chaplain here at St Nectan's.'

Ten

The red-brick semi-detached house with the neat front garden looked perfectly innocuous, Beth thought, walking past for the third time without ringing the doorbell. She could see fading net curtains at the windows and the path from the gate to the front door was paved with white and yellow diamond-shaped bricks. It all seemed normal, safe and unthreatening. Yet this was the address Milton had given her. Pacing back and forth in front of the house was ludicrous. She had to decide whether to go home or go through with it.

Clutching her handbag to her chest, Beth pushed open the garden gate and clicked up the path in her modest heels. She rang the doorbell and waited in silence, glancing down the street to where a man in rolled-up shirtsleeves was washing a dark-green Volvo. He looked up at her for a few seconds, then looked away, no doubt dismissing her as some kind of door-to-door salesperson, anonymous in her sober black knee-length skirt and white blouse. It was a pleasantly warm Saturday afternoon and she could hear kids playing somewhere behind the houses, their voices rising high and excited above the hum of traffic from the nearby A34.

The door opened and the Reverend Smith-Holland stood there in tweed trousers and an old woollen cardigan, smiling at her benignly. He was holding a small gardening trowel which he held carefully to one side as they shook hands.

'Don't mind the dirt. I just had to finish weeding the borders before the weather turns. I suspect it's going to rain later this evening.' He gestured her inside the house, ushering her into a back sitting room before pulling the curtains firmly across so that no one could see in. 'And thank goodness for that. It's been muggy for days. Quite unbearable, don't you think? Rain will be a relief.'

Beth politely refused his offer of a drink and put her bag down on the table, not sure what to say.

He gave her an encouraging smile. 'So you're Milton's new girl.'

'That's right.'

'Feeling a little nervous?'

Beth looked at him and nodded, not bothering to lie.

'Oh, there's no need to be.' He patted her hand. 'Milton's told me all about you. I won't rush things.'

'Thank you, sir.'

'I normally warm up with a little corporal punishment, in fact. Nothing too dreadful. Just some exercises to get the old juices flowing, if you see what I mean! You don't have any objections, I presume?'

'No, sir.'

'Good,' he said, nodding. 'Always best to check beforehand, though, I feel, in case of misunderstandings.'

'Of course,' she agreed, beginning to feel less nervous.

'And how are you getting on at St Nectan's? Struggling to keep up with the workload, I imagine. They expect students to do so much work these days.' He laughed, fumbling to undo the buttons on his cardigan. 'When I was in my first year at college, I don't think I went to a single lecture during the summer term. No, it was all punting and cycling and strawberry teas. Still managed to scrape my Finals, though!'

'The work's not too heavy, sir.'

'Excellent stuff. I'm very pleased to hear it.'

She tidied her hair in the mirror above the fireplace, taking the opportunity to glance at him from under lowered lids. The Reverend Smith-Holland was a tall man with shoulders which stooped slightly, a shock of white hair and watery blue eyes which seemed to dart continuously over her face and body as they chatted. She guessed him to be somewhere in his late seventies, far older than she had expected. But not incapable, she reminded herself, her skin tingling with heat at the memory of Thomas's sexual prowess. As the Reverend had invited her inside, his gaze had lingered on her breasts, braless and pushing firmly against the white blouse, the erect nipples prominent. For some men, she thought wryly, age appeared to be an irrelevance where the ability to fuck was concerned.

He had finally managed to remove his cardigan, revealing a light-blue shirt underneath, faded from many washes and fraying at the seams. The Reverend undid his top button and gave her a gentle smile, seeing her eyes on him in the mirror. 'Now don't worry, my dear, it's not all coming off. Not yet anyway. That part comes later.'

She turned to face him, her face pale but resolute. 'Where do you want me, sir?'

'That's the spirit.' His finger shaking slightly, the Reverend Smith-Holland pointed to a wooden desk near the window, the old-fashioned type with a sloping hinged lid and an in-built inkwell. 'If you could bend over the desk and pull your skirt up to your bottom, I would be most grateful.'

Beth did as she was told, unhurriedly adopting the position and pulling the knee-length black skirt up over her hips to expose the tight rounded curves of her buttocks.

'Further forwards and legs a little wider apart, please.'

Dr Milton had instructed her to wear a pair of plain white panties underneath and she had obeyed him, even though buying the horrible things in public had embarrassed her deeply. Beth considered this particular style of underwear untrendy in the extreme: they were low cut with a frilly finish round the thigh, covering her belly button and fitting snugly around her backside, and she imagined them to be the sort of comfortable knickers a pensioner might wear. But, if this was what the Reverend wanted to see when she bent over, frankly she was in no position to argue.

'That's perfect. Whatever I do, please don't get up or change your position until instructed.'

The elderly man stood behind her, his breathing uneven. For a few minutes, she heard a faint mumbling under his breath and strained to hear what he was saying, a little unsure whether to respond, and then eventually realised that he was praying.

When he had finished, his hands moved in an exploratory fashion over her bottom, tracing the taut white material as it stretched over the divide between her buttocks. 'These are very nice and clean,' he said with admiration, fingering the fabric where it clung to her skin. Then, to her surprise, his voice hardened. 'But I'm afraid you've been a naughty girl and your knickers will have to come down. Do you have anything to say in your defence?'

Beth hesitated for a moment, then shook her head. 'No, sir.'

'Very well, then.'

The Reverend Smith-Holland hooked several of his fingers into the elasticated waistband of the panties and tugged until her firm cheeks and the tiny puckered hole between them were exposed. 'You can't say I didn't warn you. You knew what to expect when you came here, my dear. Since you refuse to give a satisfactory account of your behaviour, I shall be forced to punish you.'

'What behaviour?'

'Why, coming to my house like a common whore and showing me your underwear, of course,' he said, in tones of some surprise.

'But you told me to show it to you.'

'No more of your insolence!' His hand came down hard across one of her bare cheeks, the blow stinging. 'You had a choice. You were not coerced by anyone into raising your skirt, were you?'

'No,' she said sullenly.

'The truth is, my dear, you wanted to show me your underwear. Because you need me to punish you.'

Beth felt him remove the panties entirely and raised her legs, one ankle at a time, to step out of them. She felt confused, maybe even a little bewildered for a moment. Was the Reverend right about her or was it simply another of those clever attempts to manipulate her into submission? She could not deny that no one had physically forced her into bending over and lifting her skirt, though it had felt like coercion at the time; as though she had no choice but to obey him. But that was a fantasy, as he had so accurately pointed out. Beth had chosen to visit him and whatever happened in this house would be her own choice, too. Painful and humiliating but her own choice.

The Reverend Smith-Holland came back from the other side of the room. He was bouncing a cane on the palm of his hand, presumably to test its flexibility. The gentle thwack-thwack-thwack made her heart jump and her knees begin to tremble.

'If you need to hold on to something, I should do so now,' he said. 'I'm about to start.'

'I'm fine.'

There was a short pause. 'I really think you ought to grasp the sides of the desk,' he suggested mildly, 'if only to avoid disturbing your position once the punishment is under way. Young ladies have a habit, I seem to recall, of leaping up halfway through ... and then requiring considerable assistance to regain their composure.'

Finding it strangely difficult to breathe, Beth allowed her hands to slip down the sides of the desk and grasp its sturdy wooden legs exactly as he had advised her. The hard wood hurt her nipples, her breasts pressed against the sloping lid as she stared at the heavy blue velvet curtains immediately in front of her face. Beth felt cool air on her buttocks and remembered those other times she had taken the cane; her childish trembling anticipation of the pain. She wondered how long he would make her wait for that awful first stroke. It was odd. She had never felt so completely under the control of another human being like this before, and it ought to have been a horrible experience. Yet it wasn't. There was something both exciting and reassuring about yielding up control to the Reverend Smith-Holland. The old man was going to hurt her, but he knew what he was doing. She was in safe hands with him.

Without warning, the cane bit into the soft flesh of her bottom and Beth hopped slightly, unable to prevent a muted cry.

'You must stay still,' he reminded her sternly.

She tensed as the second and third strokes fell in quick succession, forcing herself not to react to the pain with a physical movement but to gasp instead, sucking air sharply into her lungs as though she had been under water for too long. Turning her flushed cheek against the wooden desk lid, Beth tried not to think about the next stroke or the one after that. Just to let it happen and deal with it at the time. Something useful had come out of those exhausting training sessions with Milton and Thomas. She had learned that the agony of the cane might be searing but it was short lived. With practice and a little self-discipline, she could handle it.

No doubt sensing that she was still in control of the situation, the Reverend Smith-Holland abruptly alternated the rhythm of his strokes. He paused and then gave her two quick blows, followed by another seemingly endless moment where she was waiting for the cane to descend, her heart thudding.

'Your skin is really quite delectable, my dear. I must compliment you on it.'

Beth bit down hard on her lip as the cane once again sliced across the tender curve of her bottom. If she could just distract herself for a few minutes, it might not hurt so much. But all she had to look at were the heavy blue velvet folds of his sitting-room curtains, and the pain showed in her voice, now little more than a whimper. 'Thank you, sir.'

There were moments when the Reverend stopped caning her and she would tense in sudden panic, wondering whether he was poised to penetrate her bottom. Yet he never attempted to touch her, breathing hard as though too tired to continue. Perhaps he was planning to take her after he had finished caning her? She was horribly aware of her exposed buttocks, raised so submissively towards him – ostensibly to be marked, of course, but also for penetration.

That was why she was here, she reminded herself with a trembling sigh. To be initiated into what Dr Milton had termed 'the exquisite agony of anal'. She was fairly sure, from that description, that it did not sound like the sort of thing she could ever learn to enjoy. Endure, perhaps. But never enjoy.

Reverend Smith-Holland coughed and tapped her bottom with the cane, bringing her sharply back to reality. His voice seemed a little breathless. 'I see that I'm not the first man to have had the pleasure of marking your skin.'

'No, sir.'

'You've been caned before. And quite recently, by the look of these. Was that Milton or one of his friends?'

She thought back, trying to separate out each painful and ecstatic sexual encounter she had experienced over the past few weeks, but it was impossible. They had merged into a sort of chaotic jumble in her mind; a swinging circle of faces, blurred and too distant to recognise. The pleasure was what she remembered most, that high cry of release as she finally passed through some internal limit of pain and humiliation. But individual names and faces no longer adhered to the actions they had performed, the punishments meted out to her as she knelt before them in excited anticipation.

'I'm not sure, sir. Thomas, perhaps?'

She hesitated over the name, not certain whether she was allowed to disclose the names of other Club members without permission. But the elderly cleric did not seem angry.

'Good man, Thomas. Haven't seen him for a few years, though. I'm not a very active member of the

Club any more. The last time we met was that Christmas nativity they laid on, with a sweet little Virgin Mary and ... ah yes, the donkey!' The Reverend Smith-Holland gave a snort of amusement, bringing the cane down hard across her buttocks. 'How is Thomas these days?'

'He seemed very well, sir –' she hissed as the cane sliced into the unmarked flesh at the top of her thighs '– when I saw him a couple of weeks ago.'

'And did he have you on that occasion?'

'Yes, sir.'

'But not –' he tapped her bottom with the cane again, more meaningfully this time '– up there?'

'No, sir.'

'Because Milton led me to believe that I would be the first man to enter your back passage. I take it you are still a virgin when it comes to that particular peccadillo?'

She licked her lips, still gripping the sides of the desk as she tensed for the next stroke of the cane. 'That's right, sir.'

'Excellent.'

A sharp cry escaped her lips and Beth writhed against the wooden desk as he applied his cane to the tops of her thighs again. He seemed to take great pleasure in her discomfort, deliberately striking her there for the next few blows and grunting in satisfaction at her yelps. Then he returned to the more yielding flesh of her buttocks. The Reverend Smith-Holland might not be not as stringent with the cane as Thomas or Milton, she thought grimly, but he was not weak-wristed either. In fact, he had a firm hand and a disconcerting habit of placing a stroke so accurately on top of the last one that it stung far more than it otherwise would have done. She would bear these marks for several weeks, even after applying the special ointments Dr Milton had recommended to her for healing the skin. But no doubt that was precisely what the old man intended.

She was beginning to shake and there was a sheen of perspiration covering her forehead by the time the Reverend decided she had taken enough. With undisguised relief, she slumped against the desk and listened to the sound of his chest wheezing as the old man shuffled to put away the cane. Returning to her side, he smiled and wiped away the sweat on his own forehead with an immaculately white handkerchief pulled from his pocket. 'There, now, that was all very pleasant, wasn't it? But, if we don't get on, I shall be late for my dinner appointment with dear old Septimus. And I don't think he would be very understanding. He suffers from the most terrible indigestion these days, especially when he eats too late in the evening. Though perhaps if I took the liberty of showing him a photograph . . .'

Carefully, the Reverend helped her to rise. Beth moaned a little as he ran his hands over her sore bottom, presumably exploring the scarlet weals left by the cane; but she did not dare protest in case he bent her back over the desk for some additional strokes.

'Yes,' he muttered, almost to himself. 'I still have some shots left on that digital camera Milton lent me. I shall take some photographs of my handiwork and present them to Septimus at dinner.' With a gleeful laugh, he opened one of the cabinets behind him and positioned her over the desk again with a firm hand. 'He can hardly fail to forgive me then, even if I do arrive a little late. Not when the reason for my tardiness is right there on his laptop.'

Clutching the wooden desk again, with her aching and no doubt scarlet bottom high in the air, she blinked at the bright flash of the camera bulb as it went off several times. Her humiliation was almost complete, she thought tearfully. Not only had the retired clergyman caned her until she was a mess of weals, but he was also taking photographs to show to his friends. But she knew her ordeal was not yet finished. The Reverend might be elderly and a little slow on his feet, but she guessed he was not about to pass up the opportunity to be first in her bottom.

'That's wonderful,' he said at last, lowering the camera. 'Now for a quick bath and then it's down to business.'

A bath first? Beth stared at him in astonishment but said nothing, allowing him to show her upstairs to his neat and carefully organised bathroom. She stared about herself in admiration. The black-and-white tiled floor was spotless, with stacks of freshly laundered towels stored on the alcove shelves and not a bottle lid out of place. The bath itself was one of those old-fashioned freestanding tubs: stained white enamel with little blue claw feet, set on a raised level in the centre of the room. The Reverend ran warm water into the tub, liberally adding handfuls of sweet-smelling bath salts, and told her to remove the rest of her clothes and lay them over the towel rail.

Standing nude beside the bath, Beth felt ludicrously nervous. She waited for him to remove his own clothes, trying not to stare at his semi-erect cock, so unexpectedly thick and snub-nosed, or at the pale, heavily wrinkled testicles swinging behind it. Holding his hand for support, Beth stepped into the tub and sat facing the taps, hissing a little as the heat hit her tortured bottom. To her surprise, the elderly cleric bent to pour several pitchers of scented water over her head and shoulders, then rubbed shampoo into her chestnut hair, working it to a rich lather. The shampoo smelled deliciously of fresh apples and she felt the tension begin to drain slowly from her body. It felt a little as though she were Cleopatra and he was her bath slave – or, at the very least, somebody skilled in relaxation therapies, she thought wryly. Eventually, she laid her head back on the enamel tub and closed her eyes, forgetting why she was in that house and simply enjoying the gentle ministrations of the Reverend.

'Feeling better?' he asked after a while.

Beth gave him a shy smile. 'Much better, thank you. But are you sure you don't mind? I mean, the floor must be hard and –'

'Well, the floor is a little hard,' the old man admitted, interrupting her before she could finish. 'But I'm kneeling on quite a thick towel here. Besides, I like to ensure my young ladies are perfectly clean before we . . . erm . . . commune with each other.'

'Of course,' she said, with a little flush in her cheeks, suddenly remembering what she was there for.

Reverend Smith-Holland gave her an ambiguous sideways look, then dipped the white pitcher into the bathwater and poured the contents over her head in a slow, warm stream. When he stood to fetch a towel for her hair, she was alarmed to see how erect he had become since she stepped into the bath. It could not be long now before she was asked to bend over and present her bottom to him, which was a disturbing thought. Yet he was so old, she thought suddenly, worried that his health might not be up to the sort of exertion he was planning. She could not help noticing that his chest was matted with white hairs, and his belly looked sunken and flabby. Surely it could be dangerous for a man of his years to try something so physically demanding?

She accepted the towel with a nervous smile and rubbed her dripping hair with it while he waited. It seemed to take for ever, and that was partly deliberate. She was in no hurry to bend over.

At last, he took his cock in his right fist and smiled back at her. 'I think it's time we did the deed now, don't you?'

'Yes, sir.'

'Could you get on your hands and knees for me?' he asked lightly, masturbating as he stared down at her breasts. 'Fairly close to the taps, so I can squeeze in behind. Though I suppose you could hold on to the taps if it makes you feel safer. In case you slip.'

Beth nodded, biting her lip as she positioned herself on all fours a few inches from the steaming taps.

With one foot poised to enter the tub, the other still on the tiled floor, the Reverend eyed her with obvious impatience. His erection was now sturdy and throbbing. 'What's the matter?'

'Wouldn't you prefer me to sit on you, sir?' she asked awkwardly, not meeting his eyes. 'I mean, squat over you while you lie down. Erm, facing away. So that you can still –'

'Fuck you up the arse?'

There was heat in her cheeks at his coarseness. 'Yes, sir.'

'I may be old, my dear girl, but I can assure you that I'm perfectly capable of performing my duty as a man.' There was a distinct snap in his voice as he climbed into the tub behind her, apparently oblivious to the lukewarm water sloshing over the sides on to the black-and-white tiles of the bathroom. 'Now assume the position.'

The water was almost up to her chin now that both of them were in the bath together. There was barely room for so many arms and legs, she thought, wincing as his hands groped for her buttocks and spread them apart for his examination. What was he looking at? That tightly puckered hole had always seemed so dirty when she bent to inspect it in the mirror, never quite able to see what men saw in it. Like a cat's bum, she thought, disgusted by the mental image of that sphincter opening and closing under the furry tail.

She moaned with shame as one of his long bony fingers entered and probed her anal orifice. He pushed as deep inside her rectum as his finger would reach, apparently indifferent to her embarrassment. Before she could protest at such unnecessary probing the finger was withdrawn as abruptly as it had entered, only to be replaced by something infinitely thicker and more intrusive. Although it had taken his finger without too much difficulty, her narrow opening found it impossible to accommodate this new object. It was large enough to cause her serious discomfort, worsened by the fact that she had never been entered there before. She knew it was his cock, now as stiff as any young man's, that she could feel pressed against her anus, yet somehow she did not want to admit the truth. Just thinking about that hole being penetrated by a man's cock was enough to make her cheeks flare with colour and her stomach clench in hideously confused excitement. Anything rather than that, she thought rather wildly. Even the unyielding plastic cylinder of a shampoo bottle would feel less filthy being shoved up her bottom than a man's cock!

'I can't,' she cried.

'Of course you can. Now do be quiet, there's a good girl, or I shall lose my concentration.'

'But it hurts!'

The Reverend Smith-Holland paid no attention to that. Instead, he continued to press against her bottom, with awkward little grunts and gentle thrusts of his hips accompanying each attempt to enter her fully. It might have continued like that for some time, except that her hands slipped forwards on the enamel base and Beth was forced to scrabble for height as her chin dipped momentarily below the water. She widened her thighs slightly as she straightened up and that seemed to be all the encouragement he needed. With one final determined lunge, the cleric gripped her hips and drove deep into her rectal passage.

Taken by surprise, Beth shrieked, her face contorted with pain as she found herself shoved up against the hard metal taps. It hurt more than she could ever have imagined. Now that he was finally inside her, his prick felt ridiculously enormous. Like an entire cucumber had been inserted into her bottom. She screwed up her eyes and grimaced as he began to withdraw, that action being as painful – if not more so – than his original entry.

'Oh no,' she begged him. 'Please, couldn't you just . . . stay still for a moment? It hurts so much I can hardly bear it.'

Her continuing protests must have infuriated the old man beyond the point of endurance, as the Reverend gave her several harsh stinging slaps across her buttocks and his voice was stern and thundering, as though delivering a sermon from the pulpit. 'Disobedient wretch, have you no idea at all how to behave during an act of fornication? For one thing, you should never speak to the man involved unless he has given you permission beforehand. You are here to be initiated as a creature of Sodom, young lady, not to indulge in idle conversation like some ignorant shop girl.' He paused in his tirade, his bony fingers sinking cruelly into her hips as he drew her tight against his groin. 'There must be no further interruptions to this act. Do I make myself clear on that point?'

'Yes, sir,' she said, nodding tearfully.

Not giving her any time to prepare herself, the former chaplain of St Nectan's pushed himself so far inside she feared her rectal passage would split with the pressure. It felt physically impossible that he could continue without damaging her severely. Yet there he was inside her again and she was still apparently intact.

So this was anal penetration, she thought weakly, banging her forehead against the taps to distract herself from the pain in her bottom. Even her fertile imagination had not prepared her for the sore aching reality of taking a man's cock up her backside, nor this increasingly urgent need to . . .

'Please, sir, I think I'm going to soil myself!'

'Are you trying to make me lose my temper? I told you to remain silent. Now don't be such a silly girl,' the Reverend said angrily and withdrew again, only to immediately reinsert himself in her bottom with such force that the air was expelled from her lungs.

'But –'

'Clench your muscles as fiercely as you can while I withdraw, then release them when I push back inside.'

Beth groaned, trying hard to comply, her face burning hot.

'Obey me!'

Struggling to please her tormentor, she drew a sharp breath and clenched her internal muscles until they burned, biting her lip so hard she could taste blood in her mouth.

'That's much better,' he said approvingly, his voice descending to a grunt as he bent further forwards over her back, working in and out of her anus with the rhythmic fervour of a dog humping a bitch in the street.

The pain began to subside after a while, to be replaced by a warm glowing sensation which turned gradually into pleasure. She stared ahead at the bath taps, her mouth open, trying not to think about what they were doing together. But she had to admit that it was no longer quite so difficult to accommodate him. Her back passage had now been stretched enough for each forward thrust to be accepted with ease and even a sort of enthusiasm. It was a filthy activity for two humans to indulge in, she reminded herself sternly, disgusting and unhygienic. Yet somehow perfect.

The rhythm of the Reverend's thrusts steadily increased. She could hear his elbows and knees banging against the enamelled sides of the bath as he drove repeatedly into her anus. Beth gasped and strained to keep her bottom raised, aware that he could not possibly maintain such a pace for long at his age, though the elderly cleric showed little sign of fatigue. In fact, he seemed determined to finish what he had started. His fingers dug viciously into her buttocks as he hung on grimly, his weight pinning her beneath him in the lukewarm water.

He was hurting her again but this time his cruelty was not simply a welcome distraction: it was also exquisite. She felt abused and humiliated and completely feminine. She slipped one hand between her thighs and rubbed at herself – even pushing two fingers up inside that empty soaking hole where his cock should have been – and panted for more. More cock, she thought. More pain, more sweet degradation. Her breasts swung and ached, taut little nipples swollen with blood. Soon the old man would come and soak that tight unlubricated passage with spunk; shoot his load up where no man should ever enter a woman; leave her body dripping and sore from its first experience of anal sex.

Heatedly, she climbed towards her own unavoidable climax, slowly beginning to perceive what an act such as this might hold for her in the future, how a life of submission to men like the Reverend Smith-Holland could become its own reward. Then her face twisted gloriously, the pain in her anus so acute he might as well have been thrusting barbed wire up inside her, and she writhed in an explosive orgasm. Her pleasure seemed to trigger his. She felt his ageing body tremble against hers, his rhythm falter for a few seconds. Then his fingers slipped up her spine and tangled themselves in her loose damp chestnut hair, dragging her head back with deliberate brutality.

'Are you ready for my seed, daughter of Satan?'

'Yes,' she hissed greedily, pushing herself back against those heavy wrinkled balls so that he could enter her more deeply.

The Reverend Smith-Holland's grunt and sudden inward thrust made her scream with agonised pleasure. Her eyes closed as his tense swollen shaft pulsed and pumped hot fluid into her bowels.

'Fill me!'

High on the throes of orgasm, the old man administered another series of cruel stinging slaps to her buttocks. 'You filthy Jezebel,' he cried in a high shaking voice as he came. 'Receive my seed and repent your sin, you temptress, you slack-arsed whore!'

Afterwards, Beth felt his hand scrabbling about in the cooled water beneath her and heard the plug being withdrawn from the bath. She sat up in the gurgle of swirling water and looked at him shyly, her cheeks on fire as she remembered the sluttish way she had behaved.

The old man climbed gingerly out of the bath, slicked back his wet white hair and wrapped himself in a large fluffy towel. He handed her a towel as well, a look of concern on his face as he noticed how violently she was trembling. 'Did I hurt you, my dear?'

She managed a smile as she lied. 'Oh, no more than I expected. Dr Milton told me it might be painful.'

'Well, don't worry about it. I keep a special antiseptic ointment on hand for this sort of occasion.' She tried to protest but the Reverend Smith-Holland was already opening a wall cupboard set above the sink, rummaging through the assorted bottles and jars. 'Yes, here it is. Smells utterly delightful, doesn't it? Just the ticket for first-time bottoms. Now bend over and let me –'

She gave a cry as he slathered the cold salve around her sore and possibly torn anal opening.

'Sorry,' he murmured apologetically. 'It does look a little nasty down there, I'm afraid. But this cream should help clear it up in a day or two.'

'Thank you, sir.'

'So was this a useful lesson for you, my dear? Are you learning to curb your natural inclination towards disobedience?'

'Yes, sir.'

The cleric gave her a thoughtful smile, wiping his sticky hands on the white towel around his waist. 'Good, good. That's excellent news. I shall telephone Milton first thing in the morning and let him know how you got on. Though I'm afraid I shall be forced to advise your master against training you any further as a pony girl.'

Surprised and more than a little disappointed, she straightened to stare at him. 'Why?'

'Because you're too volatile to be in harness. It takes a certain type of girl to make a successful pony. And you – though quite lovely in other ways – are not suitable material for training.'

'You don't understand –' She wanted to argue her position, and show the old man how wrong he was about her character.

But the Reverend Smith-Holland had already opened the bathroom door and was gesturing her towards the staircase, his tone polite but final as he said, 'I look forward to meeting you sometime in the future, my dear. Thank you for a most pleasant afternoon and good luck with your studies!'

Eleven

There was no point brooding about it, Beth told herself firmly. She had failed some sort of unspoken test at the Reverend's house last week and now Dr Milton had told her to take off the rest of Trinity term, to forget about the Club until the start of her next academic year. No doubt someone as experienced as Charlotte would see that as a personal defeat. But it was not such a bad idea to take some time off, she thought. The tender skin on her bottom and thighs needed to heal before she was able to sunbathe in the university parks without embarrassment. Besides which, it would not do her any harm to date some boys her own age for a change.

So it was that she strolled alone into a packed student nightclub the following Saturday, in brand-new designer trainers accompanied by hipster jeans and a clinging red halter-neck. The jeans were so low cut it was possible to catch glimpses of her thong whenever she bent forwards, the silky material arching tautly up the narrow cleft between her buttock cheeks. She was not wearing a bra under her halter-neck and it only took a few seconds rubbing a chilled glass against her breasts to push those nipples high and erect.

Feeling uncomfortably damp, Beth made sure that every lad in the place had managed to get a good look before finally heading on to the crowded dance floor and beginning to swing her hips. Within less than a minute, she was surrounded. Sweaty-faced boys to her right and left, deliberately bumping into her and not bothering to apologise, their eyes glittering with lust. She looked at the hunger on their faces and smiled with an odd secret excitement, remembering how the Reverend had pushed himself into her back passage and wondering what these students would think if they knew the sort of thing she got up to outside college hours. Would they call her a whore? Push her down on to all fours and force themselves inside her? Oh, she hoped so.

Even though she was a little bit tipsy, one of them seemed quite familiar.

He smiled back at her, his hand hot on her arm. 'Hello,' he shouted above the deafening beat, his dark eyes narrowed on her face. 'I'm sure I know you, but I can't seem to remember where from. Have we met before? What college are you at?'

'St Nectan's,' she shouted back.

'What are you reading?'

'English Literature.'

He pulled her away from the crazy music, out of the crowds, into a darker alcove where the beat was just a thudding in her head and the smoke haze made her eyes sting. 'I'm reading History,' he said against her ear, his hands on her waist now. 'Perhaps we haven't met, then. I thought you looked familiar but it must have been my imagination.'

'Or a good pick-up line,' she joked, a little drunk.

The dark-haired boy was standing very close, almost part of her. His fingers stroked down her hip and he stared into her face, his voice low and husky. 'Can I get you something to drink? Or would you rather get out of here?'

'With you?'

He watched her closely, his face flushed. 'Why not?'

'I don't even know your name.'

'Do you need to?'

Suddenly she remembered where they had met before. He was one of those boys from the party at Abingdon! What they had done together flashed through her head, vivid and embarrassing. He had come in Charlotte's mouth first and then later, when most of the other boys were sleeping drunkenly on the floor, he had pulled her close and made her suck him long and slow. Such a thick heavy cock, it had filled her mouth and bloated her cheeks. That firm pressure on the back of her head had aroused her and she had dared to touch herself, coming just before he turned her gently on to her stomach and pushed into her from behind.

Beth felt a deep flush flare in her cheeks and wanted to turn away but did not dare, in case she aroused his suspicions and he remembered her, too. What did it matter, though? So he had already had her. That was not important. At least, this way, she could be reasonably sure of choosing a boy tonight who knew how to fuck.

'Yes,' she insisted.

He was touching her backside now, the splayed fingers firm and possessive. 'My name's Robert.'

'I'm . . . Clare.'

He knew she was lying, that faint hesitation had given it away, but he did not bother to challenge her about it. His smile was brief, then he was steering her towards the stairs up to the street, pushing through the crowded club with one hand gripping her by the elbow. 'I can't take you back to my place,' he said. 'It's my flatmate's turn to have guests. But there's a cinema round the corner showing late films. I think it's *Casablanca* tonight. Have you seen it?'

'Yes.'

'Do you mind seeing it again?'

'No.'

They were outside in the street now, walking arm in arm beneath the streetlights, listening to the music from the nightclub growing fainter and fainter. Robert pulled her even closer, his arm around her waist, and pushed her into a doorway for a quick kiss. His mouth was pleasantly firm, not like the other boys she had been with, and tasted of cigarette smoke. With this boy, it was easier to pretend he was a man, one of the Club who was going to hurt and fuck her. So she opened her mouth and let him tongue her. Her hands slid down to his groin, found the thick promising bulge in his jeans and caressed it through the denim.

Robert groaned against her mouth. 'Not here, someone might see. Inside the cinema. We'll get a place on the back row.'

But, when they got inside, the back row was almost full and they were forced to sit several rows forwards, having to find their seats in darkness because the film had already started by the time they arrived. They sat down and started kissing again almost immediately. The boy slid his hands beneath her halter-neck and pinched at her nipples, not as cruelly as she would have liked, but it was a start. He groped her pussy through the crotch of her hipster jeans until she was almost insane with frustration, wishing they could be alone together where she could strip off and let him touch her properly. It was not long before she was sweating with the need to masturbate.

'Robert, can you hang on for a couple of minutes?' she whispered in his ear, ignoring the sound of rapid gunfire and excited shouting from the screen. 'I need to pee. And maybe get some popcorn from the kiosk out front as well. OK?'

He looked at her suspiciously, still breathing hard. 'You're coming back, though, right? You're not running out on me?'

'Don't be silly. I won't be long.'

Safe inside the deserted ladies' toilets, Beth locked herself into a cubicle and yanked down her jeans, hastily pushing her panties to one side and feeling for the sticky bud of her clitoris. Her pussy was sodden with excitement, her shaven lips quivering beneath her fingers. It was such a relief to be able to touch herself at last, to pinch and squeeze where she needed it most. Although Robert meant well, he was not in Dr Milton's league when it came to hitting the right sexual buttons. He was cute and sexy, so what was the problem? She was not sure. Perhaps he was simply not cruel enough to satisfy her.

It was odd, but, ever since Dr Milton had shown her how good it could be when she was forced rather than asked, well, she could not get those feelings out of her head now; they were part of how she felt when she fucked, and it was no good unless they pulled her hair or pinched her breasts. But there were no men here, no one to hurt her or call her names. This was what she needed; nothing terribly erotic or complicated, just two fingers stuck roughly up inside her sex and her thumb pad rubbing, circling, pressing on the slippery hooded flesh of her clitoris. She was so wound up it took less than a minute to bring herself off.

As the orgasm hit, Beth cried out and doubled up with pleasure, bending forwards with one fist slamming against the cubicle wall and her mouth stretched wide. In her imagination, the boy – what was his name? Robert? – had tied her hands behind her back

171

with his belt and was straddling her face between two seats, thrusting himself deep in her throat while *Casablanca* played above them on the silver screen and the audience stared, torn between watching Ingrid Bergman and her own filthy little performance on the floor of the cinema.

Afterwards, she wiped her pussy and thighs with a few sheets of toilet paper and carefully tidied her clothes. She let herself out of the cubicle and paused, staring into the mirrors above the row of sinks. Her cheeks were flushed with a deep colour and her eyes were brilliant: that post-orgasm glow she had come to associate with pain. But not tonight, she realised, except perhaps in her helpless little fantasy of dominance and humiliation.

Robert had smeared her lipstick with his kissing. She reapplied it with trembling hands, giggling as she slowly realised how far she had come since that first time with Dr Milton. Breaking away from a kiss to come and masturbate on her own! Though no doubt her tutor would have preferred her to pleasure the boy first, herself second. But Milton was not here to reprimand her, she reminded herself. She would not be under his control again until the new academic year in September. This was entirely her own call.

Beth bought herself a large carton of unsalted popcorn from the kiosk in the lobby and hurried back into the darkened auditorium. Staring up at the screen, she was shocked to see how far the film had progressed since she had dived out to the toilets. Ilsa and Rick were already together in the bazaar, shoulder to shoulder at the lace-seller's stall, pretending not to feel anything for each other. It was a scene she knew word for word she had seen it so often.

After fumbling along the unlit cinema aisle, she slipped back into the seat beside Robert. 'Sorry about that,' she whispered in his ear. 'It took longer than I expected.'

Robert turned his head in the gloom and stared at her but did not reply. He must be sulking because she had been gone so long, she thought irritably, and leant over to place her hand in his lap. Not surprisingly, he was no longer erect. With a few apologetic rubs and squeezes, Beth soon stiffened him up again and moved to unzip his jeans. But they were tighter than she had expected and, after only a momentary hesitation, his hands worked to help her loosen them.

Hoping nobody in the row behind them would notice or object, she silently lowered her head to his groin. Drawing his exposed cock into her mouth, she licked and manipulated its salty mushroom-shaped head and shaft for a few minutes. Though his cock seemed a little slimmer than she remembered from that student party in Abingdon, it was now impressively hard and she sucked at it with genuine enthusiasm. Robert groaned beneath his breath and stroked at her loose hair, widening his thighs to make the sucking easier.

Sensing his growing excitement, she felt her own sex respond to that unspoken desire for more, the seam of her jeans pressing into that slippery crease like a man's finger. If she had been slightly more daring, and the cinema darker, she might have risked pulling down her jeans and climbing on top of him. But, under these circumstances, they would both have to be satisfied with fellatio.

The head of his cock was wonderfully mobile, slipping back and forth in her mouth as she worked at it. Playing with his balls, stroking and rolling them with gentle fingers, she took his cock deep into her throat and dragged her tongue back along his full length. He groaned again and his hand tightened on her head, pulling her inexorably closer. The sudden rigidity of his cock told her he was almost there, poised right on the brink of orgasm. Working his shaft with a mouthful of warm generous saliva, she increased the rhythm of her sucking until it was fast and furious. She was practically on her knees below their seats now, angling her body into the perfect position for bringing him off. His cock was bumping the back of her throat, his testicles tense between her cupped palms.

'Oh yes,' he moaned in a strangled voice.

Beth froze at the sound, her mouth stilling on his erection, her heart thudding with alarm. Was her mind playing tricks on her? That voice had sounded deep and hoarse – not a boy's voice, surely, but a man's. She let his cock slip loosely from her mouth, staring up through the gloom, and saw his face for the first time in that flickering light thrown by the cinema screen. It was not Robert!

A crazy giggle rose uncontrollably in her throat as she realised what must have happened. Somehow, in the darkness of the cinema, she had found her way back to the wrong row of seats. And now here she was, sucking like an idiot on some complete stranger's cock.

'Don't stop,' the man growled, forcing her head back into his lap. 'Not now, for God's sake. I'm nearly there.'

Responding to that note of male authority in his voice, Beth bent to her task again and obediently sucked the man's cock back into her mouth. But her head was spinning. How had she failed to spot such a massive mistake before now? she asked herself, nearly choking on another demented giggle. This guy didn't even look remotely like Robert! And what on earth must be going through Robert's head? Was he still waiting desperately for her to return? She had been absent from her seat for half an hour now, maybe more. The poor boy must be absolutely dying of frustration, stranded with an enormous erection and wondering where the hell his date had gone.

Seconds later, all thought was obliterated as the stranger made an odd noise, grabbed at her head and exploded in her mouth. Her pussy was wet before he had finished, aching to be rubbed into another blinding orgasm. She wondered if she could somehow direct his fingers to her sex and relieve her mounting frustration. But the miserable bastard jerked his cock free from her mouth without any sign of further interest, muttering something which might have been 'Sod off' as she felt the last sticky blobs of his spunk land in a haphazard fashion on her open lips, her cheek, even her hair.

Beth staggered to her feet, not even glancing down at the stranger as he tucked his damp cock back into his jeans. 'Nice to meet you, too,' she whispered, stifling a laugh.

It was time to find Robert again and finish what they had started, she thought, staring up at the flickering cinema screen. Half-disgusted, half-impressed with her hopeless promiscuity, she limped back to the darkened central aisle and dragged a hand across her cheek, trying to wipe away those telltale traces of spunk, but it was no use. Her entire body seemed to smell of come.

Some balding man in the next row along caught her eye and she stumbled, almost falling into his lap too and pretending not to notice that he was playing with himself.

With such a strong stink of spunk emanating from her face and hair and fingers, Robert surely would know in an instant what she had just done, she thought, and giggled again at the filthy position in which she had placed herself, moving from one stranger to the next through the darkened rows of a half-empty cinema.

Her eager unused sex was soaking her jeans now, and the wetness down there was becoming uncomfortable. And there were so many lone men in these back rows, she thought, almost tempted to invite one of them to fuck her. That bald man with the protruding beer belly, for instance: the one staring at her with such an avid expression on his face. He must have either heard or seen her sucking off the other stranger, because his own hand was jerking merrily away in his lap; a man like that would be unlikely to argue if she approached him, offered herself to him right now with a smile and a gesture. It would be so quick and easy, she thought with a sigh, glancing back at him occasionally as she searched the place for Robert. He was sitting alone in that row. She could just wriggle these tight hipster jeans down to mid-thigh and lower herself backwards on to his prick, both of them hidden from public view in the darkened auditorium. The man was already erect, probably on the verge of orgasm. His podgy hands would guide her into the correct position, fingering the hot slippery flesh between her legs until she moaned, entering and filling her with every urgent upward thrust of his cock.

After finally locating Robert's position, she dropped into the seat beside him with an apologetic smile and handed him the popcorn. 'I sat in the wrong place,' she hissed when he gave her a furious stare, opening his mouth to speak. 'I'm sorry.'

Robert put the tub of popcorn on the floor and grabbed her by the back of her neck, kissing her in a hostile silence. She opened her mouth and leaned into

176

him, still very aroused. It was a bit strange to be kissing a boy like this, so close up, so intimate. The members of Dr Milton's Club never seemed to kiss – not on the mouth, anyway.

She let his tongue play languidly with hers and imagined what they might do together once the film was finished. Perhaps she could take him down one of those dark little alleyways on her way back to college and beg him to hurt her.

He pulled back with a frown. 'You smell odd.'

'Do I?'

'Yes,' he said accusingly. 'What have you been up to?'

'Nothing.'

'I thought you wanted to see this film?'

'I do.'

Robert put a hand up to stroke her hair and immediately froze, his eyes narrowed on the dark matted strands nearest to her cheek. She bit her lip as he touched her and she glanced hurriedly away, not daring to meet that searching gaze. But it was too late. There was suspicion in his voice again. 'Your hair's all sticky. And so's your face. What the hell's been going on?'

'I spilled a drink on myself.'

'What?'

'Yeah. It was ... um ... vanilla milkshake.'

She could tell he did not believe a word she was saying, so she dropped her hand into his lap and embellished the story with a shy wide-eyed smile. 'You see, this guy in the lobby wouldn't stop chatting me up. He made me nervous and I spilled my milkshake. My hair and face were really sticky; it was horrid. So I had to go into the toilets to clean myself up. And that's why I was so long getting back.'

He stared at her but said nothing.

Her hand kept moving against his groin, gradually bringing the thick outline of his cock back to stiffness. It was obvious that Robert did not believe her, she thought, watching him from under carefully lowered eyelashes. But at least he was unlikely to guess that she had sucked some other guy's cock during her absence, swallowed most of his spunk and taken the rest of it in her hair. Who on earth could ever guess something that outrageous?

She unzipped his jeans again and slipped a hand inside, praying he would not suddenly realise that the smell on her fingers and face was spunk. 'Did you miss me while I was gone?' she asked provocatively as she tickled his shaft, hoping to distract him from the smell.

'Of course I did.'

'I'm sorry. Look, I'll stick to you like glue next time we go out on a date,' she murmured, leaning forwards to slip her tongue into his mouth. He did not respond and she pulled back, staring up at him in mock surprise. 'This isn't going to be just a one-night stand, is it? I thought you liked me, Robert.'

'I do,' he said reluctantly.

She worked at his cock with one expert hand, pretending to sound sulky. 'But not enough to be my boyfriend?'

There was the sound of gunfire again. They both glanced round automatically at the huge screen, watching the black-and-white images in silence for a moment.

'You don't understand.'

Squeezing the head of his cock between her thumb and forefinger, she bent down and took him very briefly into her mouth. He tasted a little musky there perhaps, but was otherwise clean. In spite of the difference in their ages, he was also much thicker than the other guy and her sex tightened pleasurably at the thought of taking him in some shop doorway on the way home tonight.

'Try me,' she muttered, licking slowly along the shaft and watching his prick jerk in response.

'I really like you but I can't go out with you after tonight. This was a mistake. I've already got a girlfriend, you see.'

She paused for a second in genuine surprise, then continued to lick along the sturdy blue-veined shaft as she worked his cockhead with her fingers. No doubt he expected her to be angry, to get up and leave the cinema. But, of course, it made no difference to her whatsoever. This particular lad could have hundreds of girls spreading their legs for him all over the city of Oxford and she would not care. All she wanted from Robert was an answer to her question: would it still feel the same, having 'normal' sex with a boy her own age – or had Dr Milton turned her into a pervert? Could she now only reach orgasm with the marks of the cane on her backside and a much older man in her mouth?

'What's her name?'

'Charlotte.'

Her mouth full of cock again, Beth could have laughed out loud. Surely not the same Charlotte who had initiated her into the ways of the Club at that party a few weeks ago?

'She's about a year older than you,' Robert continued, apparently unaware of any connection between herself and his girlfriend. 'Blonde, and a little bit ... plump, I suppose. You wouldn't know her. She's just done her Finals.'

Definitely the same girl, she thought wryly.

His cock was rigid now, its full length sliding in and out of her mouth with a gradually increasing rhythm. She concentrated on sucking it in silence, carefully digesting that information without revealing too much by commenting on it. So Charlotte was going out with Robert, was she? It seemed strange, though; the blonde had never mentioned a boyfriend to her. But, then, why would she, when she was such an active member of the Club behind his back? Even though he had actually spunked into Charlotte's mouth at that party in Abingdon – and still not recognised her! – the poor idiot clearly had no idea what his girlfriend got up to when they were not hanging out together.

But why had Dr Milton's favourite blonde chosen to go out with someone like this? He seemed so dull and conservative, a real missionary-position man. After all, that was why Beth had chosen him tonight: so she could see whether straightforward 'no-frills' sex could ever do it for her again. But she wondered what on earth he would make of Charlotte's pony-girl outfits, or those naughty little tricks she could do, like taking a horse-whip handle up her bottom and parading about with it dangling down as a tail? It was hard to grin with Robert's swollen cock nudging the back of her throat, yet somehow she managed it.

'So you don't mind?' he asked.

Letting his cock slip from her mouth with a gentle slippery plop, Beth gazed up at him from under heavy-lidded eyes and wiped her lips on the back of her hand. 'Of course not,' she murmured. 'I mean, you're lovely, but we've only just met. I came here tonight to suck your cock, not for any other reason.'

'But you said –'

She smiled. 'I was only teasing.'

'Oh.'

Her hands cupped his tense sweaty balls and she licked her lips, quite eager now for her second load of spunk that evening. It was almost like servicing one of the members of the Club, she thought, her desire making her reckless. So what if Robert realised what a shameless little whore she had become? If this boy dared to tell any of his friends what they had done together, she would take great pleasure in telling them about his darling Charlotte. And her much used cunt.

'Do you want to spunk in my mouth?' she asked sweetly.

'Yes,' he groaned.

She accepted him back into her mouth and squeezed his thick shaft between her tongue and hard palate. His hand came down to rest on the back of her head, encouraging her with the gentlest of nudges into a faster rhythm. Oh, Robert was a gentleman; there was no doubt about it. If only he knew that she had just been sucking another man's cock, she thought wildly. He might not be quite so polite then.

Her sex felt almost liquefied now, a damp stain on her jeans at the apex of her thighs, and she could not stand the frustration any longer. Furtively spreading her thighs for ease of access, she unzipped her jeans and reached inside to manipulate her clitoris and finger-fuck herself. It might be 'normal' sex but she was still excited enough to come, Beth noted with relief. Though it did give her an extra frisson of delight as she pursed her lips around his cock to remind herself that this was not only someone she had picked up casually in a nightclub, but was also Charlotte's boyfriend. That was not entirely 'normal'.

'What are you doing?' he whispered, his voice almost drowned out by shouts from the screen above them.

'Masturbating,' she told him frankly, withdrawing her fingers for a few seconds to show him how sticky they were, then shoving them back up inside herself.

181

Robert was confused. 'I didn't think ... but women hate –'

She ignored him, hurriedly bending back to her task. The film was nearly at an end; she could hear the loud thrum of a plane's propellers beginning to turn, then the car horn hooting. In no time at all it would be finished and the cinema lights would come on again. She would have to bring both of them off before that happened or die of frustration. Her mouth wrapped firmly around his cock; she sucked and licked until her tongue was sore while her fingers moved frantically between her thighs. So he thought that women hated the idea of masturbation?

Last term she might have agreed with him, and would certainly never have behaved like this: performing fellatio in a darkened cinema mere minutes after she had sucked a complete stranger to orgasm a few rows back. But Dr Milton had changed her. For the worse, though, or for the better? She might have been frigid and inexperienced before he taught her about sex, but at least she had never behaved like a whore. Now it was all she could do to forget about the Club; to pretend that all those men, so much older than her, had never been inside her mouth and her cunt and her arse.

Beth gave a strangled cry and arched against him in the darkness, climaxing violently as she remembered the aged Reverend Smith-Holland climbing into the bath behind her and pushing himself into her back passage. Her lips must have tightened around the boy's swollen member at the moment of orgasm because he too cried out and clutched at her hair, pumping his thick salty fluid into her mouth just as the famous closing words of *Casablanca* brought a scattered applause from the audience and the film came to an end.

The house lights came up as his cock was still twitching ecstatically between her lips, shiny and slick as a trout. There was general laughter and an old woman behind them gave a disapproving cough as she stood up. Beth was too exhausted to look up at their audience; she was breathless and still recovering from her orgasm. Robert was clearly embarrassed to have been caught enjoying himself in public, though. He yanked his cock out from between her spunk-flecked lips and stuffed it back into his jeans, the head a bruised purplish colour and weeping come.

She straightened up and lazily adjusted her clothes, then stayed where she was for another few minutes, sucking her fingers as the people around them began to drift up the aisle towards the exit. She knew the boy was staring but she could not help it. Her fingers were sticky and stank of spunk mingled with pussy juice.

'You look like a cat cleaning its whiskers,' he muttered, shrugging back into his jacket.

She laughed and stood up. 'Maybe, but I made a mistake there,' she said absent-mindedly, almost talking to herself.

'Did you? What about?'

She gave him a quick sideways glance and sighed, her face still flushed from the things she had been imagining as she came. None of which had been anything to do with him. 'I thought it wouldn't make any difference to my sex life.'

'Thought what wouldn't make any difference?'

Even though she had promised to concentrate on her work for the next six weeks, she had to see Dr Milton again and straighten all this out before the end of term. There was no way she could survive the whole of the summer vacation without experiencing that rush of violent trembling excitement which only pain seemed to bring.

'Needing to be hurt. Because it does make a difference. Submission is like heroin.' Stooping to pick up her bag and the uneaten tub of popcorn, Beth gave him an odd little smile. 'Maybe next time you see Charlotte you should try to remember that. Once you've learned to love pain, you can never go back to being . . . normal.'

Twelve

'Isn't that young Milton's pony?' The elderly man pointed with his stick through the cloister windows.

His friend, just as frail and white-haired, paused and stared hard over the rim of his spectacles. 'That's right,' he agreed after a lengthy perusal of her blonde mane and smooth muscular flanks, his hands trembling slightly as he bent to consult the sheet. 'Winner of the Michaelmas Derby and the Kidlington Challenge Cup in her first year of competition. This year's favourite.'

'She's certainly a sweet-stepping filly.'

'Worth a bet, Quentin?

'Humph.' The old man blinked at his friend's suggestion, licking his lips and giving the pony girl a final calculating stare before shuffling on around the ancient cloisters. 'I'm not sure that would be appropriate. I am still a Methodist, you know.'

Charlotte ignored the small crowd of admirers peering at her over the cloister wall and whinnied loudly, stamping her brand-new hoof boots in an agitated manner. Where on earth could Milton have got to? He was late coming into the enclosure and she was feeling horribly nervous. Her stomach hurt and she was having to parade about the grassy paddock with her eyes downcast, unwilling to meet anyone's gaze in case it made her feel queasy.

She always felt a little nervous before the more important races of the season, and today had proved no exception. Today was the annual Trinity Term Dash, traditionally the final race of the academic year, and probably the last time she would ever compete in a pony-girl event at this level. It was vital she performed well in this afternoon's Dash; and actually managing to add it to her collection of triumphs would be a dream come true. So, even though Milton might not believe in 'nerves' where his ponies were concerned, Charlotte was not exactly her usual bouncy self today. She shook her head and turned away with an irritated sigh, the neatly plaited blonde mane bouncing against her shoulders.

'Oh dear, what's the matter?' one of the other pony girls asked, nuzzling into her shoulder in a comforting gesture.

'My master's late.'

The pony girl, a pale and freckled redhead in her late teens, gave her a sickly sweet smile. 'Probably still in the refreshments hall. My master's just the same. Never thinks I might need a brush-down or a few words of encouragement before the race.'

Charlotte laughed reluctantly. 'I'm glad it's not just my master who can't be bothered to look after me properly. I haven't seen you around before. What's your name?'

'Lizzie.'

'I'm Charlotte,' she replied promptly, snuffling round her in traditional horsey fashion. 'Who's your master?'

High above their heads in the enclosed college gardens, the sun, which had been shining gloriously up until that moment, momentarily vanished behind a cloud. Obviously feeling the cold, the young redhead stamped restlessly in her leather harness.

Goose pimples quickly rose on her freckled arms and legs, and the girl shivered, rubbing her bottom and thighs against Charlotte to keep warm.

'Hughes.'

'Oh, poor you,' Charlotte said sympathetically, giving her a quick kiss on the nose. 'I've heard Hughes is really strict. Doesn't he beat you when you can't do the jumps and turns quickly enough?'

'Sometimes,' Lizzie admitted.

'But you don't mind?'

'If I do get beaten, it's usually because I've deserved it. Besides,' the redhead added, discreetly lowering her voice as one of the college grooms wandered towards them with a water bucket, 'no one's forcing me to stay with him.'

'That's true.'

'Personally, I prefer to belong to a strict master. Some of these new "progressives" can be quite lax with their racing ponies.' The younger girl dipped her head right into the water bucket offered by the groom and emerged with her chin and shiny red plait dripping. 'Isn't your trainer Dr Milton from St Nectan's?'

'That's right.'

'I've heard so much about him. Rumour is he lets his ponies speak in front of him, even in full harness, and only beats them for pleasure. Is that true?'

Charlotte shrugged, her tone becoming cautious. She was loyal to Milton and refused to pass comment on his rather eccentric training methods to anyone outside their usual group of friends, no matter what she thought of his idiosyncratic approach. 'Dr Milton does prefer to keep things informal between us, yes,' she said lightly. 'But I would never call him an easy master to serve.'

'Does he –?'

'Does he what?'

'Oh, this is so difficult!' Lizzie's soft-skinned cheeks seemed flushed and she stamped apologetically, looking away. 'Is he the sort who likes to use you himself?'

'Naturally.' Charlotte frowned, not quite sure where her questions were leading. 'Sex is an essential part of the training.'

'Sorry to be so curious but, when you say he uses you himself, do you mean . . . in your mouth, or –?'

Charlotte laughed softly at her flustered tone, suddenly guessing why this pretty teenage pony was asking so many intimate questions about her master. 'Milton likes to stick it in every orifice a pony girl can offer her master. And his cock is really massive, yes. Almost more than I can handle some days, especially in the arse. He can be cruel, too; don't be misled by his reputation. Sometimes he straddles me after a beating and shoots his come right up my nose; it's fantastic.' She leaned closer and her voice dropped to a conspiratorial whisper. 'And his spunk tastes of wild strawberries; I swear it on my mother's grave.'

'S-strawberries?' the younger girl stammered.

'That's right.' Charlotte sucked two fingers into her mouth and pulled them out again, gleaming with spit. 'Wild strawberries.'

'Oh!'

'Doesn't Hughes ever –?'

Lizzie swallowed hard, hastily interrupting her. 'Of course he does. And I love it, too, even when he uses the crop. Hughes may not be as exciting as your master but he's no eunuch.'

'So what's your problem?'

'Well, he's got five other girls in his stable right now, and most of them are pleasure ponies. Not racers like me. So I don't often –'

'Get ridden?'

Her cheeks on fire, the younger girl drew a sharp breath. 'Yes.'

'You must be so frustrated,' Charlotte said in a sympathetic voice. 'Coming out here so that these men can watch you race, decked out in your best harness and boots, but with your poor little pussy all aching and empty. That's awful.'

Lizzie looked at her from under pale stubby lashes, standing right against her shoulder, her body very close. They were practically rubbing harnesses now, the younger girl's breasts jutting pertly towards her as she wheeled and stamped in her high boots. The thin straps of leather which made up her harness cut beneath her breasts in what seemed a rather uncomfortable way, pushing the soft flesh upwards and out. No doubt in order to display such small breasts to their greatest advantage, Charlotte thought, noting her small pink nipples with interest.

She bent her head to blow, gently and experimentally, on the girl's breasts, and watched the skin begin to tug and tauten into a peak. 'How old are you, Lizzie?'

The girl seemed embarrassed by what she was doing, her voice barely a whisper. 'I'll be nineteen next week.'

'But you're so young!'

'Hughes recruited me in my very first week at Oxford.' The pony girl raised her head proudly, the single red braid swaying between her shoulder blades. 'I adore rowing, you see, and I've got my own single scull. He saw me out on the river early one morning during Freshers' Week and –'

'Took you back to his college rooms?'

Lizzie nodded, licking her lips at the memory. 'I was so innocent I didn't have a clue how to please him that first day. I was shocked because he wanted to put it up there, that's how inexperienced I was. But Hughes is a good teacher and I soon learned my show-pony steps and how to race. Everyone says his punishments are too harsh but I don't agree. Sometimes that's what it takes to make you obey, isn't it? The sort of punishment you'll never forget.'

'Hmm.'

Pushing closer without warning, Lizzie rubbed those small breasts against Charlotte's own fleshier pair, her mouth nuzzled into the warm line of her throat. Her hand slipped briefly between Charlotte's thighs, locating the firm mound of her sex and the smooth shaven lips below. Gasping with surprise at the teenager's audacity, Charlotte felt warm fluids of arousal begin to seep from her pussy, leaving her inner thighs moist and eager to be opened further. Seconds later, the girl's searching finger slipped inside her and was soon joined by a second and then a third, making the intrusion thicker and even more welcome.

'We can't,' Charlotte whispered, half-giggling as she wondered what the more elderly onlookers must be making of this intimate little scene. 'They'll be calling us to the starting line any minute now.'

The fingers working inside her suddenly pulled out and pinched hard at her clitoris, making her stiffen and yelp. Lizzie flashed her an apologetic smile but did not seem interested in easing her grip or removing her fingers. 'It's always better to be fairly strict with a pony, though, don't you agree? Otherwise, they might start thinking they can do what they like, regardless of what their master wants. I know it's an unfashionable idea, but it's a simple fact of life. Ponies need to be shown who's boss.'

'Let go, that hurts!'

'Does it?'

Angrily, Charlotte stared down into that pale freckled face. 'OK, Lizzie, what's your problem?'

The younger girl hesitated, then slowly increased the pressure on Charlotte's sex lips until they started to go numb with the pain. 'It's Dr Milton,' she said flatly. 'I want to swap masters with you.'

'Listen, I'm leaving Oxford forever in a few weeks. So you can have him,' she muttered, her mouth tightening as she tried not to show any sign of discomfort, 'with my blessing.'

'I know you're leaving. But he's been training that new girl Beth to replace you. How am I meant to get rid of her?'

Charlotte shrugged. 'I don't think you can.'

'I don't want to share Dr Milton with another girl. I've had enough of sharing. I mean, five ponies and one master!'

'My heart bleeds for you.'

Those fingers stabbed into her sex again; cruel little hooks, raking at the soft flesh like crabmeat. Her unprotected pussy lips stinging, Charlotte threw back her head and whinnied, dragging her hoof boot along the grass to attract attention from the crowd. She was forbidden to shout out, of course, or communicate with any of the spectators without permission. But she was damned if she was going to allow this arrogant young pony to maul her about in such an outrageous fashion. And it was hardly her fault, after all, that Milton had already chosen a replacement for her. Not that Beth was entirely the perfect choice. But at least she was not a vicious bitch with a penchant for torture.

'Shut up,' Lizzie spat, pushing right up against her until their breasts were almost entangled, leather straps and nipples and heavy silver buckles jostling for room above waist level. Her voice sounded a little desperate, though, as if she knew it was pointless to keep punishing Charlotte for a decision she had no part in. 'You'd better help me or you'll be sorry. I hear you've got a boyfriend called Robert.'

'Who told you that?'

The bell was ringing for them to take their places at the starting line. Oblivious to their low-voiced argument, the other pony girls began streaming past them, trotting friskily out of the paddock and down the narrow path on to the college green. If they did not get moving soon they would both be disqualified from the race, Charlotte thought, her eyes bulging with panic. And she could easily imagine her master's reaction if that were to happen. He would probably whip her sides and her bottom until she was the colour of a strawberry, then send her away from Oxford for good without so much as a farewell kiss. Milton could be very cold when his will was thwarted. He had already impressed on her the importance of winning the Trinity Term Dash. It would look like arrant carelessness if she did not even bother to turn up at the starting line.

'It doesn't matter who told me,' the younger girl said, her fingers still hooked like barbs in Charlotte's pussy. 'Robert doesn't know about the Club, does he?'

'No, he doesn't. But he's not my boyfriend; we've just gone out a few times. That's all.'

Lizzie ignored her, speaking in a low rapid voice. 'If you don't help me get rid of Beth, I'll tell him you're a pony girl. I'll tell him everything you get up to with Dr Milton and his friends. Is that what you want me to do?'

Charlotte tore herself away from the redhead, hissing at the pain in her poor tortured sex, but there was no time to worry about how much damage the younger girl had inflicted down there. She had a race to run and that was the last bell she could hear, warning her to get into position as fast as she could. The crowd was watching eagerly from the sides and the other pony girls were already standing shoulder to shoulder at the starting line, stamping and snuffling and whinnying with excitement as they waited for the signal.

'Tell Robert whatever the hell you like,' she shouted over her shoulder as she careered down the path towards the starting line. 'You can tell him I've fucked everyone in my college, male and female, I really don't give a toss. But I'm not missing this race.'

The sound of the starter's pistol exploded around the enclosed college green, echoing loudly off the ancient stone walls just as Charlotte reached the line. She flung herself forwards across the thick white line, hoping it was not against the rules to start from a running position, and was soon neck and neck with the other ponies. Charlotte could hardly see a thing for the next minute or so; there was loose pony hair everywhere, elbows in her face, hoof boots kicking viciously at her shins. There was a stink of female sweat and perfume and stomach-churning fear in the air: it was a sickening combination. The faces in the crowd flashed by like images from a kaleidoscope, spinning and changing, as she stumbled from an ungainly canter into an even less disciplined gallop. She could see a pony girl in front of her, a smart little chestnut with muscles of steel in her thighs and a determined spring to her step. That's the pony, she thought dizzily, who's going to win this race instead of me.

Then she caught a brief glimpse of Milton's dark face, glowering at her from the sides as though she had already lost, and she spurred herself forwards for that final furlong, grunting with exertion, the veins standing out on the backs of her hands, her whole body involved in the effort. She felt the cruel length of a whip land across her buttocks with impressive accuracy, hearing the crack a few seconds later, as though her brain had not had time to connect the two events quickly enough to make sound and impact simultaneous. It was Milton who had whipped her as she passed him; she knew that without needing to look back. She had felt his anger in every pound of body weight he had put behind that blow.

That whiplash set something alight inside her and she ran on like a flash fire, soon passing the leaders and turning her head towards the finishing line. Charlotte could hear urgent male voices on all sides now, shouting and thundering at her while she galloped through the middle as though in a tunnel of sound. Her breasts ached from bouncing hard against her chest wall and her thighs felt like they were made of rubber, strange and unwieldy. Then she was stumbling past the flag at last and into the sweet green grass beyond with the crack of applause behind her and a furious screech of defeat from one of the front runners.

Some of the other girls fell past as she slowed to a shuddering halt, glancing at her with loathing. Lizzie was among the last of them, her thin freckled limbs coated in sweat, trotting on without any sign of remorse at having nearly cost her the race. Infuriated by her apparent nonchalance, Charlotte quickly caught up with the redhead and tackled her to the ground. They rolled across the grass together, first one on top and then the other, a pair of sweating buttocks pressed hard into her face, replaced by a heaving belly and then pert breasts as Lizzie twisted and clawed at her to be free. Grabbing her before she could wriggle away, Charlotte threw the protesting girl across her knee and brought her hand down fiercely on those shiny pale-skinned buttocks.

'You said punishment was an important part of a pony's training,' Charlotte panted, beginning to spank the girl in earnest. 'Perhaps this will teach you not to get above yourself in future.'

Crying and yelping like a hurt puppy, her face scarlet with pain and humiliation, Lizzie tore at the grass in fury. Charlotte had no intention of letting her go until she had satisfied herself that the pony girl had been made to see not only how precarious her status was within this Club, but also how completely inferior to her own it was. Milton had often talked to her about the importance of enforcing authority amongst her peers as a racer, and how that included scaring them out of their wits. Part of the reason she won so often was to do with her presence on the field; how it frightened the other girls just to see her there, warming up for the race. She might be leaving dear old Oxford behind soon – and her life as a racing pony – but that was no reason to allow these arrogant younger girls to behave as though she had already gone.

The girl's buttocks jiggled beneath her hand at every slap, red and looking quite sore now. She looked down, tempted to giggle at the sight, especially since the rude little rosebud of the girl's anus was clearly visible between her outspread thighs.

'Stop it, stop it!' Lizzie kept squealing, no doubt alarmed by the force of the spanking.

'Not yet,' Charlotte replied through clenched teeth.

'Ouch! Please don't . . . oh, how dare you?'

She laughed out loud at that outraged exclamation but did not stop spanking her, adrenalin still pumping through her veins from the race. Her hand rose and fell in a hard unrelenting rhythm. 'Be quiet and take what's coming to you. You've behaved like a very naughty little girl today and it's about time somebody gave you a sore bottie.'

'I hate you!'

'Is that why your pussy is soaking wet and you're rubbing yourself against my leg?' she asked dryly.

Charlotte lowered her aim to drop a few cruel slaps on the top of each quivering thigh. The skin there was beautifully white and took her slaps like blotting paper soaking up red ink, a flushed stain spreading rapidly across the pale expanse of flesh.

There was a crowd of admiring spectators gathered around the two girls, the other ponies stamping about in their sweat-covered harnesses and watching from a safe distance as they were hosed down by one of the race officials. The hose spray rose high above their heads, a shock of cold water intended to cool the ponies off after the race and wash away the sweat. The water just managed to catch Charlotte and Lizzie as they struggled together, leaving their hair damp and their half-naked bodies even wetter than before.

With a horrible sinking feeling in the pit of her stomach, Charlotte suddenly spotted their respective masters pushing through the crowd towards them, both men frowning as they took in the awkward tangle on the grass. Feeling some explanation might be necessary, Charlotte glanced up at Milton without breaking the rhythm of her spanking and flashed him a brief triumphant smile. 'I won the race for you, Milton,' she said straight away, knowing how much her victory meant to him. 'But this pest nearly stopped me from competing, so I thought she ought to be taught a lesson. You're not angry with me, are you?'

'Oh, you liar!' Lizzie kicked her legs helplessly about in the air, still draped like a rag doll across

Charlotte's knee but trying to swivel her head towards where Hughes stood above them both, his arms folded across his chest. 'She's lying, master. I swear it on my life. I didn't do anything to deserve to be spanked. Please, master, make her stop. Ow, she's hurting me!'

'Isn't that the whole point of a spanking?' Charlotte demanded caustically and slapped her again, still staring up at her master as she waited for his reaction.

Milton smiled back, meeting her eyes with that dark intense gaze she was going to miss when she left Oxford. 'I'm sure she does deserve to be spanked, as most young ponies do,' he murmured, showing no signs of disapproval but a rather unhealthy interest in the redhead's spanked buttocks. 'However, you'd better let her go now and come with me. We are both required in the Master's tent for his presentation ceremony. But I shouldn't need to remind you of your obligations as this year's winner.'

With an unceremonious flick of her wrist, Charlotte dumped the girl off her knee and rose gracefully to her feet. There was a fine sweat coating her limbs; she could feel it trickling, slippery and warm, between her full heavy breasts and her inner thighs. A ripple of applause had broken out among the watching men as she stood up off the grass, and now, as she strode towards her master, the crowd parted to let her through as though she had some invisible force field about her body. She dropped submissively to her knees in front of him and felt his hand on her head, pulling her into the thick bulge at his groin, letting her know without words that he was far from angry with her.

Hughes was not satisfied, though. He stared at them both, his voice harsh with condemnation. 'Aren't you going to punish your pony for speaking without permission?'

'Certainly,' Milton said, nodding politely, but his tone was dangerous. 'But not until she has been rewarded for her win.'

'Well, I hope you plan to recompense me for this damage to my property. Look at my pony's haunches! She's marked to hell and not fit for anything now except dogmeat. How on earth am I supposed to ride her in this condition?'

Glancing at the sobbing figure of Lizzie, still sprawled face down on the grass with her buttocks a warm glowing scarlet, Milton hesitated and then bent to offer the younger girl his hand. She scrambled to her feet, staring up at him with amazement and gratitude in her tear-stained face. His hand ran gently over her tortured bottom, then slapped it again in a playful fashion, smiling at the girl. 'I tell you what, Hughes. If she's no longer of any interest to you, I'll take her off your hands.'

'What?'

Milton raised his eyebrows at the other man's tone. 'I'm sorry; I thought she wasn't fit for anything but dogmeat? And you have other ponies at this event, surely? I see Louisa over there, and the delightful Sarah, too, who ran so well at last year's Derby.'

'Lizzie's hardly worth your attention, though.' There was an ugly sneer in Hughes's voice. 'Not the great Dr Milton. You only train champion racers.'

'Don't distress yourself about it. I'm happy to take your cast-offs, especially when one of my own ponies has been responsible for ruining her.' Milton cupped the girl's freckled left breast and squeezed it thoughtfully, almost as though buying a bird for the oven. 'She has been thoroughly broken in, I presume?'

Hughes could barely speak; his face was almost purple. But he no doubt knew, as did everyone else at the racetrack, that he would look ridiculous if he tried to take back his pony now. Instead, the man gave an abrupt nod and turned away, crumpling up the betting slip in his hand and throwing it behind him on to the trampled grass of the college green. 'More than broken in, I assure you. Take her and use her. What do I care? She's always brought bad luck to my stables anyway.'

'Excellent,' Milton said and snapped his fingers, gesturing Lizzie – who was still trembling and astonished at her change of master – to fall in step behind him. He raised Charlotte to her feet and stroked the cooling sweat from her forehead, a hint of amusement in his voice as he bent close to her ear. 'Well done, my naughty little pony. Now it's time to find the Master and collect your reward, I think.'

There was quite a crowd gathered about the Master's tent, waiting for the winner to make her traditional appearance, and Charlotte approached the brightly coloured pavilion with the first pangs of nervous excitement churning in her belly. She had only met the Master twice before during her time at Oxford, but the memory of his powerful demeanour was enough to make her legs tremble and her knees almost buckle at the thought of pleasing him again. But, with Milton two steps ahead, and a reassuring confidence in the way he entered the tent, she was able to control a sudden girlish impulse to drop to her hands and knees and crawl ignominiously into the Master's presence, more in the manner of a slave than a champion pony.

Milton turned to Lizzie outside the tent, pushing her towards a group of young men on the sidelines. 'You will wait for us here,' he said coolly. 'And I expect to find that every one of those boys has satisfied himself inside you by the time I return.'

The Master turned abruptly as they entered, a glass of red wine in his hand. He was a tall man in his late fifties, the dark hair springing from his forehead streaked with grey, a harsh frown drawing his brows together. He examined first her flushed face and slick glowing flesh beneath the leather harness, then glanced across at Milton. There was a distinct snap in his voice. 'The race finished some fifteen minutes ago. I am not accustomed to being kept waiting.'

'My apologies, sir.'

'I trust there was a good reason?'

'A scuffle between rival ponies. I was forced to step in and chastise them before they injured each other. It was certainly not my intention to keep you waiting, sir.'

The Master lifted the glass to his lips, taking an unhurried sip of wine, then nodded. With a desultory gesture, he summoned Charlotte, watching with coldly assessing eyes as she trotted forwards and dropped to her knees in front of the older man.

'Another fine run. She's a credit to your stable, Milton. I seem to recall this is her final year, though?'

'Yes.'

'But you've secured a promising replacement?'

'With any luck, yes.'

'I'm relieved to hear it. While no one in the Club would endorse your somewhat ... unorthodox ... training methods, there is no doubt that you produce consistent results on the racetrack.'

'Thank you, sir.'

'There have been rumours lately, though. For instance, the suggestion has been aired about this Club that you do not discipline your ponies as stipulated in the rules.'

Dr Milton looked at him stiffly, hands clasped behind his back, but did not respond.

'Which is why –' the older man put down his half-empty wineglass and carefully selected a thin cane from the table at his side '– I would be extremely interested to see how well your mount responds to my preferred method of discipline. So, if you could instruct her to adopt a suitable position, I will put this pony through her paces. With your permission, of course.'

'I'm honoured by your interest, sir.'

Her heart thudding erratically, Charlotte caught Milton's barely perceptible sideways glance and rose to her feet again. Turning to face the entrance to the pavilion, she saw people gathered curiously outside and the tent flaps rippling in the breeze. Obediently, she bent from the waist, feet anchored wide apart for balance, and reached down to grasp her ankles as firmly as she could. She could hear the Master talking about her, but the words floated away from her as she waited, tense and silent, for the cane. There was cool air on her upraised buttocks and between her thighs, whispering across the shaven lips of her sex. Milton was standing somewhere behind her, too, and there were other men in suits and college gowns milling about the tent. What did she look like to these men? Her neat curvaceous buttocks were on show, bruised and displaying the marks of her last encounter with the cane. Between them, the invitingly puckered hole of her anus. Her small breasts, strapped high and proud when she was upright, hung loose in this position; two wanton mounds of flesh swinging in front of her eyes, each tipped by a hard pink pebble. The leather harness cut painfully into her shoulders, strapped across her lower back and thighs, slick and shiny now with sweat. It was a sight she knew Dr Milton would enjoy, even if he was still angry about the way he was treated at these Club meetings.

Charlotte wondered for a moment whether she would be fucked after the caning. If so, would she be

201

expected to pleasure all these men? The thought made her sex throb gloriously and she could almost taste her own arousal as she waited for the Master to strike, her mouth dry with anticipation, stringed beads of sweat trickling like liquid gold between her breasts and down her inner thighs. Her muscles still ached and trembled from the exertions of the race, and there was even faint bruising on her arms and wrists where she had struggled with that irritating freckle-faced girl, Lizzie. No doubt the watching men thought she was trembling out of fear. But let him strike as hard as he wanted. She was not afraid. There were few things she liked better than a good caning.

Suddenly, the cane whooshed through the air with a long familiar hiss and she allowed her flesh to jerk once, biting her lip.

'One,' Charlotte said clearly, counting aloud for her own benefit rather than because she had been instructed to. Counting the strokes always helped her to concentrate; it seemed to focus her mind solely on that odd silence-filled space between herself and the pain, and made it easier to bear without disgracing herself.

'Three.'

There was a tiny black ant on the floor of the tent. She watched it crawl past the narrow toe of her leather hoof boot and pause for a few agonising seconds of indecision, busy little head turning this way and that. Then it swerved away to the left with renewed purpose, threading a path towards the refreshments table where she could see several other ants also frantically milling about.

'Seven.'

The Master was breathing hard now. She felt the full weight of his strength in the next few strokes and knew what he wanted. She was expected to cry out, to struggle, to break down and beg for mercy like any of the other pony girls would do at this stage of a caning.

'Nine.'

Would that horrible little pest Lizzie do what she had threatened and tell Robert about all this?

'Eleven.'

A cold sweat had broken out on her forehead. It was dripping into her eyes but there was nothing she could do about it, blinking and staring ahead into a misty light.

Suddenly she was muttering 'Twelve' and Milton was beside her, helping her to straighten from her ignominious position.

'Is it over? How did I do?' she whispered shakily.

'You were marvellous.'

Charlotte tried to open her eyes and smile at him but everything was too fuzzy, and it made her head hurt.

'Now,' he said lightly, 'are you up to the rest of it or would you rather I took you straight back to stables?'

'The rest of it?'

He stroked her bare thigh. 'Come on, Charlotte. You know perfectly well what's expected of the winner.'

'Oh.'

Milton laughed at the tone in her voice, part rueful exhaustion, part excitement. He leaned forwards and she glimpsed some of the other men behind him, standing in silence as they waited for her to recover, the Master sipping once more at his glass of red wine, turned away from them with a slight flush on his face. No doubt the men in the tent were feeling a little impatient, one or two of them already playing with themselves beneath the discreet folds of their college gowns.

Her own dear master did not try to hurry her recovery, though. His fingers slipped between her thighs, parting the shaven lips of her sex and probing inside with a provocative delicacy that made her body twitch beneath him. Milton smiled at that helpless reaction and bent to kiss her on the nose so softly she would have done anything for him at that moment. Yet she felt oddly sad, too, as he raised his head. She would miss this easy intimacy of understanding between them once she was living and working in London. Unless, of course, she could somehow encourage Robert to share a flat with her – and perhaps treat her the same way from time to time.

After withdrawing slowly from her sex, Milton held his fingers out for her inspection, fragrant and sticky with juice, then wiped them on her cheek. 'You're impressively lubricated, Charlotte. I shouldn't worry about fulfilling your duties this afternoon. You won't have any trouble accommodating every single man here if necessary,' he murmured, his voice low and teasing. 'Far from it, in fact.'

'Are you calling me easy?' she whispered, half-laughing.

'Do I need to?'

'No,' she replied with a quick smile, feeling the hard bulge against her ribs as he shifted her lower in his arms. He was as aroused as she was. 'I know what I am, master.'

'And what's that?'

'Your slut.'

Milton dropped her on to the floor of the tent, watching her roll gently on to her hands and knees, his eyes alight with admiration as he climbed to his feet and dusted down the knees of his trousers. 'Master,' he said clearly, raising his voice. 'She's ready for you now.'

Thirteen

'What do you think of my new acquisition? Charlotte tells me she's a vicious little creature and needs to be brought to heel. But I would value a second opinion on the matter.'

Beth glanced over her shoulder at Lizzie, rowing away down the river in her single scull with long powerful strokes. It was a still morning down by the river and there was a cool pale mist drifting an inch or so above the surface of the water. Lizzie's red hair showed like a flame against the weeds growing ragged along the opposite bank, unnaturally bright and coarse. It might have seemed a little silly, but she did not like the idea of voicing her thoughts on the new girl. The two of them had been chatting together cheerfully enough for nearly an hour and she knew that Milton had not taken his eyes off them the entire time. She ought to be candid, it was true. But it was one thing to secretly like a girl and another to praise her in front of their master. With Charlotte leaving for good, Beth would soon be top pony in the stable. It would be stupid to jeopardise that status by displaying any overt preference towards Lizzie now.

'Too many freckles.'

'Hasn't she just?' Milton sounded amused, presumably unaware of her feelings. 'I could almost play dot-to-dot on those tiny little breasts of hers. And she's no racer, of course. Too awkward on her feet. But as a show pony, or even simply kept for pleasure, she would grace any man's stable.'

'She's too skinny to be a pony.'

Milton gave a nonchalant shrug, continuing to watch Lizzie as she reached a slight bend in the river some quarter of a mile away from where they were standing on the bank and began to turn her single scull back round to face them with a few expert dips of the paddles. His voice was dry, as though he was beginning to guess the hidden agenda behind her criticisms. 'She certainly doesn't possess Charlotte's delightful excess padding, nor your firm curves. But she's stronger and fitter than either of you ... and that girlish figure hasn't stopped her sucking my cock when required, I can assure you.' He smiled. 'Indeed, I expect that Lizzie would earn the Reverend Smith-Holland's approval where you failed to.'

Feeling an unexpected stab of jealousy at his remarks, Beth was surprised at herself and not quite sure why she should feel cross at the idea that Lizzie had already sucked him off. She had performed that service for him often enough now, as had Charlotte before her and no doubt countless other college girls over the years. In spite of that, Beth could not help frowning as she watched Lizzie rowing back towards them, those pale shoulders working hard above the paddles. Was she cross because her master had used Lizzie's mouth or at the possibility that Lizzie might have enjoyed it?

Milton looked down at her with an idle smile. 'What's the matter, my little chestnut pony?'

'Nothing.'

'You disapprove?'

She forced a submissive note into her voice. 'No, sir.'

'Liar!'

The hard slap across her bottom caught Beth unawares and she jumped, staring up at him with hurt brown eyes. What exactly did Dr Milton want from her, she wondered, rubbing her bottom with a rueful hand. He already had open access to her body; was he now going to insist on knowing and controlling her thoughts? That was too much. She might submit to him physically, but she was hardly unintelligent and her mind ought to remain her own.

Unfortunately, her tutor was also clever enough not to need much help in deciphering her thoughts and feelings. Those mocking eyes moved lazily from her flushed cheeks to her lower lip, caught between her teeth as she struggled not to snap back at him.

'Come on, what is it? Do you find this new girl attractive? I know you're planning to share a flat together but maybe that's not all you'd like to share. Do you see yourself in her bed, Beth?' A smile flickered across his face as he surveyed her horrified expression. 'Instead of me, perhaps?'

'That's a horrid suggestion. I never thought –'

'Didn't you?'

Beth fell silent, looking sullenly away as Lizzie reached them, water dripping from the discarded wooden paddles as the redhead made a grab for the riverbank and hauled herself smoothly out of the boat. Lizzie's face was shining with exertion, sweat glowing on her forehead and trickling between her breasts in the tiny midriff top. She was wearing tight white shorts, sitting low on her hips and so high cut at the thigh that her buttock cheeks practically oozed out of them as she bent to drag her boat from the river. Though she had tied her hair back into a ponytail, several red wisps had managed to escape, straggling about her face and slender throat. She looked lovely and dishevelled and as though she had been enjoying energetic sex; a thought which made Beth look hurriedly away, her face scarlet with embarrassment.

Milton laughed, glancing from one to the other with undisguised amusement. 'I'm glad you two girls are getting on so well. And it's an excellent plan for you to live together. It will make summer training far easier, having you both under the same roof.'

'Summer training?' Lizzie queried and, without waiting for a response, lifted her midriff top to wipe the sweat from her forehead, apparently uncaring that her small pert breasts had been exposed to the world.

She stood there like a water nymph on the river-bank, nipples stiffening in the misty coolness of the morning, and dried her face with complete nonchalance. Her nipples seemed so cute and pinkly suckable that Beth felt her mouth go dry and her heart race as she tried not to give herself away by staring. She had never found other girls sexually attractive, but, since meeting Lizzie, it was all she could do not to grab hold of the other girl and stick her fingers straight into that sweet little pussy, find out how wet she was, how hot and ready to fuck, whether she felt the same.

'That's right,' Milton was saying, reaching out to tweak one of those delectable nipples. He pinched them with idle authority, ignoring the girl's hiss of pain. 'Hughes's methods are not mine, after all. You will need to be retrained this summer, in order to take my personal likes and dislikes into account. How else are you meant to learn what makes me reward or punish a girl?'

Lizzie pulled gently away from his hand and dragged the midriff top back down, concealing her breasts once more, though Beth could not help noticing how her erect nipples strained against that tight fabric. She sounded a little out of breath, hands dropping to her hips in an oddly confrontational pose. 'Now don't get me wrong, Dr Milton. I'm really excited to be joining your stable; it's something I've been dreaming about ever since I came to Oxford. But, as far as I'm concerned, our membership of the Club is purely a term-time arrangement. During the holidays, pony girls and other college submissives should be free to do their own thing. We need to be allowed time to be ourselves. To go out clubbing and meet boys our own age if we want to.' She glanced sideways at Beth, throwing her off balance. 'Don't you agree, Beth?'

Beth stared at her, feeling Milton's eyes burning into her face and was amazed to hear herself agreeing. 'It does sound like a good idea. I mean ... I really ought to go home and see my parents this summer. Just for a week or two. And catch up on my studies.'

Frighteningly still, Milton looked at them both for a moment, then raised his eyebrows in mild hauteur. 'Is this a mutiny?'

'Not at all,' Lizzie said hurriedly, flashing him an appeasing smile. 'But we do need to set out some basic rules straight away. You see, I was with Hughes for nearly a year. So I know what it's like to be a slave. I trust you, though, Dr Milton. I think you could teach me about myself ... show me how to stretch my limits, how to submit to you without losing myself in the process.'

'It's for a trainer to set the rules, not his ponies.'

'Yes, sir. But you're only my trainer because I allow you to be,' Lizzie pointed out in an apologetic voice.

'How kind.'

'You can punish me for speaking to you like this, Dr Milton. That's your prerogative as my master. I'll submit to whatever punishments you care to choose. Cane, belt, tawse, it doesn't matter. I won't try to stop you. You can fuck me whenever you want or make me suck your cock, and obey your friends, too, if you give the order. I agreed to all that when I joined the Club. But only in term time, sir. The holidays are my own.'

He turned away from her to meet Beth's eyes, a tightly controlled fury in his face. 'And is that your opinion, too?'

She did not know where to look, torn between the desire to please her master and a sudden wish to reclaim her freedom. 'I don't want to make you angry, sir. But –'

'But you like the idea of a rebellion,' he finished for her, eyes narrowing as his head swung back towards Lizzie. His voice was like a whip. 'You've got a lot to answer for, you ungrateful little termagant. I rescued you from that vicious bastard Hughes and how do you repay me? By turning the best pony in my stable against me. I should send you straight back where you came from and hope Hughes flays the skin off your back –'

'I'm really sorry, sir,' the other girl burst out, a flush in her cheeks. 'I didn't think you'd be so offended.'

His eyes moved with cruel intent over Lizzie's body in the tight white shorts and midriff top. 'Then you're stupid as well as wilful. You both need to be taught a lesson in manners. Perhaps I should remind you that summer vacation doesn't officially begin until tomorrow. So I'm still your master for the next twenty-four hours.'

'Yes, sir,' she said, oddly docile.

Milton glanced about the riverbank with a restless searching gaze, then his eyes appeared to hit on something and he laughed beneath his breath. With a click of his fingers, he summoned Beth immediately to his side. 'Pick up one of those oars,' he instructed her, 'and stand behind your new friend.'

Lizzie gave a gasp of horror. 'Oh, not my lucky blades! Please! No one's ever allowed to touch them or –'

'Silence!' he bellowed, clearly infuriated beyond tolerance by this latest act of insubordination; and Beth was glad not to be in Lizzie's shoes as he grabbed the slender redhead and bent her over from the waist, facing the mist-covered river. One hand pushed the girl's head right down between her thighs, as the other dragged the tight white shorts to mid-thigh level. 'Hold that position until you've been given permission to rise, and count yourself lucky I haven't thrown you into the river! Good God, no wonder Hughes couldn't wait to wash his hands of you. I've never had to suffer such infernal arrogance from a submissive. Young or not, what you really need is a sound taste of the whip. But, since I don't have one to hand, your own damn paddle will have to suffice.' His voice hardened as he gestured for Beth to begin. 'Six strokes with her own paddle. By the time her punishment's finished, I suspect Lizzie will wish she'd never opened her mouth.'

Aroused and exhilarated at the thought of having to administer such a forceful punishment herself, Beth did not hesitate even for a second. She spread her legs wide and used her whole body to swing the dripping wooden paddle until it struck Lizzie's exposed bottom with a resounding thwack.

'Ow!' Lizzie jerked and cried out at the impact, both hands scrabbling to cover her bottom.

Standing back breathlessly to admire her handi-work, Beth was not surprised that the younger girl had been unable to restrain her pained little howl. The oar was heavy and solidly made, the perfect implement to mark a bottom with pleasing severity; even one as experienced as this, since Lizzie must have been accustomed to receiving a certain amount of corporal punishment from Hughes.

'Any more of that undisciplined behaviour and I'll double the number of strokes,' Milton said coldly.

Lizzie moaned. 'Please, it hurts –'

'Are you having some sort of problem understand-ing me, Lizzie? If it hurts, you bloody well ought to have thought of that before defying my authority in the first place. Now drop your hands and let Beth see the target.'

With one final miserable rub, Lizzie let both her hands fall away to expose her bottom once more to the paddle. What the girl displayed there was impres-sive. Spreading slowly across her rounded cheeks was a large block of red, glowing warmly in the centre and fading to a blotchy pink towards the outer edges. It was obvious that she had never bothered sunbathing in the nude, Beth thought with a touch of prurient glee, since the skin there was so white. White, that is, apart from some faint lines from a previous caning and this slow stain where the paddle had just landed.

Dr Milton glanced across at her, his voice sharp. It was almost as if he could read her mind, knew how distracted she had become, weighing the paddle in both hands as she stood ogling the other girl's bottom. 'Is she still in the right position for you, Beth? No bad blows, please. And no letting her off lightly either. I don't want my new pony damaged, but I would like this to be a memorable punishment for our young friend.'

Beth bit her lip and surveyed the other girl with a critical eye. 'Better shift a little more to the left, Lizzie. And bend further down,' she ordered her, after a moment of consideration, and hoisted the oar blade over her shoulder in the manner of a hockey stick. 'Try touching the grass. That may straighten your legs out.'

Much to her amusement, Lizzie obeyed her command without the slightest protest. She shuffled a few steps to the left and reached down to brush the dry grass along the riverbank, an act which straightened her legs and made her bottom instantly more accessible to the paddle. And, as she bent further forwards, those burning cheeks parted to display the neat shaven lips of her sex and, nestled above them, the tight whorl of her anus. Beth stared at that obscene little hole with a mixture of confusion and desire. Why on earth was she trembling so hard? The long wooden oar swayed precariously in her grip, still hoisted at shoulder level as she paused before the blow. That particular hole was so dirty, so irrevocably unhygienic, why could she not stop staring at it? Perhaps because, in her mind's eye, she saw herself kneeling and pressing her lips against that opening, perhaps even slipping her tongue furtively inside to taste that dark fruity orifice. Her cheeks flushing at such a disgraceful mental image, Beth swung the oar for a second time and listened with grim satisfaction to the younger girl's stifled gasps of pain.

'Sorry, did I hurt you?'

Putting her shoulder into the wide-swinging action, Beth drove the paddle home for a third and a fourth time. The wooden handle was damp and slipped a few times in her hand, but she managed to keep the blows more or less uniform in strength and position.

The girl's obediently raised bottom was soon glowing like two hot coals on a bed of snow, both cheeks marked with an area of fierce red blotches, roughly oval in shape, while the upper thighs and outer curves of her hips remained an immaculate white.

With such an angry-looking bottom, Lizzie ought to have been tearful with remorse and begging for mercy by this stage. Yet, though the girl kept jiggling about and shifting her weight from foot to foot in obvious discomfort, she was not showing any signs of having reached her limits. In fact, there was a faint silvery sheen to her inner thighs and the shaven lips of her sex, a glistening substance on the skin which reminded Beth suspiciously of pussy juice. Could Lizzie be aroused by the pain of this paddling? Or was it merely the humiliation of her position that was exciting the new girl: bent right over in full view of any early-morning joggers, breasts flopping about with a glorious lack of propriety, shorts straining about her thighs and her nether cheeks red and ripe as a couple of strawberries.

'Look, this is no good. You've got to keep still,' Beth muttered in a warning tone, fighting an almost uncontrollable urge to throw aside the oar and discover for herself just how wet Lizzie was between those trembling thighs. Her voice became cold and stern, as much for Milton's benefit as because she was enjoying her role as dominatrix. Her personal tutor was standing to one side, arms folded across his chest, watching every swing of the oar with apparent fascination; she did not want to administer this punishment in a half-hearted manner and risk finding herself on the receiving end of a paddle as well. 'I mean ... if you insist on squirming about like a worm on a hook, I might aim too low and accidentally catch your thighs. And that would really hurt!'

The defiant young redhead answered with a muffled protest and continued to wriggle. The next blow caught her squarely across the tops of her thighs and Lizzie hopped on the spot for a few seconds, snatching air into her lungs like a drowning woman, then suddenly seemed to recollect herself and sank back into a head-down position. By then it was too late, though. The oar had left its mark, both her thighs damp and painfully red just below the buttocks, and with a thin strand of green slimy weed trailing down one leg.

'Don't say I didn't warn you that might happen! Now keep your head down and stop moving. This is your last stroke of the oar,' Beth reminded her firmly. 'Though I'm sure Dr Milton will insist on another six if you can't learn to obey a simple command.'

Milton laughed softly, and his hands moved down to release a swollen cock from his jeans. 'Absolutely correct, Beth.'

Flushing as she realised that he did not intend to stop at the punishment alone, Beth swung the paddle for the sixth and final time. She barely heard Lizzie's high impassioned cry, though she saw the thin telltale fluid coursing down her inner thighs and soaking the white material of her shorts, still stretched above her knees. The girl had enjoyed her punishment so much that she had either come or was on the verge of coming.

Dr Milton was aroused enough to expect satisfaction. But which of his submissives would be required to do the honours? Beth hoped that he would not pick her for the task. Her heart was already thudding at the thought of having to perform any sort of sexual service out here, on the quiet banks of the river, less than a mile from the heart of Oxford itself. It might still be early but there were always people along the river once the sun had risen, especially in summer. On an average morning, you would expect to see college rowers beginning to appear on the river, canal boat owners pushing off after breakfast, not to mention the occasional jogger or man out walking his dog. This was no private spot where an impromptu sexual act might be overlooked as a bit of harmless entertainment and no more. If they were unlucky enough to be seen and reported, she thought anxiously, it could be disastrous for them all.

'Not here,' she said in a low voice, pleading with her tutor as he came towards her, cock in hand.

Dr Milton jerked his head towards Lizzie, who, without any sign of shame or remorse, had slipped her fingers between her legs and was frantically frigging herself to a climax. 'Would you rather that silly girl sucked me off instead of you? It's about time you stamped your authority on this stable, Beth. I know you haven't had much time to get used to the idea but I'm beginning to suspect you don't enjoy being top pony.'

'This is such a public place,' she hissed.

He looked bored. 'Need I remind you we're not on college property? The worst thing that could happen out here would be a civil reprimand. And, if anyone did see us and decide to call the police, by the time they arrived we'd be long gone. Now be a good girl and suck my cock like you've been told.'

Her face was hot as she sank reluctantly to her knees. He always made these things sound so plausible, Beth thought crossly, but accepted his rigid shaft into her mouth without further protest.

'At last she obeys me,' Milton remarked to himself in a dry voice and drew her head closer in to his groin. 'Just make sure you do a good job, Beth. Otherwise, it will be my new pony's turn to administer the punishment. And, judging by the size of her biceps, I expect a paddling from Lizzie might sting a bit.'

Lizzie must have heard him. A few yards behind them on the riverbank, crouched with her damp white shorts around her ankles and her fingers working furiously between her thighs, she suddenly reached her climax and cried out in a thin strained voice. The sound startled a flock of wild birds which broke from the tall reeds to their right and rose into the cool morning with a clatter of wings.

Beth tried to concentrate on the cock in her mouth but it was almost impossible when she could see, out of the corner of her eye, Lizzie's bottom still glowing from the paddle and the outline of those hairless lips, gaping now as the girl straddled a colony of dandelions and let go with a moan of quiet satisfaction. By the sound of it, Lizzie must have been absolutely desperate to wee for some time. Her bladder emptied itself over the towpath, gushing out at first in a loud plentiful flow. As it dissipated to a mere trickle, the pool of dark, yellow froth swirled about the dandelions and streamed merrily away towards the river's edge.

'Filthy bitch,' Milton said with idle amusement.

'Sorry,' Lizzie panted, trying to wipe her dripping crotch with a handful of burdock leaves. 'I know I should have asked permission first. But I couldn't hold on any longer.'

For some perverted reason, the sight of her new friend peeing liberally across the towpath made Beth slip her own fingers between her legs. It took a few seconds to work her way round the tight elastic of her knickers under the short skirt but, once she had pushed several fingers past that barrier, the pleasure was intense. Nor was it obvious to anyone else what she was doing down there. Hidden from her tutor's view, she was able to suck diligently on his cock while pinching and squeezing the taut bud of her clitoris. Oddly enough, his cock felt bigger and harder in her mouth than she remembered. Perhaps it was the excitement of doing it in public like this that was adding to his arousal, Beth thought, attempting to relax her jaw so she could accommodate his width more easily. It was difficult to achieve. But Dr Milton did not seem to mind the tight fit, clutching at her chestnut ponytail and making sure she took his full length in her throat.

Beth thought of that first time – so long ago in her memory that it might have happened in a dream – when he had forced her to pleasure him and then laughed at her awkward schoolgirlish response. She had changed so radically over the past couple of months that she was a different person now. Gone were those early nightmarish days when she squirmed with embarrassment at every lewd command and failed to suck cock to her master's satisfaction. Her training must be almost over, Beth told herself optimistically, since there could not be much left for her to experience. And, now that she was a fully initiated member of the Club, she did not intend to let her sexual interest in Lizzie rob her of this new and very much deserved status as top pony.

She squeezed his cock hard between her thumb and three fingers, forming a tight ring as she rolled her tongue across the fat head, letting the excess saliva roll down his shaft like treacle.

'It's not a toy so don't play with it, girl. Just give it a good sucking, I'm nearly there,' her tutor said sharply, yanking at her hair. 'You'd be such a dirty little slut if you could learn to do things properly. I can't wait to see you in action with Lizzie. I think you'll enjoy the taste of cunt far more than you realise.'

Her cheeks on fire at the thought of licking another girl's pussy, Beth drew her tongue forcefully down his shaft then back up to the tense purplish head, sucking it into her cheeks like a lollipop and holding it there under suction for a count of ten. His helpless groan told her that he was enjoying it. She reached into his jeans and cupped his balls with her free hand, ever so gently rolling each testicle in her palm, letting her fingers stroke the skin with a featherlight touch. Meanwhile, her other hand was working out of sight between her legs, much harder and faster than she would have dared to touch him, bringing her closer and closer to an inevitable orgasm.

The sound of laughter made her freeze, and she let his cock slip from her mouth as she stared beyond him up the towpath. There was a young blonde walking towards them, arm in arm with a boy. For a moment, she was terrified, thinking they would be arrested for indecent behaviour, then she recognised who the girl was – and the boy, too. 'Charlotte!' she exclaimed, hurriedly removing her fingers from her pussy and wiping traces of drool off her chin. 'What are you doing here? I thought you were leaving for London?'

'I'm on my way right now,' Charlotte said, and giggled, glancing at each of them in turn as she took in the intimate little scene before her: Dr Milton with his cock still erect and covered in shiny spittle; Beth on her knees in the dirt like a backstreet whore; and Lizzie squatting on the towpath with her legs wide apart and a stream of yellow pee draining slowly away into the river. 'I saw your car parked by the bridge, Milton, so I thought I'd come and say goodbye. This place hasn't changed much since my training days. You used to bring me down here during my first summer term. Do you remember?'

'How could I forget?' Milton murmured, kissing her politely on both cheeks as she embraced him.

'This is Robert. He's driving down to London with me. You see ... well, we've decided to get a flat together.'

Lizzie was staring, her mouth open. 'But I thought —'

'You thought Robert would dump me once he found out what a lascivious slut I am at weekends. But you were wrong, darling,' Charlotte said loudly, her eyes flashing in the younger girl's direction before turning back to her boyfriend's face. She reached up and stroked his cheek, nestling into his body as if they were newlyweds. 'Robert says it's not a problem and I can do whatever I like ... so long as I never forget I belong to him.'

Robert stepped forwards to take Milton's hand. 'How do you do, sir? Charlotte's told me a lot about you.'

'None of it good, I imagine.'

The younger man flushed slightly. 'On the contrary, she thinks the world of you.'

'How gratifying.'

The two men shook hands, regarding each other warily. Beth kneeled between them, still holding her master's cock, and wondered whether Robert would recognise her as the same girl who had sucked him off in a cinema a few weeks ago. He seemed almost as dominant as Milton now, and he had such an air of confidence that Beth wished she had pursued him more vigorously at the time.

Reprimanding herself for fancying another girl's boyfriend, Beth knelt up straight, her hand tightening on Milton's cock. Before bending to her task once more, she shot the blonde and her boyfriend an apologetic look. 'I don't want to offend anyone but I was in the middle of a blow job when you arrived. Is it OK if I carry on?'

Charlotte laughed. 'Actually, I was wondering whether I could join in. For old time's sake. Unless you object, Robert?'

An odd light in his eyes, her boyfriend took Charlotte by the back of the neck and forced her down on to her knees in front of Milton. His voice was harsh but not unforgiving. 'You want to suck your former master off one last time, you go ahead. So long as you don't mind me using this other girl as I wish.'

'Other girl? Do you mean Lizzie?'

Robert looked at his girlfriend coldly. 'Did I permit you to speak? Though, since you ask, I take it you have some sort of objection to my using her?'

It was Charlotte's turn to flush now, stammering as she lowered her eyes and turned obediently into Milton's groin. 'N-no.'

'No, what?'

'No, sir.'

'That's better. Now, Dr Milton, do I have your permission to use this little redhead?'

Milton was looking at him with a smile on his face, half-amazed, half-admiring of his way with Charlotte. It was clear from his amused tone that he thought the younger man had the makings of a formidable master. 'Go ahead, you enjoy yourself. I'm impressed by the way you're handling Charlotte; she does need a firm touch on the reins. Actually, you'd fit in well at our Club. If you ever decide to come back to Oxford, tell me where you're living and I'll put your name forward to the committee.'

'That's very kind of you, sir.'

'Not at all,' Dr Milton said easily, stroking Charlotte's hair as she nuzzled into his groin. 'Of course, we never used to accept new members under the age of thirty. But times are changing and the Club needs to change with them. Most of the girls we recruit these days are far too wilful and unacceptably outspoken. We need more young men like you, who aren't afraid to put them back on the path to submission.'

Beth's eyes flickered but she did not respond to the bait. Back on the path to submission. Yet more canings and lessons in obedience filled her mind. And he meant it, too. He could be such a bastard at times. Even as he spoke, Dr Milton removed his cock from her mouth and she stared up at the thick shiny organ as though it were an instrument of delight as well as punishment, angered by his chauvinism yet thrilled at the idea of being so completely under his domination.

Seconds later, she felt a stab of jealousy as he fed his cock between Charlotte's eager glossy lips instead and started to thrust. She had worked so hard to get him to the point of orgasm. Why should Charlotte be rewarded with his seed? Feeling a little neglected, she glanced across at Robert and felt even more left out as he gestured the half-naked Lizzie into a secluded clump of bushes, ordered her on to her hands and knees and unzipped his jeans with silent intent. Oh, how Beth remembered that cock, so firm and deliciously mushroom-shaped at the tip, and felt her mouth go dry as he pushed it between Lizzie's legs. The shaven lips of her cunt stretched wide to accommodate him and then his cock was gone, vanishing into her belly as he leant forwards over her back. Lizzie moaned and squirmed beneath him, her white shorts still round her ankles, the midriff top pushed up to expose stiff pink teats. It looked rather painful, to be honest, her pale body scratched and stung on all sides by thorn bushes and thick clusters of nettles. Yet the lucky bitch appeared to be enjoying every second of it, her face pushed unceremoniously into the dirt, her bottom raised high for each brutal thrust and her cries filling the air.

Then Milton withdrew from Charlotte's mouth and pulled Beth closer, rubbing the bulbous head of his cock across her cheek, her mouth, up against her nostrils, leaving a viscous trail of spit and pre-come. 'You like that?'

'Yes, sir,' she gasped.

'You want me to come in your face?'

'Yes!'

He grabbed Charlotte by the hair and wrenched her forwards until they were kneeling side by side in front of him with their saliva-covered cheeks touching. His cock reared up, prodding Beth in the eye, his flesh hot and slick and fiercely erect. 'I want to see you girls kissing each other. Come on, Beth, put your tongue in her mouth.'

Beth almost recoiled in horror. 'No way!'

'I've seen the way you look at other girls, Beth, so don't bother with the prissy act. Kiss her, there's no time for a debate.'

'But it's disgusting.'

'For once in your life, Beth, just shut up and do what you're told,' Charlotte told her sharply, holding her face between damp palms while she put her mouth against Beth's.

It felt so odd to feel soft lips pressing gently into hers instead of the usual hard male outline, coarse with stubble. The shock of it tingled down her backbone and ran around her hips into her groin. She could taste peppermint on the other girl's lips and perhaps a faint hint of orange juice. Toothpaste and breakfast, she told herself. So this was what it felt like, kissing another girl. And it seemed almost bearable, not as horribly intense as Beth had feared. Just so long as Charlotte kept her fingers to herself, she thought hazily, fighting her own arousal at the idea of being touched down there by another girl.

Somewhere above their heads she could hear Milton's breathing quicken and felt his cock begin to push solidly in and out between their faces, tense and ready to explode, using the gap almost like a pussy. For a moment or two, she teetered on the edge, desperate to finger herself but not daring in case they called her a lesbian slut. Then the blonde girl's tongue slipped right inside, exploring her teeth and tongue without any sign of shame or hesitation, darting moistly back and forth like a miniature cock.

Beth groaned against that invading tongue and tried in vain to wriggle away. Her pussy was throbbing. 'Please,' she said to no one in particular, her voice muffled by the kiss. 'It's not my thing; I really don't want to ... Oh!'

Hot come sprayed liberally across both of them as Milton grunted with satisfaction and climaxed into their faces, too excited to contain himself any longer. He shoved his cock first into her mouth and then Charlotte's, generously allowing them both a good swallow of spunk before pulling out and smearing the rest over their foreheads, noses, cheeks and chins until they were slimy and coated in it.

'Slap me!' Charlotte gasped, staring wildly up at him, spunk stuck in thick white blobs to her eyelashes.

Dr Milton complied instantly. He dropped his cock and his hand swung down in a ruthless arc, catching the blonde full across the cheek so that she reeled backwards with the force of the blow and would have fallen if the two girls had not been holding hands where they knelt. Charlotte cried out loud, a thin piercing scream that echoed along the river, and put her hand up to her flushed cheek where a white imprint of his hand still showed.

'Bitch!' he swore and raised his hand as if to slap her again. His face had been transformed to a stark mask of pleasure, bones showing through the flesh. 'Filthy slut!'

'I hate you, you bastard!'

'You can hate me all you want but you'll still obey me to your last breath.'

'Yes,' Charlotte moaned. 'Yes.'

Her long, shining blonde hair fell in disarray about her shoulders as she drew a deep sobbing breath and bowed her head, touching her forehead to the dirt just in front of his dark-soled walking boots. One hand slipped between her legs and the other clawed at the gritty towpath as she began a series of high-pitched wailing noises, a black filth soon gathering under her fingernails. At first Charlotte seemed heartbroken by his unexpectedly brutal treatment, a rag doll draped across the path at his feet. Then, with bewildered astonishment, Beth realised the blonde was not crying but keening with delirious pleasure.

'Oh, Christ,' she suddenly howled through her tears, throwing back her head like a wild animal, blonde hair everywhere. 'I'm coming . . . I'm coming.'

As soon as her groans and cries had died away, Milton tucked his cock carefully back into his jeans and turned to admire Robert, who had just finished filling the young redhead with come. The boy's cock slipped easily from her shaven lips, leaving behind a sluglike trail of spunk glistening along her inner thighs.

Lizzie had been sprawled face down in the dirt and nettles, her poor bottom bearing the signs of a few hard slaps as well as the glowing bruises left by the paddle, but now she pushed herself to a sitting position and gave her tormentor what appeared to be an admiring smile. 'You're good,' she whispered, looking up at him from under lowered lashes. 'Damn good.'

Charlotte was on her feet in an instant, the flush dying from her cheeks as she came back to reality and realised that her newly acquired boyfriend might be in danger. She wiped a couple of pussy-slick fingers on her skirt and hurriedly dragged Robert back to her side, pushing his semi-erect cock back inside his jeans before the other girl could start work on it again. She glanced at her watch before stretching on tiptoe to give him a lingering kiss, either oblivious to the whitish streaks of spunk all over her face or not caring how sluttish it made her look.

'It's nearly seven o'clock,' Charlotte said, adjusting her clothing as she smiled up at him. 'Time to go, sweetie. We don't want to get caught up in the rush-hour traffic.'

Beth gave up trying to look the picture of outraged innocence. Her pussy felt like it was on fire and her nipples were sticking out like steel thimbles. So what if her friends thought she was an undisciplined slut? They all seemed to have enjoyed themselves this morning. Now it was her turn. She squatted down right there in the dirt of the towpath, hitched her skirt up to her waist and shoved three fingers up inside her sex. It was not hard to build towards her climax, remembering Lizzie's bottom glowing like fire under the paddle and her yellowish pee steaming as it coursed away down the towpath; Dr Milton feeding his cock into first her own mouth and then Charlotte's; not to mention Robert humping the delicious little redhead from behind like a dog down a back alley. And, so, mouth open and eyes closed, uncaring what the world might think, Beth frigged herself to a sticky and extremely noisy orgasm.

When she opened her eyes again, the towpath was empty. Dr Milton and her friends had vanished. Bewildered, she glanced over her shoulder and froze in horror, as the sound of splashing oars grew louder. There were a few coarse shouts on the morning air, followed by stunned silence as the boat drew level and the racing eight realised they had not imagined what they had seen from a distance. Her already flushed cheeks burned with humiliation. She did not even have time to drag down her skirt before the coxswain was eye to eye with her, staring through the clearing mist. Then the entire crew of eight sturdy undergraduates – sweaty and some of them bare-chested – pulled their dripping blades back into the boat and gave Beth a spontaneous whistling round of applause that must have echoed down the river as far as the Abingdon Road.

Fourteen

It was the sunlight streaming in through the window that woke her. Beth turned over in bed, stretching lazily, and her fingers encountered warm soft flesh beside her in the bed. She paused for a moment, suddenly remembering where she was and who was lying beside her, her heart beating hard but her eyes still closed as she went through the past few days in her head. It was like a dream, except that she knew it was real. She was in Lizzie's bed, in Lizzie's flat, and her suitcase was lying half-unpacked on the floor because Lizzie had invited her to move in and they were going to live together.

She glanced at the bedside clock. It was nearly half-past ten in the morning and she could hear traffic outside in the busy Oxford street. Her hand slid carefully across a taut hipbone, wandered over the curve of a belly and stroked its way past shaven lips into a pussy which was still moist from the night before.

'Lizzie?' she whispered. 'Are you awake?'

'Mmm?' her friend managed after another minute or so, stirring at last as those fingers worked diligently between her legs. She turned into Beth's body, a slow sensual roll of thighs, hips and backbone, until the two girls were facing each other with their breasts lightly touching. Her red hair, wild and unruly at that time of the morning, flared across the white pillows as the sleepy green eyes opened and fixed on her face. 'Oh shit, have we overslept again? What's the time?'

'It doesn't matter what the time is. Term's over, remember? There are no more lectures to miss.'

'Fantastic. And no more tutorials.'

'No more days in the library.'

Lizzie smiled, widening her thighs to allow Beth easier access to her sex. 'Or private meetings of the Club.'

'No more canings.'

'Or spankings.'

Watching her face flush to an odd pink glow and wondering if she would like her pussy licked out, Beth continued to manipulate the other girl's clitoris. 'Or tests of obedience.'

'No more getting fucked in the arse by some seventy-year-old with a hard prick and a walking stick.'

Beth giggled. 'That rhymes. You're a poet –'

'And don't I know it?'

They both laughed, kicking off the sheets and stroking each other with cool fingers. Moving up to Lizzie's breast, Beth played with the rosy little nipple until it came erect. 'It does hurt, though, doesn't it?'

'Taking it up the arse?'

Beth nodded, trying to look unconcerned as Lizzie's fingers slipped down between her own thighs and parted her sex lips, stroking and teasing the fat hood which covered her clitoris.

'Of course it hurts,' Lizzie said indifferently. 'But that's what they want when they do it. To hurt us, to make us cry.'

'Do you really think so?' Oh, God, she wanted to play it cool, Beth thought – her first time waking up in bed with another girl! – but the words tumbled out

229

of her mouth in the end until she was lisping, breathless as a school kid. 'So do you hate it, then? The canings, the spankings, and the old men fucking you?'

'Hate it?' Lizzie laughed out loud. Her fingers pinched cruelly at Beth's clitoris, making her yelp and jerk away from her cradled position against those pale breasts. 'I love it, you silly bitch. That's why I do it. For pleasure, for kicks. So I can get wet and come. Isn't that why you joined the Club, too?'

'Um ...' Beth found she could barely speak any more, let alone formulate a meaningful answer. She had a good enough brain – she was studying for a degree at Oxford, for God's sake – but her body kept getting in its way. But that was not surprising, really. It was impossible to think when her pussy was aching and trembling and the juice was trickling out and running down her thighs because those wicked fingers were pushing and squeezing and rubbing at her clit and the fat swollen lips that hid it.

Lizzie bent her head and sucked hard on one of Beth's nipples. The mingled sensations of pain and pleasure were exquisite.

'It's OK,' she said, kissing her way up Beth's throat to her mouth. She ran her tongue along Beth's parted lips and made her shiver. 'You can tell me. I won't be shocked.'

'I only joined because I needed the money.'

'I see. So you don't enjoy it?'

Beth bit her lip, sensing a trap ahead. 'Well,' she muttered. 'I do sometimes, of course. Otherwise –'

'Otherwise you wouldn't do it? Because pain isn't connected to pleasure for you.'

'That's right.'

With an understanding smile, Lizzie pressed three or four fingers deep into Beth's sex, right up to the knuckle and beyond. Her wrist turned a few inches, allowing her thumb to enter, too, squashed flat against the vaginal wall. It felt like she was trying to insert the entire fist.

The manoeuvre began to hurt and Beth cried out, twisting about in her arms, her face flushed and uncertain. 'Don't!'

'Is it hurting?' Lizzie asked sympathetically.

'Yes!'

'Then you're going to absolutely love it, baby. Just relax, let it happen. It's amazing how far the skin will stretch when you're aroused. You've taken nearly my whole hand in your cunt already. Do you want me to take it out now? To stop hurting you?'

Beth lay still for a moment, her pussy throbbing and engorged and incredibly sensitive. Then she shook her head, lowering her hot face between Lizzie's breasts as if she needed somewhere to hide. She did not want to make her friend angry. Her voice came out as an uncertain whisper. 'No.'

'That's better.' Lizzie smiled. 'You know, I nearly tried to get rid of you when we first met. I didn't want to share Dr Milton with anyone. But now I see how delicious life is once we learn to –'

Before she could say any more, there was a sudden and insistent knock at the front door to the flat. Both girls sat upright in bed, nude and surprised, staring at each other as they wondered who it could be. With an exaggerated sigh, Lizzie pulled her fist out of Beth's pussy and wiped it clean on the sheets, leaving thin creamy smears of fluid behind.

'You'd better go and see who that is,' Lizzie said, slapping her playfully on the bottom. 'It's a bit early for callers, but I did ask a few friends round to the flat today. Some visiting French graduates I met at college last week. Maybe it's them.'

Obeying instinctively, Beth grabbed a clean white T-shirt from her open suitcase and pulled it over her head, wriggling it down past her bare hips. She glanced at herself briefly in the bedroom mirror before heading for the front door, glad to see that the T-shirt did at least cover her crotch, though only just. If she moved too fast, she thought wryly, the cheeks of her bottom would be clearly visible.

She pulled open the front door, a smile on her face. It was three young men, two of them swarthy and dark-eyed, the third tall and fair-haired with blue eyes.

'Hi.'

The tall one smiled back. His eyes lingered admiringly on her bare legs. 'Hi there. We're looking for Lizzie. Is this the right place?'

'Yes. Are you the French guys?'

'That's these two, Justin and Marc. My name's Tom. I don't know if Lizzie told you about us. We're all in the rowing club at college. She told us to call round today so . . . here we are!'

Beth nodded. 'You'd better come in.'

The three young men followed her silently into the flat. The shady living room was cluttered and not very spacious, even though it doubled as a kitchenette, and they had trouble finding somewhere to sit. She didn't open the curtains, knowing that Lizzie preferred them closed to ensure privacy, and bent to click the table lamp on instead. There was a muffled expletive from one of the swarthier boys as she did so and Beth straightened up, red-faced and clutching at her T-shirt, realising that her bottom must have been on full show.

Lizzie wandered casually into the living room, completely nude apart from a black velvet choker. 'Hi, guys,' she said, kissing all three of them in turn.

'It's really hot today, isn't it? Take off your jackets; make yourselves at home. This is Beth, my new flat mate. Do you like her?'

The two swarthy young Frenchmen had been staring at Lizzie with undisguised lust in their eyes but now they glanced sideways at Beth, assessing her body under the tight white T-shirt.

'Not bad,' one of them said, his voice thickened by a strong French accent.

'That's Justin,' her friend said, hurrying through the necessary introductions. 'And Marc next to him. They're both here in Oxford for a year as visiting graduates from . . . was it Marseille? And this is Tom, who's an absolute darling.'

Lizzie pushed her towards the two Frenchmen who were sitting together on the sofa. Beth stumbled and found herself caught up in a pair of strong male arms. She sat down on his knee, blushing scarlet and her heart beating fast as she started to guess what Lizzie intended. The white T-shirt rode up, exposing her upper thighs and the bare shaven lips of her sex, just peeping out from under the hem. The boy next to them on the sofa smiled, but it was obvious that his English was not as good as his friend's.

'I am Marc,' he said slowly, gesturing at her body. 'Good breasts, good mouth. You like to . . . fuck with us?'

The young man holding Beth on his knee slipped a hand between her legs and touched her pussy. She stiffened with embarrassment, not sure how to react, looking at Lizzie for help. But Lizzie did not seem to be listening. The other girl was already standing in the doorway, kissing the tall British one called Tom. She had her arms entwined about his neck and was standing on tiptoe to meet his mouth, her pale shapely legs and bottom on full display.

The boy who had just spoken glanced at Lizzie's bottom, and his eyes narrowed on the faded bruises from the paddle. He looked back at Beth quizzically. 'Someone is hitting your friend?'

'Yes.'

He frowned. 'Why?'

Lizzie turned in Tom's arms, her full mouth pouting and red from the forceful kissing. 'Because we like to be hurt,' she said with an odd little laugh. She looked at Beth provocatively and their eyes met. Do it, that gaze seemed to be telling her. Stop resisting and enjoy yourself. 'You see, we're both very naughty girls and we need to be punished.'

'Naughty girls?'

'That's right. Would you like to punish us?'

Tom was smiling down into her freckled face, pulling her nudity closer into his groin. 'I can't answer for the other two, sweetheart, but I certainly would.'

'Punish you?' The young Frenchman holding Beth on his knee tightened his grip. Perspiration broke out on his forehead as he stared down at her body in the thin white T-shirt. There was a note of disbelief in his voice. 'You mean, with hand smacking?'

'Yes, you can smack us if you like. Slap us, spank us, whip us.' Lizzie pointed to the boy's belt, a thick loop of black leather about his jeans with a snake design on the buckle. 'Or use a belt on us.'

Tom seemed genuinely interested in her suggestions, a light in his blue eyes. He was already unzipping his jeans absent-mindedly, an obvious erection pressing hard against the black denim. 'So can we mark your skin? I mean, do you mind that? I can see you're both a little bruised in places –'

'We both adore being marked,' Lizzie interrupted him, slipping her hand into the gaping crotch of his jeans and massaging his cock. 'In fact, there's a tawse in my bedroom. Would you like to use it on me before we have sex?'

Tom stammered, 'What's a tawse?'

'Oh my God, you innocent young thing,' she said, laughing and dragging him out of the room by his shirt. 'I'm going to love showing you how to use it. Beth, darling? Make sure you get seriously fucked or you're in trouble. I want to hear all about it, every sordid detail . . . OK?'

Left alone with the two Frenchmen, Beth stared down at the blue-patterned living-room carpet with a flush on her cheeks. She knew what was going to happen but somehow it felt unreal. When Milton took her to the Club, or she was visiting someone under his orders, it felt quite different to this: almost acceptable behaviour. But, now, she was taking her new sexual persona one step further along the road to independence and it was strange, uncomfortable, maybe even a little frightening. These two young men were complete strangers, yet she was about to give her body to them. What were their names again? Justin and Marc. Marc was the one watching and smiling. Justin was slightly older and he had his hand between her legs. Beth started to tremble, her breathing quickening. She was on her own now. Although it was daytime, the curtains were tightly drawn so they could not be seen from the street. Nobody would listen to her cries; no one would be coming to rescue her.

'You are strange girls, I think,' Marc commented at last after a long moment of silence, as though struggling to find the right words.

'Yes.'

'And both college girls?'

'Yes.'

He sounded troubled. 'Why you so strange?'

'I don't know.'

The older one who was holding Beth on his knee seemed much less interested in her motivation. He spread her thighs wider, his fingers still crawling over her pussy. His thick French accent was very sexy, and it made the hairs rise on the back of her neck. 'You are wet, little college girl. You want to be hurt now?'

She shivered. 'Yes, please.'

Justin yanked up her white T-shirt and Beth helped him, raising her arms above her head until it had been thrown to one side and she was sitting nude on his lap. He had large tanned hands and he ran them over her body in a leisurely fashion, eventually returning to cup and squeeze her breasts one at a time. His finger and thumb pinched experimentally at her left nipple, watching her expression as she winced. 'Too hard?'

'No.'

He increased the pressure and smiled triumphantly when she cried out.

'You like that? It hurts?'

'Yes,' she whimpered to both questions. 'Yes.'

Justin stood up, letting her nude body slip to the floor, and began to unbuckle his belt. Marc was already on his feet beside them, a large bulge in his jeans as he removed his shirt to reveal a smooth tanned chest. The two young men looked at each other over her head, speaking in rapid guttural French. She did not understand what they were saying but knew they were both aroused.

Marc knocked books and sheets of paper off their work desk with one sweep of his hand. The older one dragged her across the room and pushed her face down over the desk. Marc held her still, grasping both her arms together at the wrist. She did not even try to struggle, though, her sex warm and moist with excitement. It would be an impromptu beating, unexpected and unplanned. Something terribly exciting about that, she thought, and closed her eyes as the world spun.

The belt flailed awkwardly across the tops of her thighs and she yelped, caught off guard. The graduate adjusted his stance and brought the belt down more forcefully, this time straight across the central line of her buttocks. Beth gave a high-pitched cry but still did not move. He stepped back and made an odd noise under his breath, a mixture of pleasure and alarm. No doubt he was watching the thick red stripe come up across her pale flesh and realising how hard he had hit her.

The other boy said something in French and Justin hit her again, and then again. The third time was fierce, but the fourth was fiercer. Beth was not ready for the fifth blow, still gathering her strength and trying to control her breathing. Now she jerked under the hard leather belt; she had no choice in the matter, letting herself weep a little, too, as the excitement peaked and pain began to throb across her buttocks and the tops of her thighs. His fingers explored the stinging weals on her bottom and she tried to wriggle away, begging him in broken French not to touch her. Not yet at least. Not until the worst was over. She could not bear it. Justin either ignored or did not understand her pleas. His hand slipped lower, pushing her thighs roughly apart, shoving three fingers up inside her soaking sex so that she arched against the desk and moaned with excited humiliation.

'Oh no, please,' she sobbed.

But neither of them seemed to be listening. His friend held her motionless, pinned down on the hard surface while the older one's fingers brutally penetrated and stretched her. She was wet and dirty and ready to do whatever they told her. Her eyes were shut tight but there were bright red starbursts inside the dark lids, a feeling as though the top of her head was being blown off; and then it was too late to resist and Beth was coming under his fingers. She had no shame, gasping and writhing and groaning as loudly as a whore in front of these two strangers.

Justin stepped between her thighs, unzipped his jeans and shoved his cock into the tight channel of her anus. She moaned at the sudden entry. There was no lubrication and it hurt worse than the belting. He pushed straight into her anus and withdrew without giving her a chance to get used to the sensation. Then in again and out again. The tight sphincter tearing and protesting at every thrust. She turned her head, sinking her teeth into her own arm to take her mind off what was happening and leaving deep painful bite marks.

Then her wrists were released, her head was being lifted, and she felt a swollen purple-headed cock nudge against her lips. It was Marc, ordering her in hoarse French to suck him. '*Suce-moi, suce-moi,*' he was muttering, pre-come already winking at the slit in the end of his cock.

Her lips parted submissively and he was inside. Filling her mouth and cheeks, pushing her tongue down out of the way, as he thrust rapidly in and out of her throat. His hands grasped the back of her head, keeping her in position. She wriggled one arm underneath her body, finding and stroking her pussy without too much difficulty. The shaven lips hung open there, lewd and soaking with fluids generated by her own orgasm. She needed to climax again, could not bear the thought of these two strangers using her for pleasure while she lay beneath them, filled with cock at both ends and unable to come herself.

She rubbed at her clitoris with fierce little jabbing motions, barely able to move an inch in any direction. Oddly enough, that restriction made her pleasure even more intense. The men inside her seemed to feel it, too. Marc pulled her closer, his cock buried up to the hilt in her throat, his balls banging against her chin. Justin grunted and started to thrust more urgently, nearing the end. God, she thought wildly, it's like being sawn in half.

Marc made a noise and shouted something in French which she did not catch above her own muffled cries. His hands clutched her head; he rammed himself into her mouth one last time and spurted several creamy mouthfuls of spunk down her throat. Beth thought she would faint with the sensation, revelling in the rude disgraceful things these men were doing to her. Her fingers worked hard against her clitoris, bringing her again and again to that sudden starburst of pleasure. Her body was still writhing desperately in orgasm as Justin reached the end of his stamina. The swarthy French graduate raised her hips off the desk as though she were a wheelbarrow, sank deeply into her rectal passage and grunted into a shuddering climax.

Her cheeks flushed, she endured the pain like a climber scaling a sheer cliff, waiting for the pleasure to kick in. How on earth had she ever managed to enjoy herself in bed before Dr Milton had introduced her to the Club? Lizzie could say what she liked about him, but her tutor would always hold a terrible fascination for her. He alone had shown her what was possible in a world of discipline and power, that her true sexual self was not only submissive but also utterly amoral.

In the past, she had always been in charge; she had been the one to say when and how. None of her boyfriends would have dreamed of slapping her face during orgasm as Milton had slapped Charlotte's, or pulling up her skirt and spanking her before sex. But, now, she knew, felt it like an ache in her bones, that what she really wanted from sex was to be used, to be dominated, to be hurt.

Her own fingers dug cruelly into her sex and Beth came with a cry of ecstasy, slumping to the floor as the men withdrew from her body, trembling all over and feeling inexplicably bereft. Would she really have to wait all summer before she saw Dr Milton again?

Milton paused outside the gentleman's outfitters, gazing at their display of camel-coloured jodhpurs with a black leather riding crop lying so innocently beside them. He was already missing Charlotte. It had been several months now since their last trip down to the basement of this shop, to fit her out with a new harness and matching hoof boots. He had intended to make an appointment for Beth and Lizzie over the summer, so that they too could enjoy the latest designs in pony wear. But all that was impossible now. Those disobedient little girls had chosen to go their own way during the holidays and he had little option but to look elsewhere for his pleasure.

'Dr Milton?'

He turned, recognising the petite blonde immediately. She was one of his first-year students, whom he suspected of having performed rather badly in Moderations, though there was still time for the girl to recover and go on to gain at least a good Second. 'Wendy, are you still up in Oxford? I thought you and Ruskin had plans to take Australia by storm this summer?'

'Yes, such a shame, our plans fell through at the last minute,' the girl told him, speaking with a delightful lisp. 'So it looks like I'm stuck here in town for the holidays.'

'That's terrible.'

'How about you, Dr Milton? Are you off on your hols?'

Milton hesitated a moment before answering, sensing a possible opportunity in the air. He looked at the girl more closely than he had done before, his eyes narrowing on that heart-shaped face, the sweet bow-like mouth, and then dropping to the firm high breasts jutting so invitingly from beneath her midriff top. Not for the first time, he wondered whether she was still a virgin or if that weak-wristed idiot Ruskin had managed to break her in. Wendy had definitely been a virgin when she arrived at Oxford. There was no other explanation for the way she blushed whenever she had caught him looking at her breasts in one-to-one tutorials. He had been tempted then, seeing how provocatively innocent she was, to pluck that particular fruit himself. But she had also looked like the sort who would flee in tears once the deed was done, and probably spill the entire tale to the College Dean. So he had let the pretty little blonde go and followed more experienced prey, like Beth. But, now, perhaps, she was a little more soiled around the edges.

'I haven't made my mind up yet.'

She glanced in the shop window, her eyes widening as she took in the jodhpurs and leather riding crop. 'Is that what you were looking at, Dr Milton? Do you ride?'

'Absolutely.'

Wendy clapped her hands in sudden childish delight. 'Oh, how marvellous. I love horses. I go riding whenever I possibly can. I hadn't thought of you as an equestrian type. But, of course, you can never tell just by looking.'

'No, indeed,' he said dryly.

'Well, if you like riding, too, perhaps we could –' she stammered, coming to a halt as she realised what she had been about to ask.

Milton allowed himself an ironic smile, once more looking down at her mouth as the blonde fell into silent confusion. Now what would Beth and Lizzie say if they could hear this rather interesting exchange, he wondered wryly. No doubt, they would be as mad as cats; his pony girls were such intensely possessive creatures, and it was a disagreeable female trait which he had never been able to understand. The more the merrier, that was his motto.

His spirits began to rise along with his cock. Just because he had been banned from enjoying his two new training ponies until the start of Michaelmas term, that did not mean he would have to spend a lonely, ponyless summer. Wendy would be in town the whole time, she had said so herself. And, since one glance at a riding crop had been enough to nudge her mind towards sex, perhaps it would not be too hard to recruit her to the Club. Milton imagined that pretty mouth opening and stretching to accommodate his erection, which was already pressing against the crotch of his trousers, and knew he had no choice but to pursue this conversation to its natural end. Besides, those shapely ankles and feet would look superb in hoof boots.

'Are you suggesting that we go riding together?'

She looked up at him then, her face hotly flushed. 'I'm not sure what I was saying. Except that I don't want to bore you. I mean, you're probably not as keen on horses as I am.'

'Not at all. Ponies are my life, Wendy. I spend almost all my free time training and riding them.'

Her blue eyes flew wide in that heart-shaped face.

For a moment, she resembled a china doll, her perfect pink mouth gaping in awe. 'You're joking? You're a trainer? You actually train ponies?'

'Yes,' he said, growing in confidence by the second. 'In fact, I belong to a sort of . . . Pony Training Club.'

Wendy stared up at him with a fanatical glow in her cheeks and he suddenly knew the girl was ripe for it, ready to have her legs spread and her buttocks marked and a fine hand-stitched saddle slapped on her back. That would teach Beth and Lizzie to flout his authority as master, returning next term to find a new pony in the field. The thought had him instantly rigid.

'Gosh,' she exclaimed, her lisp growing more pronounced. 'I'd be so excited to see you in action, Dr Milton. Maybe even ride some of the ponies you've trained.'

'I have a few photographs at home,' he said modestly.

'Oh, I'd love to see them.'

Milton held out his arm to her and Wendy hesitated for a split second, her eyes skimming the firm bulge in his trousers, then took his arm and hung on to it as they walked down the street, gazing up at him with her pretty lips moist and slightly parted.

'Do you think,' he asked idly, 'that your boyfriend would mind if we went riding together?'

Her smile was all innocence. 'I doubt it, Dr Milton. I've never been riding with him either.'

NEXUS NEW BOOKS

To be published in April 2005

CONCEIT AND CONSEQUENCE
Aishling Morgan

Conceit and Consequence follows Lucy Truscott and her three female cousins through a series of romantic entanglements – some more bizarre than others – with spankings and other assorted humiliations inflicted on the girls by the bossy Lucy on the way. Smuggling, swashbuckling and sodomy mix in a plot that's tighter than Mr D'Arcy's breeches.

£6.99   0 352 33965 9

NO PAIN, NO GAIN
James Barron

No Pain, No Gain is a collection of short stories united around their narrator's search for satisfaction through sexual submission. The pseudonymous author, a film-industry insider, has spent his own life questing after strong and beautiful women who will dominate him - sometimes for money, but mostly for love. Inspired by the results of his search, *No Pain, No Gain* turns the usual male memoir of sexual conquests upside-down and inside-out.

£6.99   0 352 33966 7

PLAYTHING
Penny Birch

This classic book in the Penny Birch series features bad girl Penny's dirtiest antics yet. After going a whole month without doing anything naughty, she is desperate to be even more filthy, despite her imminent departure to Brittany where she is instructed to set up a university field course. Once there, her academic responsibilities get pushed aside for more deliciously rude indulgences. This time, however, she will encounter a French voyeur called Tom, whose penchant for dirty fun will shock even Penny and her playmates.

£6.99   0 352 33967 5

If you would like more information about Nexus titles, please visit our website at www.nexus-books.co.uk, or send a stamped addressed envelope to:

  Nexus, Thames Wharf Studios,
  Rainville Road, London W6 9HA